Hansjörg Schneider, born in Aarau, Switzerland, in 1938, has worked as a teacher and journalist, and is one of the most performed playwrights in the German language. He is best known for his Inspector Hunkeler crime novels. Schneider has received numerous awards, among them the prestigious Friedrich Glauser Prize for *The Basel Killings.* He lives and writes in Basel.

THE BASEL KILLINGS

Hansjörg Schneider

Translated by Mike Mitchell

BITTER LEMON PRESS
LONDON

BITTER LEMON PRESS

First published in the United Kingdom in 2021 by
Bitter Lemon Press, 47 Wilmington Square, London WC1X 0ET

www.bitterlemonpress.com

First published in German as *Hunkeler macht Sachen* by Ammann Verlag, Zurich, 2004

The translation of this work was supported by the Swiss Arts Council Pro Helvetia

Copyright © 2010 Diogenes Verlag AG, Zurich

English translation © Mike Mitchell, 2021

The poem "Poesie" by Manfred Gilgien is quoted from: Manfred Gilgien, *Strassen-Tango*. Copyright © 2005 by Verlag Nachtmaschine, Basel
The poem "Salz" by Rainer Brambach is quoted from: Rainer Brambach,
Gesammelte Gedichte. Copyright © 2003 by Diogenes Verlag AG, Zurich

A CIP record for this book is available from the British Library

PB ISBN 978–1–911394–547
eB USC ISBN 978–1–913394–554
eB ROW ISBN 978-1-913394-561

Typeset by Tetragon

swiss arts council
prohelvetia

THE BASEL KILLINGS

Peter Hunkeler, inspector with the Basel City criminal investigation department, divorced with one daughter, came out of the Milchhüsli onto Missionsstrasse. It was early in the morning of Monday, 27 October, half past midnight to be precise – he'd looked at the clock on the wall of the inn before heading outside. There was a shimmer of white in the air, cast down from the street lamp in the fog. The end of October and already the town was grey and wet, just like the beginning of December.

Hunkeler felt a need to pee. The sudden cold, he thought: inside it had been nice and warm. Not just because of the heating but also because of all the people sitting round the regulars' table, one next to the other, like beasts in the cowshed. He wondered whether to go back inside to the toilet. Then he heard a tram approaching from the right, from the city centre. The soft sound of the wheels on the rails, metal on metal, a round light, the outline hardly discernible. A ghostly gleam gliding through the fog. Then the lighted windows of the number 3, a man with a hat on in the front car, a young couple in the rear. The girl's light hair was draped over the boy's shoulder. The tram disappeared in the fog, heading for the border. A sudden screech of the wheels – the light on Burgfelderplatz was presumably on red.

Hunkeler waited until he heard the tram setting off again. He crossed the road to the Turkish pizzeria and looked in through the window of the Billiards Centre. He saw the artist Gerhard Laufenburger sitting at the round table with his girlfriend Nana, beside them little Cowboy with his Stetson on his head and his black dog. He didn't want to see them that evening, so he headed off towards Burgfelderplatz.

After he'd taken a few steps he came to the Cantonal Bank on the corner that had a little tree in a tub outside. He thought the plant was ridiculous. Either a tree or no tree, rather than an apology for a tree. But now the little tree was just what he needed. He went over to it and pissed on the slim trunk. Bloody prostate, he thought, by now he couldn't even hold his water for the few hundred yards to his apartment.

He turned his head and saw a dark figure sitting on the stone bench in the corner, leaning against the wall. He went over to see who it was. It was Hardy, the old vagabond who always had a diamond in his left earlobe. He appeared to be asleep, mouth open. Hunkeler sat down on the damp seat beside him, grasped the collar of his jacket and pulled it up. He looked across the square, where there was nothing but fog. After a while he heard the sound of a car approaching. Two bright headlights appeared and slowly went past.

"Shitty weather," Hunkeler said. "Shitty town, shitty time of year."

He looked back at Hardy, who wasn't moving. His false teeth had a strange white glow.

"My Hedwig," Hunkeler said, "is a lousy bitch. When you need her, she isn't there. At the moment she's away in Paris, studying the Impressionists. A sabbatical, that's what she calls it, for three months, until the new year, to recharge her batteries. Being a kindergarten teacher is obviously an extremely stressful job, normal holidays aren't enough for you to recover. You need an extra three months' further study in Paris to be able to withstand the psychological pressure of the brats. That's a quarter of a year."

He spat on the wet asphalt, three yards away, and lit a cigarette. He took a drag, coughed and leaned back against the wall.

"I'm finding it a real effort getting through this dreary time," he said. "Not smoking too much, not drinking too much beer, not going to bed too late. I could use a sabbatical too. Just imagine, Manet's women in the park with their lovely hats and white blouses and the sunlight falling through the foliage. Monet's water lilies. Van Gogh's blue church. And now just look across this square. What do you see? Just muck, and so grey you don't even recognize it as muck."

He spat out the cigarette in a wide curve; it landed by the tree. He watched the glow gradually die out.

Hardy still wasn't saying anything. He'd leaned his head back, his eyes half open. It almost looked as if he wasn't breathing.

Hunkeler suddenly felt a chill on the back of his neck. He got to his feet, grabbed the man's upper arms and tried to pull him up. But he was too heavy. At least Hunkeler managed to heave him up so far that his head tipped back, as if it wasn't firmly attached any more. A sharp wound appeared across his throat, going from one side to the other. The left earlobe had been slit. He had a closer look to see if the diamond was still there. It wasn't.

He let the man's corpse drop back and went to the little tree to throw up. He didn't want to, but he had to. Beer ran out of his mouth, dripping down. Odd, he thought, why am

I being sick on the tree and not simply on the ground – as if that would make any difference?

He took some fast, deep breaths, like a dog panting, forcing the stuff back down that was coming up. He wiped his chin and forehead with his handkerchief; they were suddenly dripping with sweat. He could feel himself swaying. For a moment he thought of running off, going to the Billiards Centre and joining Laufenburger and Cowboy as if nothing had happened. But then he took his phone out of his pocket and called the emergency number.

The ambulance was the first to arrive, with its siren sounding and its blue light flashing through the fog. It came from the cantonal hospital on Hebelstrasse, down towards the Rhine. The doctor, a youngish man with rimless glasses, leapt out. He went over to the slumped figure of Hardy and grasped him by the chin, making his head tilt to one side. He had a close look at the wound on his neck and his left ear.

"Broken neck," he said. "Strangled. What's this with his ear?"

"He wore a diamond in the lobe," Hunkeler said.

"There's no diamond there any more," the doctor said, carefully leaning Hardy's head back against the wall. He took a cigarillo out of a tin, lit it and looked across the square, a nauseated expression on his face. The first onlookers were standing there in the fog.

"Turn that bloody blue light off," Hunkeler said.

The driver nodded, got into the ambulance and turned it off. The crossroads were grey in the light, which was so diffuse you couldn't tell where it came from. It was quiet, an almost unnerving silence. The men could all feel it: no one was moving any more. The onlookers stood there like spectres, no one came close.

Then a light flared up, sharp and brutal. It was directed at the dead man, tearing him out of the protective darkness, his white teeth, the cut on his neck. It was fat Hauser, the newshound, a reporter, always first on the scene. He lived just round the corner on Hegenheimerstrasse.

Hunkeler went over and grabbed him by the arm, but Hauser was young and strong.

"I'll break every bone in your body," Hunkeler said, "if you press that button again."

"Not necessary, I've got what I need." Hauser wriggled out of his grip and disappeared in the fog.

Hunkeler went over to the onlookers. He knew them all. Nana was there from the Billiards Centre and little Cowboy with his dog. Luise in her leopard-skin jacket. Dolly with the long legs, little Niggi, pale Franz, Richard the foreign legionnaire. They'd all been sitting at the regulars' table in the Milchhüsli. There were also a few old people there from the surrounding apartments – they'd presumably also heard the siren.

"Hardy's dead," Hunkeler said. "Someone broke his neck."

He'd no idea what else he could say. No one moved, no one cried. Out on the street a taxi slipped past.

Then Hermine appeared out of the fog. She lived directly opposite, in an apartment over the pharmacy she managed. She was over fifty but still had a model's complexion, like Dresden china. She was wearing slippers and had slung on a blue dressing gown. She went over until she was three paces from where Hardy was slumped, stopped, put her hand over her mouth and seemed to be swaying for a moment.

"You must get away from here," the doctor said. "It's a crime scene, no unauthorized person is allowed. Actually, that should be your task, Inspector. You should know what is to be done."

"She's Hardy's lover," Hunkeler said. "She wants to say farewell to him."

"No," Hermine said, "I'm not saying farewell to him. We'd only had an argument, it wasn't a farewell for good. Why is he dead?"

"That I don't know. Go now, have a cognac."

Putting his arm round her skinny shoulders, he took her to the others.

"Take her with you. Give her something to drink, put it on my tab. The square will be cordoned off, there's nothing more to see here."

Luise nodded. "Come on, you lot. We can't do anything more for Hardy now."

They vanished in the fog, heading for the Milchhüsli.

The police squad finally arrived, a good quarter of an hour after Hunkeler had called. It consisted of Detective Sergeant Madörin, Corporal Lüdi and Haller, with his cold curved pipe in his mouth. They got out, a bit too slowly as it seemed, and went over to the dead Hardy.

"He's dead," Lüdi said. "Strangled."

They looked round the foggy square, nauseated by their profession, the work that was waiting for them.

Haller scratched his neck ostentatiously. "A stupid business," he said. "What have you been getting up to?"

"I haven't been getting up to anything," Hunkeler said. "This is my way home. I just happened to come across him."

"You said on the phone that you knew him. You know what he's called."

"He's called Bernhard Schirmer. Known as Hardy. He used to have a diamond in his left earlobe."

"I didn't see a diamond in his earlobe," Haller said. "I saw a bloody gash."

"Your way home?" Madörin asked. "From where? The Milchhüsli over there isn't exactly a top-class establishment. Nor the Billiards Centre. That's where the Albanians go."

"That doesn't bother me," Hunkeler said. "I drink my beer where I want."

He was trying to give his voice the sharpness he usually had at his disposal. But he couldn't summon it up.

"I had a drink in the Milchhüsli and studied the Barbara Amsler file. That case just won't leave me in peace."

"Night work then?" Madörin grinned. "Which file was that exactly?"

"I call the emergency squad," Hunkeler said, "and you take more than quarter of an hour. What's going on?"

"Calm down," Lüdi said. "We can't tear along through the fog. You really ought to know that."

"Hauser was here," said Hunkeler. "He was faster than you. He took a photo."

"And you allowed that?" Madörin said nastily.

"I didn't see him coming, because of the fog. What's more, I feel as depressed as if it was just before Christmas."

13

"It's this shitty fog," Haller said.

They stood there and waited. No one sat down on the stone bench, it was too damp.

Then the crime scene squad arrived, in three cars. They parked on the pavement. The spotlights were set up, the square was cordoned off, the usual work began.

A chubby man with a reddish face came over to Hunkeler and grasped him by the arm. It was Dr de Ville, from Alsace, head of the section.

"*Hélas*, Hünkelé," he said, "why did you have to go across this of all squares on your way home? The man could quite happily have stayed sitting there until the morning. No one's going to bring him back to life again."

Hunkeler took a cigarette out of the packet and put it between his lips, but seeing Madörin's venomous look he put it back in the packet. Then he went to find the cigarette butt he'd spat out at the tree and picked it up.

"The crime scene must stay the way it was," Madörin said. "Who's actually in charge of the squad here?"

"I threw this butt away while I was waiting for you and the ambulance. I'm in charge of the squad. And my instructions are to let the forensic team get on with their work. Lüdi and Madörin are to go over to the Billiards Centre and take the customers' details."

"If it was one of them," Lüdi said, "he'll have been across the border long since. And no one will know him."

"No one is to leave the place," Hunkeler said, feeling the sharpness returning to his voice, "before their names and addresses have been taken down. Haller and I will do the same in the Milchhüsli."

*

As Hunkeler went into the Milchhüsli, he felt a slight dizziness. He stopped and clutched his forehead. He could see the bar with no one sitting at it. The darts machines on the walls with no one playing at them. The regulars' table, which was fully occupied, the pall of tobacco smoke over it. He felt as if he was going back to a long-past time that he could hardly remember any more but which had him in its grip and wouldn't let him go. Most of all he would have liked to turn round at once and stride out towards the border and into Alsace. To tramp over the wet meadows, through the clayey woods, up the rise to Folgensbourg, across the plateau to the village where his house was. He would have opened the door, called the cats, lit the stove and gone to bed, pulling the blankets up over his head. Then the crackle of the logs, the purring of the cats, the calls of the owls in the trees outside.

He took his hand off his forehead, as if he'd just been wiping off the sweat, went over to the bar and ordered a cup of coffee from Milena. He watched Haller sit down at the regulars' table, light his pipe and take a notepad out of his pocket. That was all so pointless, so boring, so stupid. He saw Hermine whimpering in Luise's arms.

"Hardy's dead, isn't he?" Milena said as she put the cup down in front of him.

"Yes."

"Who did it?"

"I don't know."

Milena was Serbian. She had two children who were at school, whom you could sometimes see doing their homework in the kitchen. She was paler than usual. She gave Hunkeler a long keen look. Then she shook her head slowly. This slowness was one of the reasons he liked her so much.

15

"I can't imagine," she said, "that there would be any reason at all to kill Hardy. He wouldn't hurt a fly."

He stirred the two sugar lumps in his coffee, equally slowly.

"You never know who can hurt whom," he said. "Did you notice anything out of the ordinary this evening?"

She thought, then shook her head again. "It's the end of the month. A few had already had their money, they paid for rounds. A lot was drunk, but no more than usual for the time of the month."

"Was Hardy in here? I mean before I was?"

"Yes, at eight, as always. He was drinking apple juice until nine. Then he set off on his walk, as he did every evening. He doesn't drink alcohol any more, since Hermine threw him out of her apartment. He couldn't sleep any more. Every night he walked round the block where she lives, as if he wanted to guard her. But you know all that, of course."

She lowered her eyes and brushed a strand of hair out of her face. "Now he's dead," she said.

"Was there anything that struck you while Hardy was here, between eight and nine? Was there anyone here you've never seen before?"

She thought about it, her expression brightening. "Yes, two middle-aged men. Powerfully built, well dressed, ties and all that. They had coffee. One certainly weighed more than two hundred pounds. The other had a thick chain on his left wrist, solid gold."

"Do you know where they came from?"

"They were speaking Turkish. Presumably they'd been collecting money from the Turkish pizzeria opposite. I'm pretty sure of that actually, I know that kind of gentleman.

They were laughing very loud, that did strike me. They left immediately after Hardy."

Hunkeler looked across at the regulars' table, where Haller was writing something down in his notepad. No one was speaking, they were just waiting tensely for the questions.

"Do you think the two of them killed Hardy?"

"No. They were pros. They wouldn't just go and kill an old man like that."

He took out his notebook and wrote down: *Two Turks, professionals, one with a solid-gold chain on his left wrist.*

"It wasn't them," Milena said. "They only use violence when there's no other way."

"I know. Still, it's remarkable for two Turks to be drinking coffee in a Serbian cafe. Isn't it?"

"Not necessarily. That's all ancient history, we have to forget it."

She took a bottle of vodka out of the fridge, put schnapps glasses on a tray and filled them.

"Do you want one too?"

"No."

He watched her take the tray over to the regulars' table, looking a bit slipshod but still charming.

"How's Hedwig?" she asked, once she was back behind the bar. "Still in Paris?"

"She's doing fine, excellently."

Now she did smile, with a trace of mockery, or so it seemed to him.

"Let me give you a piece of good advice. Go home and have a good sleep. You've got dark rings round your eyes."

*

Outside he crossed the road and saw that Gerhard Laufenburger was still in the Billiards Centre. Nana and Cowboy were there as well. Most of all he'd have liked to go home, but there was still something he wanted to know. Skender, the Albanian landlord, came over to him as soon as he went in.

"Listen, Herr Hunkeler," he said, agitated, "this is all a misunderstanding. We are peaceful people. We don't kill anybody. Our religion forbids it. Recently everyone seems to have come to think we Muslims are bandits and murderers. That is an insult."

"I know," said Hunkeler.

"You're the boss. Send these two policemen away. They're bad people. They treat us like dogs and want to know our addresses."

Hunkeler looked across at the billiards tables, which were empty. Crushed together at the coffee tables beside them were the Albanian customers. Young folk, mostly men, a few couples.

"Next please," Madörin, standing before them, said in his sharp officer's voice. "Precise name, precise address, precise telephone number. And no sly tricks. Anyone who lies will have problems. We check everything."

Lüdi was sitting beside him, stony-faced, noting down everything he heard.

"I liked Hardy," Skender said, "especially after he stopped drinking alcohol. Who would kill an old man like that?"

"He wasn't that old," said Hunkeler, "he was around sixty."

"We are a place for my Albanian countryfolk but also for people from here. We are tolerant, we serve alcohol, even though the Swiss sometimes drink too much. But these are decent premises, we don't need the police."

"I'm sorry, but that's how it has to be. It won't be any use, but we have to be doing something." He grinned, tried to wink with his left eye. It wasn't really a success, he was simply too tired.

Hunkeler sat down beside Nana at the round table. Laufenburger had brought his Siamese cat, which was purring in his lap. Cowboy's black dog was lying asleep on the floor. In the twenty-foot-long aquarium a few fish were calmly swimming. A video clip was running on the TV in the corner but no one was watching it. On the table was a half-full bottle of red wine. Hunkeler would have liked a glass, but he ordered coffee.

"Why did you stay sitting here?" he asked. "Surely you heard the ambulance?"

"I couldn't get away because of the cat," Laufenburger said.

"But you usually take her everywhere with you."

Laufenburger lowered his eyes, picked up his glass and had a drink.

"I didn't like Hardy," he said.

"Why are you saying that? You can't have known it was anything to do with Hardy."

Again Laufenburger took his glass. His hand seemed to be trembling slightly.

"Nana ran out to see what was going on. She came back in straight away and said Hardy was dead. Then she rushed out again."

He raised his head and looked Hunkeler straight in the eye.

"Hardy always used to get on my nerves. He wasn't quite clean. Didn't you know that?"

"What do you mean?"

"Crooked things, fiddles. Why was he always going away?"

"He told me," Hunkeler said, "that he had a hut in Alsace. By Morschwil Pond, I think."

"He had, had he? And how did he pay for that? And his diamond was worth a good twenty thousand francs. Where did he get that?"

"He was a truck driver," Cowboy said, "before he got stomach cancer. They cut out half of it. He had a large pension. At least, he always had enough money. And he'd always worn the diamond."

"If you believe that, you'll believe anything," Laufenburger said.

"Who actually was it who told Hermine?" Hunkeler asked.

"Me," said Nana. "I've got a mobile phone."

Hunkeler looked at her. Her name was actually Natasha and she was a Belarusian. A fifty-year-old woman, hair dyed blonde, a bright, finely featured face, a trace of freckles. He looked at Laufenburger, his ridiculous sailor's cap, the silver chain round his neck, his nicotine-stained fingers. He suddenly hated this guy, he hated himself.

"How can you stick it out with this wreck?" he asked.

"He's not a wreck," Nana said. "He's just drinking too much at the moment. But I cook for him and sometimes he eats a bit. I love him."

Hunkeler dumped the money for his coffee down on the table and left. He was now really furious. He hated these pubs, he hated this town, he hated his profession. Riff-raff the lot of them, he thought. Do nothing, don't work, sit around drawing their pensions. And are even loved.

Over at the crossing he saw the forensic team at work in the floodlit fog. Two young guys were kneeling down beside the little tree examining the ground. Hardy's corpse was on a stretcher.

He walked past without any greeting and turned onto St Johann's-Ring, heading for Mittlere Strasse.

He had a restless night, even though he was dead tired. He curled up in the foetal position, which usually gave him a sleep that dissipated all his worries: hands over his temples, knees drawn up, wreathed in the warmth of the blanket. And he did manage several times to submerge and dock with things that were unknown to him, with the old familiar realm of the undefined, where he felt at home. But he kept on waking with a start, having to emerge from the protective world of dreams. It was a painful rising that took place at breakneck speed and was almost physically painful. And then he would see Hardy's face tipping to the side once more.

Hunkeler had had too much coffee. He wasn't used to coffee late in the evening. He'd ordered an espresso when he went into the Milchhüsli at ten and sat at a table by himself because he wanted to reread Barbara Amsler's farewell letter. Again. Barbara had been a whore who paid tax on a regular but not particularly high income as a prostitute. Having grown up in Schinznach Dorf in Aargau canton, she'd had a difficult youth; her father had originally been a farmer and wine-grower, and later had worked at the power station down on the Aare. Her mother had been an incomer called Rosa Minder; both parents were dead.

Barbara had run away from home at a very young age, with almost no education, and had been in various children's homes and institutions. Then she'd come to Basel and worked as a cashier at a grocer's. On 14 August, aged just thirty-two, she'd been found in Allschwil Pond, strangled with a noose of white raw silk. Allschwil Pond was in the Basel Rural Area. And since the place where the body was found determined who had investigative responsibility, the Basel Rural CID was in charge. However, as the murder had possibly taken place in the city, Inspector Hunkeler had also been called in.

It was in her apartment in Schneidergasse that he had found the letter he called her farewell letter. It said, *If you kick me, I will long for you. If you hit me, I will crawl back to you. If you kill me, I will stay with you for ever.*

Hunkeler had read these lines time and time again, as if they held the key to the murder case. He'd got caught up in this case in a way that was rare in his career. And he refused to even contemplate the idea that he couldn't solve it. The North Italian Enrico Casali, for whom Barbara had worked in the Singerhaus and the Klingental over in Lesser Basel, had a cast-iron alibi. And her colleagues had no information to offer at all.

Hunkeler couldn't forget her slim face with the full mouth that reminded him of a plant. He himself came from the Aargau. He had a soft spot for those kinds of women, who were dear and gentle like the valleys from which they came.

In the Milchhüsli he had gone over to the regulars' table at eleven and drunk three small beers. He'd needed company, human warmth. He'd left the place after twelve and found Hardy's dead body. Around two he'd had another coffee in the Milchhüsli and then one more later on in the Billiards Centre. And that had clearly been too much.

He could feel his pulse pounding. It wasn't something he was used to. Usually he slept like a log; sleeping was one of his strengths. Now his heart was thumping, as if he'd been climbing a mountain. Was it old age, was his circulation collapsing?

He heard the nearby clock tower striking; he counted: one, two, three, four times.

He got up, went to the telephone and dialled a Paris number. He let it ring fourteen times until Hedwig answered. "Yes?" she said, almost in a whisper.

"I need you," Hunkeler said, "right now. You have to talk to me."

"What's wrong? I was fast asleep. Call me in the morning."

"No, don't hang up. I need your voice."

"What do you want with my voice? You must be joking."

"Are you alone?"

She giggled; she'd finally woken up. "No, I'm with someone. With a dream."

"I'll kill the guy!" he screamed.

Hedwig laughed, taking her time. "I'm with Seurat and Sisley. They're pure light."

"Seurat I know. He's the one with all the dots. He can't even draw a decent line. Come over to me."

"In the middle of the night? Are you crazy?"

"Hardy's dead. Someone broke his neck."

Silence. She was shocked.

"Are you still there?" he shouted.

"Yes. Is he the nice alcoholic, the one with the sexy voice?"

"Yes. Him. But he hadn't had a drink for two months."

She waited, he heard her sitting up.

"So that's it for Paris next weekend," she said coolly.

"Yes. But I'll call you every night."

"Listen," she said after a pause, "I do like that kind of call now and then. But I'll be switching off my phone the next few nights. I'm taking this sabbatical to have a good rest."

She hung up.

He went out onto the balcony and looked down into the courtyard. He could see nothing but fog. All that could be heard was a quiet rustling. It must be the last autumn leaves of the maple tree.

It was already nine when he woke, but that didn't bother him. There would be difficulties anyway, you could bet your bottom dollar on that. There had been huge restructuring when the public prosecution office had moved out of the Lohnhof and into the Waaghof. Anyone who couldn't – or wouldn't – adjust to the new structures was sure to be faced with difficulties sooner or later. And one of those people was old Inspector Peter Hunkeler.

However, he didn't feel as old as he was. But that was presumably one of the main difficulties associated with getting older. The image you had of yourself lagged behind the reality.

He paused for a moment while he was soaping his face in the bathroom to scrape off the grey hairs, and looked at himself in the mirror. He knew the face he saw very well; after all, it was his own face. He quite liked it, though not particularly. It was just his own face looking at him from the mirror.

He picked up his razor and started, as always, at the bottom right. That face would last the few years until he was pensioned off, at least he hoped so. And until then he had no intention of letting himself be substantially restructured.

Out in the street he decided to leave his car there because of the fog. He went into the Restaurant Sommereck and sat down beside Edi at the regulars' table and ordered coffee. He picked up the papers and leafed through them both, but there was nothing about Hardy. Hauser the newshound hadn't been that quick after all.

"I've got a lovely piece of Alsace ham there," Edi said when he brought the coffee. "The farmer's wife fattened up the sow on nothing but kitchen scraps and potatoes. It grazed in the meadow, wallowed in the stream and was smoked in the fireplace. With fresh white bread it's superb."

"No thanks," Hunkeler said. "I don't like ham in the morning."

"Pity," Edi said, cutting off some slices from the ham and stuffing a few in his mouth. "Pity about Hardy. Who killed him?"

Hunkeler shrugged. He drank his coffee slowly.

"If you ask me," Edi said, "it'll have been those Albanians from the Billiards Centre. They all have a knife on them and they use them at every opportunity."

"Hardy wasn't stabbed."

"And the cut on his neck? Where did that come from?"

"How should I know? Don't chatter so much this early in the morning."

"Early in the morning? It's almost ten."

Hunkeler paid and went out. He squeezed through between the cars waiting at the red light. Their wipers were on, even though it wasn't raining. The drivers ignored him, seeming to be asleep with their eyes open. He crossed the forecourt of the Cantonal Bank and saw that it wasn't cordoned off any longer. So they thought they wouldn't find anything else. Or they didn't want to find anything else.

He got onto a crowded number 3 and went to Barfüsserplatz.

When he went into the Waaghof, Frau Held waved to him from the reception desk. He went over and gave her a friendly greeting, as friendly as was possible for him on that wet morning.

"What have you been up to?" she asked. "People are saying you were boozing last night in Basel's worst dive with a man who's dead now."

"So that's what people are saying, is it?" He leaned forward and once more regarded the beautiful curve of her lips. "I'll tell you a secret. I was in the Milchhüsli in Missionsstrasse last night. That's Basel's jolliest bar – that's a tip. You must go there sometime. Perhaps we'll met there and share a bottle of wine."

He winked his left eye, she giggled.

In his office he sat down on the wooden chair he'd brought from home. He looked round the room. There were no pictures anywhere – he really liked white walls. In one corner was the swivel chair that could be adjusted to give the correct position for your back. On shelves along the walls box files, beside the computer on his desk two exercise books, piles of handwritten scraps of paper. He felt as mute as a fish in an aquarium. He leaned back, put his feet on the edge of the desk, first the right one, then the left, tilting the wooden chair. He put his arms round his knees and rested his head on them. That always felt good, despite his beer belly. He breathed out, waited for the moment of emptiness, then breathed in again, without stopping. He liked that, the flowing transition, he concentrated on that alone.

Someone knocked on the door. He didn't react. He heard them come in. He recognized Madörin's footsteps.

"Am I disturbing you?"

Hunkeler released his knees, took his feet off the edge of the table and let his chair come down again.

"Yes, you are."

"I don't know what's wrong with you," he said. "I'm really worried about you. There was a time when I liked you very much. I've learned a lot from you, you know that. But for some time now you've been letting yourself go. You're letting yourself fall and you've fallen quite a long way already. And you won't let anyone help you, not even your closest colleagues."

"What's got into you?" Hunkeler asked. "You don't usually talk this much."

Madörin shook his head with the sad look of a devoted hound. "Your sardonic wit won't help you any more. Nor your sharp mind." He got up, seemed about to leave, but stood there for a moment longer. "As you know, Suter's attending a psychology congress in Baden-Baden. I've informed him. He'll be back at 2 p.m. The meeting will be at four. It would be nice if you took part in it."

"Are you crazy?" Hunkeler screamed. "What do you think I'm doing here?"

"In your place I wouldn't shout so loud," Madörin said. "I think you're mistaken about your situation. The fact is that someone peed on the trunk of the tree outside the Cantonal Bank. And they spewed up as well."

He quietly opened the door and went out.

Hunkeler watched how the door was shut – very slowly, as if someone was leaving a sickroom. What was going on? Of course they'd established that someone had peed and thrown up. And of course they suspected that it had been him. But what was so bad about that? Was he an old model who had to be pestered until they got rid of him?

There would have been no problem taking early retirement. He'd have enough to do in his house in Alsace. Moreover, he had a woman he loved and who, so he believed, also loved him, even if at that moment she was in Paris gazing adoringly at the *pointillistes*.

A sabbatical, huh! The things they thought they could do, these kindergarten women, the liberties they could take! Those spoiled state employees dancing ring-a-ring o' roses with cute kids? He wasn't dealing with children himself but with strangled whores and old men with broken necks. He could do with a sabbatical as well.

He grinned – a bitter grin, for it had just occurred to him that he too was a state employee. A state cripple, safeguarded against crises and destitution, secure in the Helvetian net of prosperous uprightness. That was presumably the reason why he kept on plunging down into the world of the lost nightbirds. Because he needed human contact. Because he wanted to live. Because he wanted to breathe.

No, he wasn't going to let them freeze him out. He was still in charge of the Barbara Amsler case, even if he couldn't solve it.

He took the farewell letter out of his jacket pocket and read: *You have shown me what love is. What you have shown me will stay with me. You are part of me. If you kick me, I will long for you. If you hit me, I will crawl back to you. If you kill me, I will stay with you for ever.*

Hunkeler took out his phone and called his doctor.

"I need two appointments," he said. "One with a urologist and one with a heart specialist."

"Why?" the doctor asked.

"My ticker's going haywire and I have to pee all the time."

"After how many beers?"

"Yesterday it was after three small glasses. I didn't even manage to get home."

The doctor thought it over. He knew Hunkeler very well; they'd been at high school together.

"An inspector who urinates in the gutter," he said drily, "should be pensioned off."

"It wasn't in the gutter, it was on a shitty little tree in a tub."

"Why does it always have to be a tree?"

"How should I know?"

"Then come over here and talk to me."

"No," Hunkeler said, "I need specialists. I want to know what's going on. Leave the details on my home answerphone."

He hung up and sat there calmly for a while. Yes, that was right. Perhaps the damage could be repaired, for the moment at least.

He left the Waaghof and went the few steps to the high-rise building. There he took the elevator up to Harry's sauna. He had three sessions in the steam room, a quarter of an hour each. He couldn't relax, he could feel his heart pounding again.

After his third time in the steam room he climbed the stairs up to the roof terrace. He went over to the balustrade and looked down on the Heuwaage and the City Ring. He could hear the rumble of traffic. There was nothing to be seen, just the flash of brake lights now and then. He wrapped himself in his towel and lay down on one of the damp loungers. He tried to think of nothing other than the fog, to feel nothing but the damp coolness, to remember nothing but the present moment.

When he woke, he felt good. He'd had a dreamless sleep, he could tell that from his deep breaths. He felt pretty chilly, but that was the way it should be after all the sweating. Remarkable, he thought, how quickly a human body can recover, if you give it time.

At four on the dot he was in the conference room with the whole team, awaiting the meeting. They'd just briefly nodded to him when he came in. That was always the way in a new murder case, no one felt like talking.

At quarter past, Suter, the state prosecutor, strode in, in a pale-blue suit and a pink tie. A man in the prime of life, decisive and in every respect a decent fellow. Without hesitation he went over to the desk, placed his right hand on it and made sure he had the attention of all those present.

It was outrageous, he said, that nowadays even older people from the lower orders cannot be safe from being attacked and killed while sitting on a bench. As far as he knew – without wanting to anticipate the investigation, of course – the victim was a harmless man with a disability pension, an alcoholic who frequented the bars in the surrounding area. It was a human right, he insisted, to sit down in a bar and have one too many. It was above all a privilege for old, lonely people. And it was important that the police should use all means to preserve that privilege. He would say nothing more on this particular case at the moment; he would leave that for one-to-one discussion.

That meant with Hunkeler, everyone was clear about that.

Then Dr Ryhiner, the forensic physician, spoke. As always, he was in a hurry and spoke quickly in a monotone. Of course, the autopsy had not yet been completed, so it was unclear for example whether there were any toxic substances in the dead body. On the other hand, it was clear that the victim had been strangled, and so violently that one of the cervical vertebrae had been broken. Death had been instantaneous, presumably half an hour before midnight. All the indications were that the victim had not put up any resistance. The man must have fallen asleep on the bench and been taken by surprise while sleeping. It had not yet been established what kind of cord had been used. It was possible that fibres from the murder weapon would be found in the wound, but that was still undecided. What was clear was that there had been something like a ring in the left earlobe. Apparently a diamond, as he had heard. The earlobe had been cut open and the diamond removed, which could have been the motive for the crime. It had in all probability been cut open after the death of the victim, and with a pair of sharp scissors.

It reminded him, Lüdi said, of the murder of Barbara Amsler. Her left earlobe had been cut open, because, as was well known, there had been a pearl in it.

That was a parallel, said Dr Ryhiner, indeed.

Then the head of the forensic section, Dr de Ville, spoke. He had not discovered very much yet, he said, there had been too little time. What struck him was that the victim's wallet was still in his jacket pocket, what's more with six hundred francs in it. If someone stole diamonds, they would also steal money.

"So not murder in the course of robbery?" Suter asked.

That he couldn't say, de Ville went on. The forecourt of the Cantonal Bank was a busy spot. It was more or less impossible to see precise traces such as the imprints of shoes. There was, however, something they had been able to establish clearly. In the first place, someone had peed on the trunk of the little tree. And secondly, someone who had been drinking beer had vomited in that same place.

They all fell silent and stared at the table. Suter put his finger down between his collar and his neck, as if he needed air.

"That was me," Hunkeler said. "As I've already explained, I'd come from the Milchhüsli. I couldn't hold my water, however much I tried, so I went over to the little tree, the way one does. That's how I came to see the dead man sitting there. When I took hold of him and his head fell back, I felt sick and spewed up."

"*Mais mon Dieu*, Hünkelé, why didn't you go to the toilet in the bar?"

"Because the urge to pee came on so suddenly," Hunkeler said, "perhaps because of the cold. What's more, I've got problems with my prostate. What's so bad about that?"

"We'll talk about that later," Suter said. "Please continue."

De Ville hesitated. Clearly he had something more to say about that business, but he let it go.

Furthermore, he said, the usual stuff had been found on the ground – cigarette butts, crumpled store receipts, chewing gum and even eight pumpkin seeds. They'd been still quite fresh, not at all crushed by shoes or softened by the wet.

There was a pause; now it was the turn of the officer in charge of the investigation. And that was Hunkeler. No one in the room seemed to feel at ease.

He'd known Bernhard Schirmer for years, he said for a start, trying to speak in a calm, objective way. He'd met him every so often in the bars on Burgfelderplatz. He was well aware that these were not appropriate establishments for a detective inspector. As they would recall, some time ago the Turkish pizzeria had been blown up by a bomb. Despite that, he was fond of those bars, and he would take the liberty of patronizing them now and again.

Moreover, Hardy Schirmer had been a pleasant individual. A truck driver who'd taken early retirement, a friend of the pharmacist Hermine Mauch but with an apartment of his own. After an argument with Hermine two months ago he'd given up beer and spent the nights wandering round the district. It could well be that he'd fallen asleep on the bench. It could also be that it was murder in the course of robbery, as the diamond had been worth around 20,000 francs. However, he warned them not to tie the investigation down at this early stage. He knew from experience that figures such as Hardy often had a colourful life behind them. Hardy hadn't been some miserable idiot. A plain murder in the course of robbery seemed too simple to him.

It wasn't a good speech; he had something in his throat, his neck, his brain, that stopped him from thinking and speaking precisely.

Suter called on Madörin. He had been waiting quite a while and was visibly nervous. There was something that seemed quite probable to him, he said. The perpetrator wasn't to be found in that shabby band of local dives but more likely in the Billiards Centre, in the Balkans. He hadn't got very far in his investigation, but some of those there yesterday evening were clearly without regular jobs. Despite that, they all had enough money to spend half the night playing billiards.

The perpetrator had probably made off after the deed over the nearby border to France. And naturally no one in the Centre knew anything. They were all thick as thieves. It was of course well known that the drug-trafficking business was controlled above all by Albanians and Turks. But when you asked those guys a question, they suddenly couldn't understand German.

Moreover, yesterday evening there'd been two Turks around in the area, they'd been collecting protection money in the Turkish pizzeria. He couldn't prove that, but he was sure it was the case. They were called Turkoğlu and Sermeter, but those were very likely to be assumed names. Guys like that would change their names and passports every six months. The two of them had been well dressed, and one weighed more than two hundred pounds and the other had a solid-gold bracelet round his wrist. They would also have to be questioned about the crime.

It was unbearable that such criminal riff-raff, who often enjoyed refugee status, should go round free in the city of

Basel. He knew, basically, that that was a political question and therefore shouldn't play any part in police work. But it was a truth that had to be told again, which he had duly done.

Again there was a pause. Madörin's speech had been a little too sharp for most of them. That was the way he was, doggedly determined and pig-headed. And that was precisely why he was sometimes successful.

Everyone knew it was going to be a difficult case to solve. They probably wouldn't succeed without some lucky chance. A corpse on a bench on a foggy night, that was what a policeman wanted least. It could have been any passer-by who had happened along and seen the glitter of the diamond.

To finish, Suter spoke again and said what everyone had been expecting.

He'd thought this over carefully, he said, and had come to the conclusion that in this particular case it would be best if Inspector Hunkeler handed over to someone else, namely Sergeant Madörin. In this case the possibility of bias could not be excluded, since Hunkeler had, of course, been friendly with the victim. In addition, he had enough on his plate with the Barbara Amsler case, which was unfortunately still not solved. He wanted the Inspector to devote all his strength, energy and intelligence to solving that murder. Moreover he would ask Herr Hunkeler to come and see him in his office after the meeting.

It was a similar room to Hunkeler's, just somewhat bigger. The same desk, the same adjustable chair, the same shelves.

In one corner two leather armchairs with little tables, on the wall a coloured Jean Tinguely print.

Suter invited him to sit in one of the armchairs.

"Would you like a coffee? I can have it sent up from the cafeteria. You may also smoke." He pointed affably at the ashtray.

"No thanks," said Hunkeler.

"Right then, now we're going to talk to each other for once. Man to man, I mean. We've known each other for twenty years now."

Hunkeler remained silent. He did think of crossing his legs, but that would have meant he'd slip back even further into a supine position.

"I know what you think of me," Suter said. "You consider me a careerist. Someone who subordinates everything to his personal advancement. Basically, you're right. From the very beginning I wanted to get on. Not simply for the power that would give me, though, but for a purpose. I want to help see to it that this town has a sensible administration of justice."

"We all want that," Hunkeler said. "And I'm not in the habit of moaning about my superiors in public. If I do, then I do it in private."

There was a knock on the door. It was the Italian bringing the coffee from the cafeteria. Suter leaned forward, and it cost him a great effort: he couldn't really sit up in the armchair either. He carefully dropped the sugar cubes into his cup. He tore open the milk carton, splashing part of the contents over the table. But he didn't let that bother him either. He took a sip and put his cup back down. Then he raised his head and gave Hunkeler a very straight look out of his grey eyes.

"I like you. I hope you know that. Even though we are very different kinds of people. Permit me to tell you briefly my opinion of you. You are a rural kind of person, a peasant almost, a man from the country who has ended up in the city. You are a hedonist who appreciates the pleasant sides of life. You are very intelligent. You have a good nose for things. And you like mingling with simple folk."

"I'd agree with that. But that's not forbidden."

"Please don't misunderstand me. I've told you often enough already that I value your work very much. The very characteristics I've briefly sketched enable you to solve serious cases that we, with our upper-middle-class, urban cast of mind, if I may say so, can't get into."

God almighty, Hunkeler thought, the complicated sentences this guy can make!

"If you want me to take early retirement, then please say so. Don't waste your valuable time on me."

Suter raised his hands in a dismissive gesture. A brief, subtle smile appeared on his face.

"I like a glass of beer now and then myself," he said. "And sometimes I have one too many, during carnival or after a successful first night at the theatre. But there are limits. If, in the village you come from…"

"It isn't a village. It's a small town."

"If you're going home in your small town after a bar crawl and pee on a tree or a dung heap, presumably no one will have anything against that. But here in Basel, in a public square, one that's also the scene of a crime, it's simply unacceptable…"

"I know it was wrong. I've arranged a consultation with a urologist. I hope I'll be able to overcome my weak bladder."

"Why do you insist on going round drinking in low dives?" Suter asked with amazing openness. "Isn't it possible to go somewhere more respectable, the bar in the Art Gallery for example?"

"If I feel like it, I go to the Art Gallery as well."

"I know. I've been told."

"What have you been told?"

Suter shook his head indignantly. He leaned forward again and picked up his cup.

"Sometimes I wonder," Hunkeler said, "what the point of my being here in Basel is. I've been living here almost forty years but I've never felt I really belong. Why, for example, shouldn't I frequent a bar? Here in Basel everyone lives nicely separated from each other. I don't understand these invisible boundaries. Nor do I understand the reserve, the almost timorous distance people stick to. If someone shows an emotion here, then they've had it."

"There is something to that," Suter said, putting his cup back down. Then he sank back in his chair again. "How is your enchanting partner, by the way?"

"She's in Paris for three months."

"Oh really? How would we manage without our women, eh? Go and see her for a few days."

"I think I'm needed here. There are two murder cases."

"True, you're working on the Amsler case. Although it does look as if it's going to remain unsolved. The head of the Basel Rural District Police, Füglistaller, is of that opinion too. Please keep your hands off the Schirmer case. And I have to make a formal request for you to observe the rules of respectable behaviour appropriate for an inspector. With no exceptions."

"I'll do my best."

"Good," Suter said with an extremely friendly smile. "I for my part will always stick by you loyally. I wish you every success in your work."

He stood up from his chair. Hunkeler also pushed himself up. He took Suter's hand but avoided shaking it.

That evening Peter Hunkeler sat for a long time in his kitchen on Mittlere Strasse. He'd made some tea, a whole pot full. He drank it slowly and thoughtfully, each time with a shot of cold milk. He could have read a weekly newspaper or sat down and watched TV, but he didn't want to. Now and then he looked down into the rear courtyard, into the fog enveloping the houses opposite.

Once he called Hedwig. He heard her voice on the answerphone. He waited for the tone, then he said, "I love you. Please don't forget that."

He wondered whether he should heat up a frozen pizza. He didn't bother and went out. He walked down the Ring and past St Johann's-Tor to the Rhine. He opened the door of the St Johann's bathing house by the Rhine and stood by the balustrade, where he always had a coffee in the summer. Down below a wild duck quacked; he'd obviously woken it up. He saw it float past, hardly visible on the water. His body was still warm from the sauna, and he wondered briefly whether to go and have a quick swim. He decided not to and went out again, closing the door behind him. Slowly he walked upriver along Treidelweg, passing the moored ferry, the river police ship, the firefighting boat. He crossed Mittlere Brücke and went back down to the river on the other side. The path was covered in leaves but they didn't rustle, they were too damp. Nothing could be seen of the cathedral across the river. He didn't encounter anyone, he was alone. He liked that, this walking through the dark.

He returned to Greater Basel over the Wettsteinbrücke and went into the Art Gallery bar. He was amazed how many people were there, at their loud voices, their cheerful faces, the scent of the huge bouquet of flowers coming from the table with its white cloth.

He sat down at the regulars' table, joining the landlord, two women, a doctor, a pastor who, as usual, was sad because he'd come from a funeral. He ordered some cold Vaud sausage with spring onions and a glass of Rioja. He ate, drank and listened to the conversations. When they laughed he tried to laugh along with them.

"What's wrong with you?" the landlord asked. "Why aren't you saying anything?"

"The weather's like November," Hunkeler said, "and I don't talk much in November."

"Is Hedwig still in Paris?"

"Yes, until the end of the year."

"Go and see her. You'll be there in five hours, she'll cheer you up."

"Perhaps I will pop over," he said.

He suddenly felt a wild longing for Hedwig welling up inside him. He came close to crying. He finished his glass, paid and went out.

*

Around eleven he went into the Singerhaus on Marktplatz. He went up to the first floor, where there was striptease. Sitting by the dance floor, where a naked woman was doing things with a rope, were businessmen, Americans apparently. Some were watching the woman, bored, others talking quietly among themselves. An oldish man beside them was reading a newspaper. Sitting by the bar at the back were two whores, whom Hunkeler knew: Angel, who came from Seville, or so she claimed, and Maria la Guapa from Colombia. Enrico Casali was also sitting there and, at the end of the bar, were two powerfully built, well-dressed men. One certainly weighed over two hundred pounds, the other had a solid-gold chain round his wrist. They had cups of coffee on the bar.

"*Hola, hombre*," said Angel when he sat down beside her, "*qué pasa, por qué vienes aquí? Quieres hacer el amor?*"

"No," Hunkeler said, "I'm here on business as usual."

He ordered a beer from Ismelda behind the bar.

"*Oi*, this business," said Angel, "it wears you out. Barbara la Gitana *está muerta*. She's dead. You won't bring her back to life. What do you say? Grass has grown over it. Buy us some champagne, we're both parched."

"If you like," he said. "Just a small bottle."

He watched Ismelda take a bottle out of the fridge, uncork it, fill the glasses and put the bottle in an ice bucket. A nice image, he thought: two beautiful women and a good bottle in an ice bucket.

The two men at the end of the bar had stopped talking. They slowly drank up their coffee, eyes on the bar. Then one put some money down.

Hunkeler poured his beer into the glass, carefully: he wanted it to have a nice head. Out of the corner of his eye

41

he saw Casali go over to the two men and talk to them quietly. They nodded, smiled briefly across at Hunkeler and one ordered two beers.

"Cheers," said Maria la Guapa, and Hunkeler clinked glasses with the two women.

Then Casali joined them. "What's up?" he asked. "Do you want to talk to me?"

"Yes," Hunkeler said, "if you've got the time."

"Of course I've got the time. A foggy Monday evening – nothing's going on."

They sat down at one of the little tables in the corner.

"What were you whispering to those two men just now?" Hunkeler asked.

"I told them you're a detective inspector and were looking for my girlfriend's murderer."

"And that calmed them down?"

"Yes, of course."

"What kind of men are they?"

"They're Turks. They work for a Turkish firm."

"Protection money, that kind of thing?"

Casali blew a speck of dust off his left cuff, in which there was a pearl. "How should I know? It's no concern of mine. At least they both behave decently. I don't imagine the police can prove anything against them?"

Hunkeler nodded. He knew that too.

"Yesterday, shortly before midnight," he said, "a man was murdered on Burgfelderplatz."

"I know," Casali said.

"The interesting thing about it," said Hunkeler, "is that the victim was a sixty-year-old former long-distance truck driver."

"That is indeed interesting."

"Why?"

Casali gave his charming smile. "But you know why. Swiss men who can drive long-distance trucks are much sought-after. I'm sure you know the route from Turkey to Switzerland across the Balkans."

Again Hunkeler nodded. He knew that as well. "Have you heard anything in particular?"

Casali thought. He had chiselled features, dark hair, light-blue eyes. All in all an elegant figure. And cold as an ice bucket.

"Nothing in particular, no."

"There's one other thing about this murder case," Hunkeler said, "that's also interesting. The man was strangled. With a cord or a thread. His left earlobe, in which there was a diamond, was cut open. With a pair of scissors apparently."

"And the money he had with him?"

"The money was still there."

"So not murder in the course of robbery," Casali said.

Something strange was happening to his face. The man stayed the way he was, quietly sitting on the red artificial-leather bench, his eyes fixed on the dance floor. Nothing moved in his face, neither a nostril nor a corner of his mouth. And yet it was suddenly a different face. Pale, pallid, snow-white in the beam of the revolving spotlight. He slowly took a packet of cigarettes out of his pocket, stuck a cigarette between his lips, lit it with a silver lighter and took a drag, his eyes still fixed on the dance floor. He did that mechanically, with precision, without hesitation, but strikingly slowly. When he blew out the smoke the blood returned to his face.

"That's certainly striking," he said, putting the lighter back in his pocket.

"I'm still assuming," Hunkeler said, "that it wasn't you who killed Barbara Amsler."

Casali smiled, a delicate smile round his thin lips. "As you know, I'm not a violent man. I'm the manager here in the Singerhaus and across the river in the Klingental. Barbara was my girlfriend. I loved her."

Hunkeler smiled back, as sweet a smile as he could manage. "I know. But you should leave the case to the police. You should work together with us."

"But I'm happy to do that, very happy. Now you must excuse me. I have business to see to in the Klingental."

He stood up, gave a brief bow and went to the bar. There he whispered something briefly in the ear of the beautiful Angel from Seville and went out.

Hunkeler stayed there watching Ismelda draw the beer for the men from Turkey. One waved to the two whores, but only Maria la Guapa went over. Angel gave Hunkeler a questioning look and he nodded. She came, slowly, she had all the time in the world. She sat down next to him, putting her hand on his knee.

"If you want," she said, "you can spend the night with me."

"That's not possible, I don't pay for love."

"*Hombre*, you have no problems otherwise?"

"I don't know," he said. "I'm an old man. And my girl-friend's away."

"But she's coming back?"

"Yes, I hope so. At the end of the year."

"You see, you need *una mujer*."

44

They went up to her room, which looked out over Marktplatz. He got undressed, lay down under the red plush blanket and curled up.

"No," she said once she'd got undressed too. "Get rid of the blanket. Just stretch out nicely there."

He felt her pull off the blanket and lay on his back. She knelt over him, kissing him slowly, almost lethargically, so that he could feel her hair on his face. Then she sat on him and took him inside her. Now he could feel her hair on his chest. In the mirror on the ceiling he could see her moving her beautiful bottom.

"Why did you do that?" he asked once it was over.

"*Por amor*, old man. And because you'll find Barbara's murderer."

She was still lying on top of him; she pulled the blanket over herself.

"And because Enrico said you should sleep with me for free."

"*Hombre*, would it bother you if that were true?"

"No, in fact it wouldn't. Only a satisfied policeman is a good policeman for Casali. Come on now, let's get some sleep."

He was woken by the clock in the Rathaus tower; it struck six times. He heard Angel, who was in his arms, snoring quietly. He looked at her neck, shimmering in the light from outside. You old goat, he thought proudly, you'll never forget how to do it. Then it occurred to him that it was bribery of an official. If it should come out, he'd be dismissed on the spot. That cunning Casali, that son of a bitch, now had something he could use against him. He carefully pulled his left arm out from under her neck. He went over to the window and looked down on the square. A little truck rolled up; he saw the rear lights and the yellow Alsace licence plate. Two figures got out, a woman and a man. The man climbed up onto the loading platform and pushed some crates over to the edge. The woman took them down and carried them over to the stall, one after the other. Then the man climbed down, got in and drove off. The woman stood there for a moment and looked across at the stall, then the crates. Clearly she was wondering whether to unpack the vegetables right away and set them out or to have a quick coffee at the Restaurant Hasenburg. She disappeared to the left, in the direction of the Hasenburg.

He got dressed, as quietly as he could, and went out of the room.

At nine he was driving out of town heading for the border. The cars were crawling along, the fog was so thick. Once he only just managed to avoid a truck that seemed to be taking building rubble to the gravel pits just outside town, by braking sharply and pulling over into a parking bay on the right. "Bastard!" he shouted, fist clenched. Then he had to grin at his rage, his enjoyment of swearing.

He knew that he had any amount of time. He'd take Suter's advice next weekend or the one after. He'd get out at the Gare de l'Est, inhale the familiar smell of the *Métro*. Have a coffee in the Café Buci. Eat oysters with a bottle of Chablis. And then crawl into bed with Hedwig.

At the border crossing he nodded to the Swiss guard, standing there, miserable in the fog. He could go to hell, and by the fastest route. All these men in uniform, these Suters and Madörins could go to hell, all these honourable men who'd suckled on uprightness with their mother's milk and never gone off the straight and narrow.

After Hésingue, while he was going up the road through the rolling fields, which he was aware of despite being unable to see them, he thought of Angel. It occurred to him that she'd said something important. Yes, she had said "*por amor*" and that he'd find Barbara's murderer. Where had she got that from? Did she know more than she was letting on? And then she'd said something else that had struck him. He tried to remember what, but couldn't.

He took his left hand off the wheel and sniffed it. It smelt of Angel. *Por amor*, what a great night it had been!

Up on the plateau at Trois Maisons, the sun forced its way through, a white light that almost tore the fog apart. He hesitated briefly at the turn-off to the village where his house was, but then continued straight ahead. Where was he heading? To Paris maybe? He could have got there by evening.

After Tagsdorf he turned off right, heading for Morschwil Pond. The fog was so thick that the facades of the houses could hardly be seen.

He turned off onto a field track, got out and peed on an apple tree that hadn't been pruned for ages. Up in the fog the white mistletoe berries were gleaming. On the ground were rotting apples, a wasp crouching on one. It had a strangely yellow gleam.

Then he heard a car approaching. It was coming from the direction of the pond. He saw the light of the headlamps and ducked behind a tree trunk. It was a small red Suzuki van with Basel plates, but he couldn't read them. In white on the side he could see the first three letters of a name: ALB... At the wheel was a young man with black hair. He only saw the man briefly, but he seemed familiar. Then the van was gone.

Hunkeler waited until he couldn't hear the engine any more. He got in his car, opened the window and had a cigarette. He spent quite a long time thinking about it, not really sure what to do. Why shouldn't a red van with a Basel plate actually drive along here? After all, Morschwil Pond was rented by Basel anglers.

But what about the man driving it? Did he look like a Basel angler after some Alsatian carp? No, he looked more like a man from the Balkans. And now Hunkeler remembered. The man had been sitting in the Billiards Centre the previous evening.

Hunkeler decided to be cautious. He got out and locked his car. He waited to see if he could hear anything. Nothing, no birds, not a sound. He went along the track, cautiously, keeping an eye on every bit of gravel. He entered the woods. Here the vehicle tracks were deeply embedded in the clay. There was water in them, and he walked in the middle between the tracks.

Then he saw the hut. It was a dark shape on the edge of the woods, standing out against the light fog. Beside it, Hunkeler knew, was the pond.

He waited a good five minutes. Once he heard something drop into the water. Or it could have been a fish jumping out, it was impossible to say.

When nothing moved, he slowly went out from under the trees to the hut. The door was open; he looked inside.

There were two tables there, benches, three bunk beds, a blue bottle of gas with a stove over it. There was no one there.

He looked across at the side of the pond. There was a man there sitting on a folding chair, a rod in his hand. He was wearing a black coat and a black hat. The man seemed to be asleep.

Hunkeler went over.

"Come closer," the man said. "I've been able to hear you for some time now, but it doesn't bother me."

"What doesn't bother you?" Hunkeler asked.

"All the people sneaking around here. You hear every sound in the fog. The guy who was here half an hour ago didn't think I could hear him. I heard his car, which he parked in the woods. I heard him go into the hut and fetch the bag, then go off into the woods again. I heard him start the engine and drive off. You were somewhat quieter, but I still heard you."

The man kept staring at the pond. Beside him he had an open tin of red maggots.

"What kind of man?" Hunkeler asked.

"I don't know."

"You didn't recognize him?"

"I didn't look. I have to keep my eye on the float out there."

He pointed at the water, where there was a red float.

"Are you after carp?"

"Yes."

The man had to be around seventy. He hadn't turned his head one single time.

"What kind of bag was it? Was it Hardy's bag?"

Now the man did turn his head. Bright, watery eyes, stubble.

"Are you a policeman?"

"I'm a detective inspector and I'm called Hunkeler. I'm investigating the case of Barbara Amsler, who was strangled in the middle of August."

"I heard about it. Alois Bachmann."

He looked out over the water again. The rod lay calm in his hands.

"Both were strangled," he said. "Hardy and Barbara. And both had something in their earlobe. I wouldn't mind having Hardy's diamond, that was quite a dazzler on his ear."

He gave a hoarse giggle. Then he spat into the water.

"It was a black travel bag," he said. "It belonged to Hardy. He brought it back from a trip to Zagreb. He deposited it here in the hut. It was his property. Hardy was my friend."

"Do you know what was in the bag?"

"Underwear, pyjamas, that kind of thing. Probably also some kind of drug that he was going to sell. From his trips to the Balkans. But you'll know that. Anyway, are you allowed to pursue your investigations on French soil?"

"I'm not pursuing any investigations. I'm just having a little chat with you."

Again Bachmann giggled. Then his body suddenly tensed, his look became fixed. The float out on the pond went down. The man counted out loud to twelve. Then he pulled the rod up, making the line vibrate. He slowly turned the reel and pulled a fish, a silvery gleam under the water, to the bank. He pulled it up onto the sand: it was a carp. The man bent down and tore the hook from its mouth. Then he watched the fish leaping up with powerful thrusts of its tail, trying to save itself. You could see the golden scales on its thick-set body, its wide-open mouth, its dark fins.

"An eight-pounder," the man said. "I pull them out and make them dance. Some need up to ten minutes before they're back in the water."

"You don't eat them?"

"I haven't eaten any carp since my wife died. I watch the way they open their mouths wide, as if they were gasping for air. Of course, it's not air they're gasping for but water. It only looks like that. My wife died in the middle of August, by the way."

He shook his head as if he thought that was funny.

"Someone strangling a person's just unacceptable. We all need air."

The fish lay there quietly, only its rear fins quivering slightly. Then it shot up, several times, fell into the water and disappeared. The man giggled, picked up the hook, put fresh maggots on it and cast the line.

"I wouldn't help you if Hardy wasn't my friend. But throttling, that's just unacceptable."

They both watched how the float was pulled into position by the weight and stayed there.

"It could be that you were lucky just now, when the man was here. He could have killed you as well."

"That wouldn't have bothered me. There's nothing worth living for any longer. I sit here fishing the whole day. It calms me down. I'm not afraid of these Albanians anyway. They're show-offs, there's nothing behind it."

"Is it your opinion Hardy was killed by an Albanian?"

"I know nothing about that," the man said. "I don't care about anything any more. You don't need to come back. If you want, you can have a look round the hut. The bag was under the rear bunk bed. Go now."

He leaned forward, resting his lower arms on his knees. He seemed to have fallen asleep in a second.

Hunkeler went into the hut and looked under the bunk bed. There was no black bag there.

He drove back down into the valley of the Hundsbach to his village, in second gear, keeping well to the right on the bends: Schwoben, Hausgauen, Hundsbach, Franken, Jettingen. By the side of the road he could see sweetcorn as high as a man, with withered leaves and yellow cobs. At one point the headlights of a corn harvester shone across the road, he saw the red monster in the fog. At St Imber's Cross, where he ought to have turned off, he continued straight ahead to Knoeringue. Münch's inn wouldn't be closed, he knew, it was Tuesday. He parked outside the inn, right beside the church. There were a good dozen vehicles there, cars and vans of suppliers and tradesmen who had come from the surrounding area to have lunch.

Before he went in he looked at the maxim that had been carved into the lintel of the house opposite:

> Sure is Death, unsure the Day.
> And know the Hour no man may.
> Therefore do Good. This thought hold fast:
> That every Hour may be thy Last.

A good maxim, he thought. And somehow comforting. For how could you live if you knew the hour of your own death in advance?

He waited a moment. Again there wasn't a sound to be heard. The fog seemed to swallow up every noise. And yet Alois Bachmann, waiting for his golden carp, had heard everything.

The restaurant was almost full. All men, some in overalls by which you could distinguish the carpenter, the plasterer, the chauffeur. The tables were covered with white paper, carafes of Côtes du Rhône and water. Lively chatter, some French, some Alsatian.

The *plat du jour* was semolina soup, veal tongue with capers, stewed apples as dessert. "Yes," Hunkeler said, "with soup and dessert. And a glass of wine."

He sat on the right, beside the entrance. He watched the landlord's wife bringing in the bowls and plates from the kitchen on her powerful upper arms, the waitress, no more than five foot tall, serving the men, putting the soup down in front of him and ladling it out.

So, he thought, as he finished his soup, you spend the whole night walking round the block where your woman lives. She's thrown you out for drinking too much beer in the local bars. You try living in your own apartment, but it's too empty, especially at night.

You stop drinking beer. You want to keep a clear head, as you know you need this woman. And since she also needs you, she'll forgive you after a few days or weeks and let you back in.

That was all normal and logical. And Hunkeler helped himself to a couple of slices of the veal tongue.

One evening you go to the Milchhüsli as usual and have an apple juice. Two Turkish mafia guys are there as well. They're playing darts and laughing too loud, but you guess that's not important. At nine you go out, do one or two circuits, but you can't keep going round in circles. So you sit down on the corner outside the Cantonal Bank, looking across at the apartment where she lives. You see the glimmer of the TV in her sitting room, a pale light that makes you feel jealous. You know you have to wait. You wait until the light goes out. The sitting room's dark, Hermine's going to bed.

That's the way it will have been, every evening the same. He took a mouthful of wine. It had a sour taste, but it was what everyone drank there.

It must have been like that every evening for two months. Apart from that particular evening. You're not looking across at Hermine's room, since the square is full of fog. You roll yourself up in your jacket, you lean back in the corner and you fall asleep. Never to wake again because someone strangles you while you're sleeping and cuts the diamond out of your ear. With a pair of scissors.

Was that still logical? No, it was unexpected and surprising. Who would do such a thing? What sort of person crossing the square shortly before midnight would have scissors on them anyway?

Hunkeler nodded as he pulled over the bowl of stewed apples. That was it, the scissors. That was the striking point, the detail that stood out.

The stewed apples were sprinkled with cinnamon and heavily sugared, and the tartness was refreshing.

Right. Then there were the other things, his journeys across the Balkans, the black bag in the anglers' hut. They were astonishing enough. Who would have believed Hardy was still working at his old job, going to Zagreb or Split, to Sarajevo or Tirana, to bring back a truck full of Bulgarian bolts or Turkish secateurs and get them safely across the border with his Swiss passport? And somewhere among the bolts or secateurs would be a few kilos of heroin. Who would have thought the old tramp had even managed to siphon off part of the stuff for himself, hide it in a hut in Alsace and sell it on his own account?

Hunkeler was almost certain that was the way it must have been. The man had disguised himself as a washed-out alcoholic living on a modest disability pension. Quite a guy then, that Hardy. He'd even managed to give a clue and have a diamond stuck in his ear. And no one had suspected anything.

Hunkeler grinned as he sipped his coffee with a sense of well-being. Bitter and sweet, those went wonderfully well together. It had been a long time since he'd felt so happy with himself. He'd eaten well. And he'd thought things over well. In the first place it wasn't very likely that he'd been murdered by the people for whom he'd made the journeys. They would have done it differently, more professionally, they'd have got rid of the corpse, at least for a few days or weeks, in order to gain time. In the second place there was the possibility that the scissors that had been used to cut his earlobe would give them a clue sooner or later. A clue that would possibly take him back to the Barbara Amsler case.

He was only marginally interested in trips to the Balkans and drugs. That was a lot of effort, he was too old and tired for that. He knew from experience that such cases usually remained unsolved. Those people were usually two or three steps ahead of the police. That was something for Detective Sergeant Madörin, that sharp hunting hound who would get his teeth into it. Moreover, Hunkeler wasn't even in charge of the investigation.

The second point interested him even more. He'd almost given up. True, he'd read Barbara Amsler's farewell letter again and again, he knew it off by heart. But so far the letter was all he'd had to go on, nothing else.

He'd get going on it again, patient and dogged, as was his way.

Hunkeler drove back to St Imber's Cross, turned off, crossed the stream and parked outside his house. There were still a few leaves on the walnut tree, the nuts were on the ground.

He went to the house, opened the door and let in the two cats that had heard the noise of the engine and run over. He went into the living room, put some kindling in the stove and lit it. He did the same in the kitchen, adjusting the damper so that it would warm the tiled stove. He put on some water to make tea and opened a tin of cat food. He added some beech logs and sat down at the kitchen table.

He looked out into the garden. The cherry tree and the meadow could still clearly be seen, the pear tree was just a silhouette and the poplar had disappeared in the fog. He saw the cock scratching about under the willow, the hens beside it, he could hear them cackling. He poured the water for the tea into the pot, waited and then filled a cup for himself. He just sat there for quite a long time, until one of the cats jumped up into his lap.

After he'd drunk three cups, he went out across the meadow to the old pigsty, where the hen coop was. There were three eggs in it. He collected them and put them on a plate in the kitchen. Then he fetched a basket from the sty and started collecting up the nuts. There were so many he had to get a second basket. He took them into the living room and put them on top of the stove to dry. He got undressed, went to bed, pulled the red-and-white check blanket over himself and fell asleep. He vaguely felt the two cats snuggling up against the back of his knees.

When he woke it seemed to be dark outside. He heard the sparrows making a racket in the hornbeams, therefore it must be early evening. He could hear the noise of the milking machine in the cowshed opposite, the jerky sucking, the clatter of a chain.

He got dressed and went across the road. The farmer's wife was busy. Six cows, four teat cups, one milk basin, two carrying frames with containers for the milk. One bull, three calves, a small dog squatting in the gangway and watching. From behind you could hear the pigs squealing and grunting. Hunkeler sat down on the bench in the shed.

"I took three eggs," he said. "I'll see to the hens this evening. And tomorrow morning as well."

She took the cups off the four teats of the cow's udder, picked up the basin and emptied the milk into the container in the frame. Then she went to the next cow and attached the teat cups again.

"I just do the same as always," she said. "When your car's parked outside in the evening, I know you're here. Otherwise I look after the hens. I'll pay you for the eggs, there aren't many at the moment."

"No, I want to pay you for your work."

"So we're quits if that's all right by you."

"It's certainly all right by me."

He always sat there in the evening, when he had time. He loved the sounds of the cowshed. The cows chewing, snorting, the sound of the dung landing in the manure gutter. But this evening it was different.

"What's wrong?" he asked. "Where's your husband?"

She pushed a strand of hair back under her headscarf and looked across at the dog, which immediately started to wag its tail.

"The dog doesn't really like it in the cowshed," she said, "he's got too sensitive a nose. But he still follows me round everywhere."

Hunkeler waited. He knew she was thinking about what she should and shouldn't tell him.

"He's at the inn in Jettingen. He's playing cards with his colleagues. They have no animals at home, they've taken early retirement."

Taking the fork, she lifted the dung into the cart, carefully, so that she took as little straw as possible.

"What we're doing here, what we've been doing here all our lives, my husband and I, isn't worthwhile any more. They wrote to tell us that. We're to give up producing milk. They've offered us a paltry pension. They're not going to take our milk any longer."

"And now?"

"He's at the inn. If he's going to be pensioned off, he says, then he wants to play cards too. Do you think that's right?"

"No," he said. "It can't be justified, because there's no justice."

"Don't say that, Monsieur. What does the *bon Dieu* say about that? *Ce n'est pas juste.*"

No, it wasn't fair, that was what he thought too.

"So what do you do with the milk?"

"We feed it to the calves and the pigs. You could make butter and cheese out of it. Aren't there enough people going hungry in the world?"

Hunkeler nodded. Yes, there were enough people going hungry. And there could also be enough butter and cheese to satisfy that hunger.

His phone rang. It was Lüdi. "Listen," he said, "something's happened that I want to tell you about."

"Just a moment, hold the line. I'll only be a minute."

He went back across the road and sat down in the kitchen.

"I'm ready now. I'm sitting in my kitchen in Alsace."

"I don't want to disturb you in your idyll," Lüdi said, and his hoarse bleating laugh could be heard.

"It isn't an idyll. They're not collecting the milk from my neighbours any longer."

"All the worse for him. Milk and butter and cheese, it's enough to make you cry. Tastes good, doesn't it?"

"Get on with it."

"Shortly before two this afternoon a red Suzuki van exploded on the Dreispitz industrial estate. Madörin drove over there immediately. He found the front licence plate. And do you know what?"

Yes, Hunkeler did know. But he said nothing.

"The van was registered to a firm called Albolives that appears to import olive oil. The firm belongs to an Albanian family called Binaku. The father's Ismail, the son Gjorg. And that Gjorg was sitting in the Billiards Centre last night."

"Well well, what a coincidence," Hunkeler said. "Where is he now?"

"He's disappeared. We've put out a warrant for his arrest. Madörin's had his father taken in, he's seventy-two. The magistrate wasn't very keen, but Madörin's determined to keep him inside."

"I want to see him," Hunkeler said.

"That you can, we've got him here. But there's even more. Hardy Schirmer regularly drove trucks from the Balkans back to Switzerland for this Albolives firm, about every two months."

"How did you find that out?"

"Hermine told us. It's her opinion that those trips weren't clean."

"What was he transporting?"

"Olive oil. First-class stuff, mostly from Greece and Turkey. Here Albo olive oil costs a good forty francs per litre."

"And in a few bottles with special labels there were presumably those plastic bags with the white powder. Is that what you think?"

"Yes, that's exactly what I think."

"Just a minute," said Hunkeler, "I need to think."

"What are you thinking about? Do you know something?"

Yes, Hunkeler knew far too much. He ran over things quickly in his mind. It was no use, there was no way out. Alois Bachmann knew he'd been at the pond, and he'd tell people about it.

"Hey, are you still there?"

"Yes," Hunkeler said. "As you know, I'm not involved in the case. What's more, I've been more or less put on ice. Well, this morning I took a walk, by Morschwil Pond. A

Basel angling club, of which Hardy was a member, rents it. In the fog I saw a red Suzuki van drive off. I couldn't quite read the writing on it."

"Now you know what it was," Lüdi said drily.

"A man who was fishing there – he's called Alois Bachmann – told me several things. Just before I arrived, he'd heard a man creep up and go into the hut, fetch something and then go. He said he didn't look because it was nothing to him. However, he was sure the man had taken a black bag that belonged to Hardy. And he was equally sure that this bag contained underwear and drugs. He also told me about Hardy's Balkan trips. He told me everything he knew. And now I've reported all this to you. I've done what I'm supposed to do, haven't I?"

"Depends how you look at it. When exactly were you at the pond?"

"How should I know, I didn't look at my watch."

It was no use, it had to come out. He heard Lüdi's quiet laugh.

"Shortly before midday."

"You're a little late with it," Lüdi said.

Hunkeler thought feverishly. "Suter expressly forbade me to get involved in the case," he said. "That's why I didn't report it."

"No, that's no good. If you'd reported it right away, we could perhaps have intercepted the van."

"There was no signal. The battery was flat. I had to charge it first. Then I was going to call, but you beat me to it."

"It sounds a bit weak," Lüdi said, "but OK, I'll help you. We'll sort it out. The next meeting is tomorrow at 4 p.m."

"Thank you, my angel."

He put his phone back down on the table. A blasted thing it was, unavoidable, inescapable, he hated it. He could only hope that Lüdi's call hadn't been checked.

He went out into the corridor and unplugged his landline. He wanted to be unobtainable for as long as possible, ideally for the rest of his life. He was in a sticky situation again, in the soup up to his eyeballs. Of course he should have reported his visit to Morschwil Pond immediately. The Suzuki would possibly not have blown up, and Gjorg Binaku might have been caught.

But he hadn't wanted to. He gave a bitter laugh as he went out across the meadow to the old pigsty. The hens were there already, waiting for their food. Hunkeler took a handful of grains out of the brown-paper sack by the door and scattered them over the floor. He watched them pecking and cackling. He put the light out and bolted the door.

He cooked the eggs and ate them. Then he fetched a bottle of beer from the shed and sat down at the TV. He zapped around until he found a black-and-white film with Jean Gabin. A fairly young woman, so much he deduced, had had a daughter by a doctor. The doctor had gone off with another woman, which drove the younger woman to despair. She was admired and loved by an old writer, but she refused to get involved with him despite claiming to love him. In reality, though, she was sleeping with various other men. When Hunkeler started watching, her daughter had just disappeared. A kidnapping, Jean Gabin suspected. But who was the kidnapper: the doctor, the writer, or some person hired by the mother as a trick to get the doctor back?

Hunkeler would have liked to find out; the film was so good he would have liked to follow it through to the end.

However, as his eyelids were closing, he switched off the TV, opened the window and went to bed.

At nine the next morning he drove back to Basel. He'd slept for over ten hours. The high road through Trois Maisons was almost empty, the early morning frenzy of commuters was over. He drove at a leisurely pace through the fog, he wasn't in a hurry. He knew that he was going to have to be patient, look round, ask around, for days, for weeks on end.

At half past nine he went into the Sommereck. Edi was sitting in his usual place, two Zurich tabloids in front of him.

"Look," he said, "just read that. It's horrible. That's yesterday's edition. You can clearly see the cut in his ear."

Hunkeler ordered a cup of milky coffee. He didn't feel like looking at the newspaper.

"Why didn't the *Basler Zeitung* have that?" Edi asked. "An old man has his neck broken and a diamond torn out of his ear right on your doorstep. And all the *BaZ* has is a brief report. And the rock is said to have been worth around 30,000 francs. Where did Hardy get that? Fat Hauser has been saying he was carrying drugs in the trucks. Do you know anything about that?"

Hunkeler shook his head, had a drink, then reached for the newspapers after all. In the previous day's edition there was a big picture of Hardy, dead and with the wounds to his throat and ear. In the latest edition Hermine could be seen, stony-faced. Beside it was a longish report on Bernhard Schirmer. Clearly a decent fellow who had taken some hard knocks in life but who, thanks to his unrelenting energy, had always managed to get back on his feet again.

The wreck of the burnt-out van was also to be seen. Hunkeler glanced through that report as well, looking for the name Binaku. It wasn't there. Even fat Hauser hadn't been that sharp.

So those smart guys from Zurich were thinking of making it into a substantial story.

Edi came out of the kitchen with a plate. "That's hare pie from the Markgräflerland, straight from the hunt. With spring onions and gherkins it's a revelation. Would you like some too?"

"No, not so early in the morning."

"It's almost ten. At that time a man needs something in his belly." He hacked a piece off, put it in his mouth and closed his eyes in rapture.

"All this guzzling's going to kill you," Hunkeler said. "Can't you give it up?"

"No, I don't want to. Eating's such a joy. And I want to die joyfully. This diamond," he went on as he cut off another piece, "it was very striking, of course. But no one suspected Hardy was such a sly bugger. I did realize that he wasn't a true alcoholic. I do have an eye for that. He did always have a glass of beer in front of him, but he could sit there for an hour with the same glass. An alcoholic couldn't do that."

"Did he come here often?"

Edi wiped a few drops of sweat off his forehead. Clearly the pie was making him warm.

"Not very often. The last time was about ten days ago. He was here with two of those mafia guys."

"What did they look like?"

"Just the way those guys do. Well dressed, a bit overweight but in good trim. They looked around here as if the place already belonged to them."

"Did the smaller one have a solid-gold chain on his left wrist?"

"There, you see," Edi said, "I was sure you knew the pair of them."

In his apartment Hunkeler sat down at the kitchen table and thought things over. He knew that there were lots of problems awaiting him at 4 p.m. Most of all he'd have liked to make off, get on the train for Paris right now. Seurat and Sisley, he thought, the pure light.

He went into the sitting room to fetch a book on modern painting. He opened it at the *pointillistes* and looked at a river by Seurat with a sailing ship and a rowing boat, and a landscape by Sisley consisting of single spots. He saw the landline phone on the table. There were two new messages. The first was from Hedwig: "Where have you got to, Peter? Is anything wrong?" The second was from the head of the Basel Rural District Police, Füglistaller.

He called Hedwig. He got her answerphone. "No," he said, "I'm fine. I've been over in Alsace and had a great sleep." Then he called Füglistaller and arranged to meet over lunch in the Spitzwald restaurant.

He went back down onto the street and drove to Allschwil Pond. He knew the place very well, he'd already been there several times. There were two benches from which you looked down onto the water. It was there that the angler had been standing on that 14 August, the one who had been after carp with a strong line. But he was presumably shocked when he started to pull in the line. What had taken the bait couldn't be a carp, it was too heavy, too sluggish. A catfish perhaps, he thought, expecting long and vigorous resistance. But there was none. He slowly turned the reel, always prepared for some fierce thrashing of the tail. It was Barbara Amsler's corpse he pulled out.

She had appeared down there, her white body coming out of the darkness, her arms, her legs, her hair. The angler was so shocked that he didn't pull her right out. But she couldn't sink back down again, the hook had caught in her dress.

Hunkeler couldn't help himself, he stared into the water, as if another woman's body would appear there. He felt the hairs rise on the back of his neck, he felt the drops from his wet hair rolling down his cheeks. Then he tore himself away.

He decided to take a walk along the stream, through the woods, and go up the back way to the Spitzwald restaurant. He fetched his raincoat and umbrella from the car and set off.

He passed the parking area of the Basel Rifle Club, which had its shooting range where at weekends they aimed at targets three hundred yards away. Shooting, an old tradition, said some, an important part of Swiss culture. An unnecessary disturbance of the peace, thought the others, stupid men blasting away. Hunkeler, who had learned to use a carbine during basic training, couldn't care less.

Parked were around thirty cars with caravans. They'd been there for five weeks now. That too was a contentious issue, as the caravans belonged to a clan of Romanian

Gypsies. Travellers, some thought, an ancient culture that had to be helped, given places to stay. Foreign riff-raff, others thought, ruffians and thieves.

Hunkeler couldn't care less about that either, especially as the place was in the Basel Rural District.

There were lights on in two of the caravans. He saw a girl sitting on a step eating an apple. In front of her a dog was wagging its tail.

Behind the trunk of an aspen tree further over by the river Sergeant Hasenböhler of the Basel Rural District CID could be seen. He had a pair of binoculars and was watching the girl. Hunkeler went up to him quietly and tapped him on the shoulder.

"You won't see anything in this fog," he said, "you'll have to get closer."

"Oh God, Hunkeler," Hasenböhler said, "you gave me a nasty shock there. What are you doing here?"

"I'm going for a walk, up to the nature reserve. Then I might have a run round the keep-fit trail. To keep fit. So that we can have a go at these damned Gypsies together, yes?"

"You just go ahead and make your jokes. You're well off, you are, you're not responsible for keeping this place clean. They just throw everything away in the woods, shit behind every tree. And I bet that apple the girl's eating was stolen, probably from the Migros supermarket at the crossroads over there. They pinch anything they can lay their hands on."

"It's just petty larceny, and apples still grow on the trees."

"Are you pulling my leg?" Hasenböhler asked. "They don't just make off with apples but with TV sets as well."

"Walking past the checkout with them hidden under their clothes, right?"

"Oh, bawl me out if you have to," Hasenböhler said. "Just go and have a walk, just go."

Hunkeler followed the stream through the foggy wood. He came to a horizontal bar on the fitness course. A man of around sixty was hanging from it, jerking himself up several times. At every pull-up he made a squeaky noise.

A quarter of an hour later he reached the nature reserve, which consisted of a system of several ponds. The largest was down in the valley. Hunkeler went to the edge and tried to see something, a frog, a toad, a newt. But they were presumably already enjoying their winter sleep. A pair of tufted ducks swam past, the female in front, the male behind. He saw its crest.

Füglistaller was already sitting at the table when he entered the Spitzwald Inn. They were the same age, and they liked each other very much. They ordered schnitzels with French fries and cucumber salad and half a bottle of Beaujolais.

"That idiot Hasenböhler," Hunkeler said, "is standing behind an aspen tree outside the Rifle Club, watching a girl eating an apple. What's the point of that?"

Füglistaller poured them some wine. "If we do nothing," he said, "people go on about us not doing our duty. If we *do* do something, then there's an outcry that we're racists. Just let Hasenböhler get on with his observation. Then people will be happy."

"Actually, it would be an ideal place for them. They have to be somewhere or other."

"People are the way they are," Füglistaller said. "Most of them don't like Gypsies. At most in operettas."

"O play to me, Gypsy," Hunkeler hummed, "the moon's high above, play me your serenade, the song that I love."

He cut off a piece of his schnitzel, shook salt over his fries. They were just right, crisp on the outside, still soft inside. They ate slowly, deliberately, in silence, the way they always did when they were together. They needed time to get attuned to each other.

Then Füglistaller started to talk.

"What have we got on the Barbara Amsler case? We know about her childhood, her background. We know that she'd been living in Basel for eleven years. That she had an apartment on Schneidergasse. That she'd been working as a prostitute for six years. That she picked up clients in the Singerhaus and the Klingental. That Casali was her pimp, though he won't admit it. That she was liked by her colleagues, which is rare among whores. That she paid her taxes punctually.

"Moreover, we know that at eleven in the evening of that 11 August she was approached by an oldish man. That shortly after one in the morning of the twelfth, she left the Klingental with that man. That for the next day and the two following days she was unobtainable. And that late in the afternoon on 14 August she was pulled out of Allschwil Pond by an angler. That in all probability rape can be excluded, but not normal sexual intercourse. That she was strangled before she was thrown into the water, and it was done with a length of raw silk. That her left earlobe was cut open with scissors, that the pearl that was there has disappeared. That she left behind a letter in her apartment that indicated a great love."

He emptied his glass and ordered another bottle.

"We've worked well together," he said, "as so often before. We've established a description of the man who approached her. Around sixty, dressed in the usual jacket and tie, not tall, not small, not fat, not thin. Light eyes, thin lips, complexion on the dark side. No rings on his fingers. He spoke some Basel German, but not pure. The only striking thing about him was his mop of grey hair. Angel, who was also in the Klingental, thought it was a wig. He paid for champagne but only drank a little. According to Angel, he was certainly nervous but managed to conceal his nervousness. Have I left out anything important?"

Hunkeler pushed his plate away. He wasn't enjoying the food any more.

"So you're going to give up," he said.

"No," Füglistaller said, pouring himself more wine, "I refuse to give up. But we had three men assigned to the case, and with you it's four. And nothing's come of it. We have no suspect. It could have been any sixty-year-old of average height I came across in the street. As you know, we have a new case now that some of the press is giving headline treatment. Bernhard Schirmer, the Albolives van that blew up on the Dreispitz estate. The Albanian, Gjorg Binaku, who's disappeared. And Bernhard Schirmer drove trucks back from the Balkans for Albo. We're not going to let that rest. Albo is registered in Binningen, that's in our area."

"I assume," Hunkeler said, "that Suter asked you for this."

"True. But I still make the decisions myself, and that seems to me to be right."

Hunkeler picked up his glass and slowly emptied it. It was a superior Beaujolais, but it still didn't taste right.

"Frau Amsler and Hardy both had their earlobes cut open," he said. "Who would do that kind of thing? If it was the same man who did it twice, then he'll do it a third time. If we want to stop that happening, then we have to find the man who murdered Barbara Amsler and Hardy Schirmer. Don't you agree?"

"Yes, that's what we ought to do. But I'm short of men."

"I've been put on the sidelines," Hunkeler said. "I assume you've been informed."

"Yes. And I'm not happy about that, I can tell you."

"Still," Hunkeler said, "I can't abandon the Amsler case. I refuse to. And I'm sure the Schirmer case is linked to it."

"Right," said Füglistaller, "you're keeping at it. And if you want to know anything about Albo or Gjorg Binaku, I'll help you."

At three Hunkeler went into the Waaghof. He felt good, more relaxed than he had been for a long time. He'd found an ally in Füglistaller, who'd supply him with information. The old guard, he thought, the old soldiers, they stuck together through thick and thin.

Then it occurred to him that he'd had quite a lot of wine. Three halves had been on the final bill. That was a litre and a half, a bottle for each of them. He never drank that much at lunchtime. In the evening certainly, in the evening yes, then off to bed for a good sleep. At lunchtime no, at lunchtime one glass and then back to work.

He had a wry grin on his face as he walked along the corridor to the cells for people awaiting trial. He was definitely a bit tipsy.

The guard, Alfred Kaelin, was sitting asleep at his little table. There was a crossword puzzle in front of him.

"Alfred Kaelin," Hunkeler said, "wake up."

The man, around fifty with a prominent beer belly, woke with a start, horrified. "Inspector," he said. "Sorry. Surely I didn't fall asleep?"

He quickly picked up the crossword puzzle and put it in the drawer.

"I would very much like to talk to Herr Binaku," Hunkeler said. "What's his first name?"

"Ismail. Ismail Binaku. He speaks excellent German. But you're not allowed to talk to him."

"And why not?"

"Because you've been specifically excluded from this matter. I'm sorry, but those were Herr Madörin's express instructions."

"I've been the inspector here for years," Hunkeler said. "And I wish to talk to Ismail Binaku, who has been detained here. At once. And in private."

"Go on then, on your head be it."

Kaelin stood up and led the way back down the corridor, where he opened cell number nine.

"The door is to stay open," Hunkeler ordered. Kaelin nodded and withdrew.

In the cell an old, well-groomed man with white curly hair was sitting at the table reading a book.

Hunkeler introduced himself. "I would like to talk with you," he said.

"Go ahead." The man pointed to the bed. Hunkeler sat down.

"What are you reading?" he asked.

"*Broken April*, a novel by Ismail Kadare. It's about blood feuds in Albania."

"Why are you reading the book in a German translation when you're Albanian yourself?"

"Because I love the language of Goethe and Heine above all else. My father was Albanian, my mother came from Graz. We lived in Sarajevo. I went to the German school there. Is that what you wanted to know?"

He really was a well-turned-out gentleman, a handsome old man.

"I'm seventy-two now. I've been through quite a lot. I've lived in Cairo and Beirut. I set up an olive oil business here in Basel thirty years ago. But I've never been in prison before."

Hunkeler looked round. The bed, on which he was sitting, a table, a chair, the door to the lavatory and shower. The barred window.

"I'm not involved in your case," he said. "I'm here purely out of curiosity. I'm wondering who killed Bernhard Schirmer."

"I heard about that. But Albo has nothing to do with it. I swear to that," he said, putting his hand over his heart.

Hunkeler looked at his outstretched hand. Clean, manicured nails, a gold ring with a black stone in which a bird was engraved.

"What kind of bird is that?"

"That's a falcon, our family coat of arms. The falcon sees everything. And it kills with one strike of its claws."

"Does your son Gjorg have a ring like that?"

"Of course, we all wear one."

"You do know that they are looking for your son. He should come and give us information about the red Suzuki, about its load, for example."

Binaku gave an obliging smile.

"You're asking out of pure curiosity, are you, Inspector?"

Hunkeler smiled back, sweet as honey.

"The red Suzuki had a consignment of olive oil," Binaku said. "Olive oil is the most valuable product of the Mediterranean. A people that possesses olive trees will never perish. My son and I deal in that product."

"Who, then, could have an interest in blowing up that product?"

"In the Balkans," the handsome man said, "one animal hunts another. The skies are swarming with birds of prey. The powerful eagle pursues the falcon with wings widespread. The Berisha family. The ground is teeming with poisonous snakes. The Prela family. The falcon grasps them and throws them in the air."

"Is that why you're reading a book about blood feuds?"

"I'm reading it because Ismail Kadare is a great novelist. You ought to read it too, Inspector. Then you would understand certain things better."

Hunkeler noticed how hot he was getting. The room was presumably overheated. Moreover, the man seemed to have a strange power over him that he could hardly resist. Was it his dark, calm voice, was it his assured, almost serene look? But what was the point of all this stuff about eagles and snakes and blood feuds?

"May I smoke?" he asked.

"Please don't," the old man said. "I can't stand it."

"It's too hot in here," Hunkeler declared, standing up. "And I need a cigarette. Come with me."

Binaku remained sitting in his chair. He smiled politely.

"Am I allowed to leave this cell?"

"We'll go to the cafeteria. I presume you won't run off?"

"What an idea, Inspector! A falcon doesn't run away from a dog."

Now what does he mean by that, Hunkeler wondered, whom is he referring to as a dog? He was about to turn round and ask the handsome old man. He briefly saw him about to make a short, swift movement.

When he came to again, he was lying curled up on something hard. He felt that immediately. He opened his eyes and saw a plank bed, a chair. And a cell door that was closed.

Then he felt the pain. It was in the left side of his chin, it was everywhere in his skull. He cautiously moved his tongue. There was something that didn't belong there. And at the bottom on the left there was something missing that really ought to have been there.

He sat up and spat out two teeth. It had been a powerful blow, a clean right hook from the handsome old man, right on the chin. He started to grin, but then he felt the pain in his temples again.

He lay down again and tried to breathe calmly, to concentrate on the situation he found himself in. It was bloody awful, he saw that at once. He held his breath so that he could hear better. He could hear nothing, not even from outside. He took his watch out of his trouser pocket: it was shortly before four. So the meeting would go ahead without him. Now he did grin; that was OK by him.

Then he remembered his mobile phone and what was inevitable, inescapable. He rolled over on his belly, pulled himself up onto the bed with both hands and sat down. It was a painstaking business, but he managed it. He wondered whether to call the police emergency number. No, he didn't want that, he didn't want to see any laughing policemen just now. He punched in the number of Frau Held at the reception desk.

"It's me, Hunkeler. I'm sitting in number nine. The door's locked. Come and get me out, please."

"My God," she said, "why aren't you at the meeting? But Herr Binaku's in number nine."

"Not any longer, I'm stuck in here now. I suspect that Herr Binaku walked politely past you a quarter of an hour ago."

"Was it that handsome old man?"

"What do you mean, handsome? He had a bloody hard right hook. And Herr Kaelin has presumably fallen asleep over his crossword puzzle again. Would you please be good enough to give him a kick up the backside so he'll come and unlock the door."

"The things you get up to," she said. "I'll come at once."

She took him to the cantonal hospital in her own car. At first she'd wanted to call an ambulance, but he'd said no. Then she got Dr Ryhiner out of the meeting. Then Lüdi and

Madörin had come running over. Then Suter had appeared and given poor Kaelin a dressing-down. Hunkeler had been spared that, his face looked too battered.

It was all useless, Ismail Binaku had vanished.

Hunkeler shut them all out. He didn't want Ryhiner's help, he didn't want Lüdi's concern, he didn't want to see Madörin's anger, he just wanted to be driven to the cantonal hospital by Frau Held.

The diagnosis was concussion: ten days in bed, then two weeks' convalescent leave.

That evening he was lying in a single room in the cantonal hospital, having been given a strong sedative.

He called Hedwig.

"Listen, I've a confession to make, but it's not that bad."

"If you've been unfaithful," she said sharply, "keep it to yourself. Is it an affair?"

"No, not an affair. Someone knocked me out."

"Oh really?"

She seemed relieved. She thought for a while, then he could hear concern in her voice. "Is that why you're talking in such a funny way?"

"I'm talking in a funny way because two of my left bottom teeth are missing. And I've got concussion."

Now she did become furious. "You are and always will be a lout. Why can't you use your aggressiveness productively? Why do you have to get into a fight?"

"I wasn't in a fight. I was punched. A prisoner on remand gave me a right hook. It was enough to make me see stars."

"And the prisoner?"

"He's disappeared."

"My God, Peter, what have you been getting up to? And now you think I'm going to drop everything here and come and look after you?"

"Yes," he said, "as soon as possible."

She came the next evening. Hunkeler was already in bed, in his green nightshirt. He'd tried to eat the evening meal, semolina with cinnamon accompanied by plum puree. He'd pushed the plate away, he didn't want it. Moreover, the places where the teeth were missing hurt.

Then the door opened and Hedwig came in. She came over to his bed; she was wearing a new, black-and-white-check jacket.

"How are you then?" she asked, her voice full of concern.

"Not well. But what's that jacket?"

"I bought it in a boutique on the Boulevard St Germain. Do you like it?"

"Come here," he said.

She bent down to give him a kiss. He embraced her, pulling her down onto the bed.

"Are you crazy?" she said. "We can't do that in a hospital bed. It'll roll away."

"Let it roll," he said, "that won't bother us."

Peter Hunkeler was sitting at the kitchen table in Alsace. It was 7 November, nine o'clock on a Friday morning.

He'd had a copious breakfast, the first time he'd had an appetite for a week. Two fresh eggs he'd got from the hen coop. Four slices of bacon he'd bought in the Jettingen butcher's. Accompanied by white bread and a pot of tea. He'd been careful to chew on the right side, the left still hurt. He lit a cigarette, his first for a week. Things were going quite well.

He picked up the letter the senior public prosecutor had sent him. Even though he knew it by heart, he still read it through again. Suspended from duties with immediate effect, his office to be cleared out and keys handed in by a week on Monday.

He got up, opened the stove door and put the letter on the fire. So what now, old man? Should he buy some Bermuda shorts, a Hawaiian shirt and a sombrero and get on a flight to Tenerife? Or just get the train straight to Paris? Or stay stuck in the fog here in Alsace, buy two donkeys and look after the hens? No, he wouldn't do that. At least not while there was some guy running round in Basel strangling people and slitting their ears open.

He took out his notebook and checked out his appointments.

Monday, 10 November: clear out office and hand in key.
Friday, 21 November: cardiologist, Dr Naef.
Saturday, 22 November: dentist, Dr Steinle.
Monday, 24 November: urologist Dr von Dach.

He was faced with a general overhaul, a major service for an old wreck. Moreover, he was his own master now.

He gave a sly grin. Basically it suited him very well that he was now a man of leisure. They hadn't been able to find the least trace of the culprit, the ear-slitter, with the usual police methods. The investigation into the Amsler case had been shelved. Füglistaller had withdrawn his men. And their efforts in the Schirmer case would peter out after weeks or months, of that he was quite sure.

He felt slightly dizzy and held onto the table and waited until it was over. Why had he lit a cigarette again? Could he really not give up this stupid habit?

What had just come into his mind? Had the word "slitter" not just occurred to him? What did it mean? Slit, slitter, slit-ear?

His head wasn't clear enough for him to think this right through. He went over and lay down on the bed. He picked up the novel he'd bought, *Broken April* by Ismail Kadare. He started to read, but after a few sentences the book fell out of his hand.

He was woken by the roar of a corn harvester driving past his house. The bed was trembling, woodworm sawdust trickling down from one of the ceiling beams. He saw the light of the headlamps sweep across the room. The rattling died away down into the valley.

He decided to take a walk. Cool, damp air, muted light, slow strides, that would do him good. He put on his boots and his old jacket, and a felt hat on his head. He followed the trail of the harvester, whose huge wheels had torn up the clay. He entered the wood. There was only a little light, giving the damp tree trunks a dull gleam. He heard the creak of a branch. He saw two men disappear behind the trunks of the beech trees – the fog seemed to have swallowed them up. Then they could be seen again, though not very clearly, two dark figures.

He'd stopped immediately when they'd appeared. They were wearing black jackets and were carrying white plastic sacks. He heard them talking, in a language he couldn't understand. They only noticed him when they were right in front of him. They started, hesitated and walked past without saying hello. He saw that the sacks were full to the top with snails. He watched them as they disappeared into the fog; they didn't look back at him.

He went through Knoeringue and followed the country road via Muespach-le-Haut to the Cäsarhof. He went in and ordered Münster cheese with caraway seeds and mineral water.

Why had he been so startled in the woods, why had he suddenly become so timorous? Was it the punch from old Binaku or was it being suspended without notice? What kind of men were those two, what were they going to do with the snails?

There were three old women in the inn, nicely done up in flowered dresses and permanent waves. They were eating cakes and drinking coffee. They were telling each other in the local dialect, a mixture of French and German, what was happening among their relatives: *d'Fröi vo mim neveu, dr mari vo minere Schweschter, dr beaufrère, la nièce, dr Onggle.* Everything was clearly as well as it could be in the extended family.

He decided to go and see Stallinger, the old actor, who lived in Heiligbronn near Leymen. He walked straight on through the woods, taking care not to lose his way. He walked slowly, he didn't yet feel really fit, but walking was doing him some good.

It was already starting to get dark when he reached the track to Heiligbronn. So his sense of direction was still in working order, he thought with a satisfied grin. He avoided the puddles in the gravel. Strange, he thought, all this water; after all, it hadn't rained for a long time.

He saw a dark animal going along the path in front of him. It wasn't in a hurry, it hadn't noticed him. Then his boot struck a stone. The animal stood up and looked at him. It was a badger, he saw the dark stripes on its snout. Without moving, they stared each other in the eye for some time. Then the badger went back down on all fours and disappeared, heading towards the edge of the woods.

Hunkeler had watched it, spellbound. It was an animal out of a fairy tale, a magic animal. He looked the way it had gone, heard the rustling. Then all was quiet again.

He was still looking across to the edge of the woods, which could be made out as a bright line in the fog. He tried to establish what he could see there. He walked over slowly, going through nettles and damp undergrowth. He came to a car. Someone had driven it across the meadow into the scrub, the tracks could clearly be seen. Someone had removed the licence plates. Someone had poured something over the vehicle and set it alight. And someone had been sitting in the passenger seat while it burnt.

He took the packet of cigarettes out of his pocket and lit one. He looked up into the empty crowns of the beeches, saw the branches disappearing into the fog. At the third puff he felt dizzy. He threw the cigarette away but picked it up again, extinguished it and put it back in the packet. No, he thought, please not again. Who was that following him?

He took out his flashlight and shone it on the wreck. Apart from the skull, teeth and bones there was little to be seen. He shone the light all around the area. The bark of the surrounding trees had burst open, the heat had presumably made the sap boil.

His eye was caught by something that had been cut into one of the trunks. Someone had taken the trouble to carve the shape of an animal into it with a sharp knife. A writhing snake, its tail down, its mouth wide open, pointing up, its tongue forked.

Hunkeler went out of the woods and into the meadow. He walked slowly, trying to breathe calmly. He didn't want to see any more snakes or falcons, or any eagles. He'd had enough of burnt-out and blown-up cars, of strangled and charred corpses. That was nothing to do with him any more, he had that in writing from the senior prosecutor. Finding the wrecked car was a stupid coincidence. It was the fault of the badger, the mythical creature, sly Master Brock. Had it all been a dream? And what would happen if he forgot the dream?

After a few hundred yards he came to Heiligbronn Chapel, where Stallinger's farmhouse was. After a cursory knock on the door he went in. The old actor was sitting at the table in his lounge with a volume of poems open in front of him. He was pleased when he saw Hunkeler.

"Listen," he said, "what a magnificent poem I've just read:

"Shipped Oars

Drops fall from my shipped oars
Slowly into the depths below.

Nothing to distress me or irk me now:
A painless day just dripping down.

Below me – oh, vanished from the light,
My fairer hours still dreaming bright.

Yesterday is calling from the depths of blue:
Are some of my fellows still up there with you?

"It's by Conrad Ferdinand Meyer. When you get as old as I am it's only the present moment that matters. The quiet, the light, the fog. Will you have a drop of wine?"

"Over here at the edge of the woods," Hunkeler said, "there was something burning recently. A huge fire. Didn't you see anything?"

"I did. It was two days ago, in the middle of the night. It really blazed. It will presumably have been the lads from Leymen. When they come out of the inn at midnight and don't want to go home yet, they make a fire now and then."

"No," Hunkeler said, "it was a car that was burnt. And there was someone in the car. Call the police immediately."

"Sorry? There was someone in the car? That's none of my business. You call if you think it's necessary."

Officer Herbst from the Leymen force drove up after half an hour. He was very nervous. They'd never had a charred body in the area. He'd reported it to Mulhouse, he said.

They'd send specialists over that evening, he couldn't do much about it himself.

Though resisting, he let them take him over to the wrecked car.

Around seven, six firefighters from the Leymen brigade came, with gleaming helmets and hatchets at their sides. They too went briefly over to the edge of the woods to have a look.

At eight they were all sitting in the actor's living room with red wine, ham and bread. It was *scandaleux*, they said in their mixture of French and Swiss German, to burn a car with a man in it over there in the woods, *affreux*, horrible, a disgrace. Who would do such a thing? Doubtless those people from North Africa, *ces Arabes*, riff-raff they were, hoodlums, they were sick to death of *ces salauds*.

At ten they decided to pop over to Bertelé's for a quick drink. Only the actor and the gendarme stayed behind, with two of the firefighters, who were to show the specialists, who would arrive soon from Mulhouse, the way from the road to the crime scene.

Around midnight the firefighters drove Hunkeler back to his house. You've a lovely place here, they said as they had another beer in the kitchen. A bit *très vieux*, a bit of a ruin, but cosy. It had been a nice evening, it had been pleasant *d'avoir fait la connaissance*.

The next morning the telephone out in the corridor rang while Hunkeler was having his breakfast. It was a Monsieur Bardet, *chef des services techniques*. Could he come round? He had a few questions.

Bardet was a tall, gangling guy of around thirty. He spoke perfect German, he'd studied in Karlsruhe, he said. They sat in the kitchen drinking coffee.

Could he please tell him, Bardet said, precisely how he'd found the wrecked car. He'd heard he was a Basel policeman. And a Basel policeman finding a car with a charred corpse in it, just across the border with France, was a bit odd.

"I'm an inspector with the Basel CID," Hunkeler said, "but was suspended a few days ago."

Bardet lit a second cigarette. Clearly he was a chain-smoker. "Why?"

"Because I made too many mistakes."

"A man of your experience makes too many mistakes? Oh, come off it."

"Two people were strangled in Basel. There's a theory that one of the victims, a man called Bernhard Schirmer, who had clearly been working for an Albanian drug organization, had been executed by that organization."

"And you don't believe that theory?"

"No."

"Ten days ago," Bardet said, "the Basel police put out a warrant for a young Albanian called Gjorg Binaku. His van had been blown up. With explosives or some kind of fuel?"

"I'm old and stupid, I don't know."

"And that's why you were suspended," Bardet said with a grin.

"I've come here to Alsace to recuperate. I was knocked out by the father of that Gjorg Binaku. I'd gone to see him where he was being held on remand. He hit me and escaped. I assume there was a warrant put out for him as well."

"True, his first name's Ismail."

"I went for a walk through the woods yesterday. I saw a badger. I followed it and then found the wrecked car. Pure chance."

"Really?" Bardet asked, with a cold, inquisitive look.

Hunkeler poured more coffee. "Yes, it was."

"We haven't got any photos, neither of the father nor of his son. Which doesn't surprise me. Those kind of people don't like being photographed. How might he have looked?"

Careful, old man, he told himself, he's a smart guy. But he still told him.

"On 28 October I went to Morschwil Pond for a walk. There I saw a red Albolives Suzuki driving away. At the wheel was a young man with black hair. It struck me that I'd seen him before. On the night Bernhard Schirmer was murdered, that is: he was sitting in the Albanian Billiards Centre. And it was the Suzuki that later exploded."

"Why was it blown up? Could it be connected with the goods it was carrying?"

Hunkeler thought about it. Should he or shouldn't he?

"An angler at Morschwil Pond," he said, "a Baseler called Alois Bachmann, told me a man had taken a black bag from the anglers' hut, which had belonged to Bernhard Schirmer. There were some kind of drugs in the bag."

Bardet lit his third cigarette. "And that all came out by chance, did it?" he said. "That Madörin doesn't tell us anything at all. But I've already realized that there's something fishy about it. You can smell it. We presumably won't be able to identify the corpse, not even with DNA. We've nothing to check it against. The car's a red Punto. We've got the chassis number." He looked at his hands, which were spread out on the table. He seemed to be checking his nails, first the left hand, then the right. "What about the snake someone scratched into the bark of the beech tree?"

Hunkeler hesitated. But then he told him that as well.

"Old Binaku has a ring on his right hand. He is, by the way, a handsome, well-turned-out man with perfect manners, when he doesn't happen to be knocking someone out. In the ring is a black stone with a falcon engraved on it. He said the falcon was the symbol of his family, that his son also wore a ring like that. He talked about three families who were in conflict with each other. The clan of the falcon, the clan of the eagle with wings outspread and the family of the poisonous snakes."

Bardet stubbed out his cigarette and looked out of the window at the fogbound meadow.

"Blood feuds then," he said. "I know nothing at all about those."

He stood up, his head almost touching the ceiling beam.

"Wasn't Red Zora Albanian? Yes, I remember now. Red Zora fled with her mother from Albania to Croatia because all the men in their family had been killed. Haven't you read the book by Kurt Held?"

Yes, Hunkeler had read it. But he couldn't remember it.

"The guys ought to shoot each other down in the Balkans," Bardet said. "What are they after over here?"

"Serious money," Hunkeler said, "like the rest of us."

Bardet grinned, he really was a jolly guy. "Thank you. I'll be in touch. Keep your eyes open. There's my number." He put it down on the table.

"I don't think it's a good idea," Hunkeler said, "for my name to be mentioned in this case."

"In which case? Some guy out for a walk happened to find the car. Unfortunately, we don't know his name."

They grinned at each other.

That evening Hunkeler went into the cowshed across the road. He sat on the bench where the farmer was already sitting. His wife was milking.

"We might just as well dump the milk in the cesspit," the man said.

Hunkeler picked up the pitchfork and started to load the cart with dung.

"It's the same with all of us," he said, "we're just old buggers who're in the way everywhere."

"How was it in the war, how was it back then?" The farmer flushed; it was an outburst in which he was suddenly giving vent to his rage. "Back then the Germans came running after us. They took us to Karlsruhe and put us in uniform. We were blockheads from the countryside, they said, and they'd send us to the Eastern Front. I ran away, home. Now no one's coming for us any more. Back then they gave you clothes and boots and a rifle. How much do you think that cost? Now the state gives you just enough to keep you from kicking the bucket. But for these criminals from North Africa, the state pays everything. Health insurance and the rent and school for their children. Did you hear about the charred corpse in Heiligbronn? Who does something like that, eh?"

Hunkeler nodded. Yes, he had heard about it.

"When I get my pension, and that will be soon," he said, "I'm going to buy two donkeys. A male and a female.

Keep your ears open to find out where there are some to be bought. Then we'll breed donkeys here."

"If you like. At least you don't get milk from donkeys."

Hunkeler stood between the handles of the loaded wheelbarrow. He pulled them up, pushed the barrow out over the plank and up to the dung heap. There he tipped it out.

His heart was thumping, he could feel the beats right up in his neck. He looked across to the walnut tree with his house behind it. He gave a satisfied grin, he'd made it with the wheelbarrow. And he liked what he saw.

At nine that evening he called Hedwig. She was, she said, sitting in the Bistrot Saint André in the market of the same name, in the African quarter. It was much livelier and merrier than in the Quartier latin.

"The colours, the scents, the general chatter," she said, going into raptures. "Here they're delighted at every red tomato, every white cauliflower, every corncob. And then the fish, the scales, the bright fins, the crabs. Incredibly beautiful. Only they have dead eyes. How are you? When will you manage to come and see me at last?"

"Soon," Hunkeler said. "At the moment I've got rather a lot of free time."

A pause, clearly she was thinking.

"Why have you suddenly got some free time?" she asked. "What about that old man who beat you up?"

"He's disappeared."

Now she had her suspicions. He could tell from the way she held her breath. "What's going on?"

"I've been suspended. I have to clear out my office and hand in my keys."

"And since when have you known that?"

"A few days ago. The senior prosecutor sent me a registered letter."

"And you're only telling me that now?"

"I had to spend a bit of time getting used to it first. I wanted to be nice and calm when I told you, as I am now. I'm trying to see the positive side of it, as you keep telling me."

"What did I tell you?"

"You said we'd have a lovely life together."

"But not with a coward who doesn't dare tell me the truth."

"But I've told you now," he shouted. "Now are you happy?"

She hung up.

He sat down at the TV and zapped around a bit. He found nothing he liked. He opened the window and lay down in bed. He heard the screech owl in the poplar calling and the response came back from down in the valley.

At nine on Monday morning he parked outside the entrance to the Waaghof, right in the no-parking zone. He saw Frau Held waving. She handed him a bag of *läckerli* on which there was a picture of the Rhine with the ferry and the cathedral.

"Nice of you," he said. "I like Basel gingerbread."

"You take care of yourself. I wish you a happy retirement. And don't keep on getting up to things like that."

She blew her nose and even wiped away a tear, almost making him lose his composure.

"Do you know what?" he asked. "Come round to the Milchhüsli at midnight one day. The lonely pensioners are all sitting there then. We'll dance a waltz together."

"Oh, come on," she said, beaming, "it's ages since anyone took me out dancing."

He went up to his office, sat down on his wooden chair, tipped it back and tried to put his feet up on the edge of the table. He couldn't manage it and he didn't want to either. He picked up the jotters and a pile of notes on the table and leafed through them. He stared at the scribble with which he'd filled the pages. You could presumably call it untidy. But for him it was all in order.

He opened the drawer, took out a plastic bag and stuffed the papers into it. Then he looked at the photo at the bottom of the drawer. It showed Hedwig and himself in Crete, after they'd driven a hired scooter over a mountain pass and down to the beach. It must have been a good twenty years ago, they'd only just got to know each other. The white wall of the hut where they'd slept, an open door, a green-painted window shutter. In front was the scooter, the two of them beside it, and Hedwig's hand on the saddle.

Was that all over now? He knew she felt insulted that he'd kept quiet for a few days about being dismissed. But he hoped her love would hold out.

He stuck the photo in the bag and looked round. It was a hole, a cage. Thirty-two years in the service of justice and you get a kick up the backside. He spat on the floor three times, one after the other. He put the key down, picked up the bag and the chair, and went out.

He knocked on Lüdi's door.

"I was expecting you," his colleague said. "Come on in and sit down."

Hunkeler put his chair down and sat on it.

"A lousy business," Lüdi said. "We couldn't do anything, we weren't even asked."

He laughed, an almost soundless laugh, it was clear he didn't feel like laughing at all.

"The senior prosecutor wants to take it further, at least that's what he said. Madörin was furious. He wasn't going to let you screw things up for him. However did you get that crazy idea of going to see Binaku when he was in prison awaiting trial? He was no business of yours. And then you let him thump you."

"I wanted to talk to him, which I did. Now I know something you lot don't."

"Oh, do stop, right?" Lüdi was getting really angry. "Keep your paws off it. There are legal proceedings in progress against you, for serious insubordination. At least wait until it's over. We'll see that it's swept under the carpet. You'll be pensioned off honourably."

"That's the last thing I want."

"What do you want then?"

"I want to find the man who slits open earlobes."

Lüdi gave a hoarse giggle. "Huh, the ear-slitter of Basel, not bad." Then he became serious again. "As you very well know, you won't find him. Because there's no even vaguely recognizable connection between the victim and the perpetrator. You won't be able to sort out the business with the Albanians either. Because that's a foreign, self-enclosed world. No one here in the CID can speak Albanian. And they all keep their mouths shut anyway. We could perhaps lock two or three of these guys away for a few weeks, but we'd never find out what was going on. You can spend hours searching the computer, there's nothing there."

"There's a family of the falcons," Hunkeler said, "a family of the eagles and a family of the snakes."

"Aha, so that was you." Lüdi shook his head, then giggled again, this time with pleasure. "You really are a bomb waiting to go off. So Bardet got it from you. He informed us."

"No," Hunkeler said coolly, "I got it from him."

"And you expect me to believe that?"

"Yes, please. Otherwise I can't go on working."

"Right, let's assume I believe you. Bardet was talking about someone going for a walk and getting lost in the fog near Leymen and just happening across a burnt-out Fiat Punto. I was asking myself who the crazy guy going for a walk could be. But that's the gendarmerie's business, isn't it?"

Hunkeler nodded.

"I am of course wondering what's actually got into you. If you go on like this, you'll be locked up for endangering an ongoing investigation. You could take things easy just now."

"Alone I'm powerless," Hunkeler said. "What I need is access to your computer."

Lüdi stood up abruptly, went over to the window and looked out. "I really am an ass," he said after a while. "I'm much too nice. Why do I help you? Can you tell me that?"

"Because you can't stand these pig-headed know-alls who've no idea, either. And because you're a sensitive man."

Lüdi went back to the table and wrote down a number, blushing slightly.

94

"I've got another phone. Until now only my friend had the number. It's switched on while I'm asleep. From midnight to seven in the morning."

"Thank you, my angel."

Shortly before midday Hunkeler went into the Sommereck and sat down at the regulars' table.

"What I have here," he said, "is a large bag of Basel *läckerli*. They've been made according to an old recipe, with honey and almonds and cinnamon. If you dunk them in your coffee they go soft and you get the whole aroma."

"They taste great without coffee as well," said Edi, tearing the package open and stuffing a handful in his mouth.

"What's actually going on in the Basel CID?" he asked as he put the coffee cup down. "It seems a senior inspector's been dismissed."

Hunkeler dipped a *läckerli* in his coffee and waited until it was soft. He chewed it on the right-hand side of his mouth, it was OK there.

"Where did you hear that?"

Edi pushed a tabloid over to him. "Two stranglings in ten weeks," it said there, "a van blows up, a prisoner on remand escapes, a burnt-out car with a corpse in it is found across the border in Alsace. Are the Basel police fast asleep? From what we hear, at least they have fired a long-serving inspector."

There was nothing in the *Basler Zeitung*.

"Typical," Edi said. "The *BaZ*'s degenerated into a government mouthpiece. Anything that's to be swept under the carpet isn't in it. Do you know the inspector who's been fired?"

Hunkeler shook his head.

"Thank God. I was afraid it might be you."

"Why me?"

"Well, you are long-serving. And the packet of *läckerli* could have been a farewell present from the city of Basel to a retired official."

"Are you crazy?" Hunkeler cried. "What kind of a world is this we live in?"

"Calm down, calm down," said Edi. "I didn't intend to insult you."

Hunkeler went across Burgfelderplatz. He stopped briefly outside the pharmacy on the corner and looked at the display offering vitamin supplements to ward off influenza. The flu, he thought, what a wonderful, old-fashioned illness. Socks soaked in vinegar on your feet, a warm compress round your chest, lime-blossom tea in your belly and a thermometer in your mouth. He spat on the ground, three times again, and waited until he'd calmed down. What did they think they were doing? How could they chuck him out just like that, without so much as a by-your-leave?

He went up Colmarerstrasse to Hauser's press office. Hauser was sitting at his laptop.

"Just a moment," he said, "I've almost finished."

Hunkeler sat down on one of the two plastic armchairs and lit a cigarette.

"Please don't smoke," Hauser said.

Hunkeler tapped off the ash onto the worn carpet.

"Didn't you hear what I said?"

"No. Did you say something?"

Hauser looked across, shook his head and continued working. Hunkeler would have liked to wring his neck. A duel, man against man, that would have been good. He didn't do it; he knew a policeman would never stand a chance against someone from the media. They had the power to reproduce their arguments, opinions or slander a hundred thousand times over. He dropped his cigarette on the carpet and watched as it continued to glow and then died out.

"You're a bastard," Hauser said. "Do you really want to fall out with me?"

"Yes, because you've no sense of decency. You've not a shred of decency."

"Decency? What's that?"

"First you publish a picture of Hardy's dead body. And I'm willing to bet you touched it up a bit."

"That's part of our profession."

He came away from the laptop and sat down in the other chair. Fat belly, shirt soaked in sweat, tie askew, bright, sharp eyes.

"That's exactly what I'm talking about," Hunkeler said. "Your profession has no sense of decency."

"Oh God, Hunki, let's not start talking about that again. That's just the way things are. People want murder and violence and blood. You wouldn't sell a single paper with good news. You know that's the way things are. And you also know that it's not my fault."

Leaning forward, he took a toffee out of a bowl on the table.

"At least I've seen to it that my colleagues didn't put the name of the inspector who's been fired in the paper. They did want to do that."

He popped the sweet in his mouth.

"Where did you hear that?" Hunkeler asked.

Hauser stopped sucking, spat out the sweet into his right hand and threw it into the wastepaper basket.

"It's too sweet," he said. "It's a scandal what's going on round here. Hardy was my friend. Sometimes my profession is so shitty you can hardly bear it. Hardy understood that. He comforted me when needed, he listened to me at night at the bar. I miss him. I refuse to accept his death without doing something about it."

He looked at the sweets in the dish but didn't take another.

"If we had to rely on the official channels of information, we couldn't produce our newspaper. We have our own informants. We only have them because they know we will protect our sources under all circumstances."

"Madörin?"

"Why Madörin?"

"Because he's desperate to get rid of me."

"I assume he won't manage that, will he? Surely you're not going to give up, or are you?"

He grinned, a pretty unsavoury grin, Hunkeler thought. Most of all he'd have liked to thump him in the face.

"Calm down now, Hunki," Hauser said. "Don't ruin your life. I'm the lowest of the low. Come and have a drink with me instead, if you feel lonely. And have a look at the pharmacy down there. There's something fishy about it."

Hunkeler got up and left without a word.

*

At eight that evening he got into his car to drive to Alsace. He switched on the engine and the headlights. A drive through the night, he thought, at first along the lighted streets of the town, then up over the plateau, turning off to the left and parking underneath the walnut tree.

Then he switched the engine off again, he didn't want to drive. He walked up St Johann's-Ring towards Burgfelderplatz. He stopped briefly outside the Sommereck and looked in. Edi was sitting in his seat, looking grumpy. Beside him four pensioners were playing cards.

A bit further on was the newly built old folks' home with the Café Oldsmobile, which was open to the public. There were a few old people in it, each with a table to themselves. Some were in wheelchairs.

He wondered whether he would one day be sitting at one of those little tables himself, a peppermint tea in front of him, making an effort to hear whether there was a voice of memory inside, speaking to him. He put the thought aside, he had other things to do at the moment.

At the square he saw the little tree in the fog, the stone bench in the corner. He went over, sat down, turned up his jacket collar and pulled his cap down. He leaned back in the corner, crossed his arms over his chest.

The fog seemed to have thinned a bit. The traffic lights could be seen turning to green, a car setting off. The building diagonally opposite across the square could just be discerned, you could see the bright gleam of the pharmacy's window display. He couldn't make out Hermine's apartment. Either she wasn't at home or the light of the TV was too weak.

He ought to have a look at that pharmacy, Hauser had said. What had he meant by that? Who did it actually belong to? Only a few years ago there had been a bar on the corner there. Then the house had been sold and the new owner had set up a pharmacy. That was the way things were. Bar landlords didn't earn much any more. But pharmacists did.

He saw the number 3 heading into the town. There was a woman in the front car, no one in the rear.

He noticed he was getting chilly. The cold was creeping up his body from the stone bench. What was it that made an old man spend hours sitting there? How could someone go to sleep there?

Once three young women went past. They had linked arms, they didn't look across at him. They were speaking a language he didn't understand, they were wearing headscarves.

Later an oldish, dark-haired man came from the right. For a moment he slowed down and seemed to look across, but then he just went on.

Several cars went past. They waited for the green light, then accelerated away. From one of them, the windows of which were open, came loud music. Obviously young guys out for a spin.

The number 3 drove past at regular intervals. First it came out of the town with a few people in it, braked at the red light, set off again at green, disappearing in the fog. A few minutes later you could hear it coming back from the border, mostly empty.

His phone rang. It was Hedwig. "What's going on?" she asked. "Why haven't you called?"

"Why? What time is it?"

"Half past nine. You said you would call every evening at nine."

"And you said I was a coward."

"Of course you're a coward, if you don't resist. You can't simply accept your suspension. And you shouldn't keep on having fights with men who are stronger than you. You should take care of your teeth, I don't want a toothless man."

"I've already told you I wasn't having a fight," he shouted. "I was hit."

"Serves you right," she said coolly, "if you don't keep your eyes open. And there's one more thing I'm going to tell you. If you don't call me at nine on the dot tomorrow, that's the end for us."

She hung up.

He put the phone back in his pocket. He just loved that woman. He knew he would always love her.

Hunkeler got up and stretched his back, which had seized up. He saw the number 3 appear, coming from the border. Sitting in the rear carriage were Turkoğlu and Sermeter, in light-coloured raincoats. Why were they travelling through the night? What had they been up to out there at the border?

No, they weren't important. It was a very faint trail he was following; he mustn't let himself be diverted from it.

He crossed the street and briefly had a look at the sex cinema's display. Naked women, their lips apart with longing, that wouldn't have been bad on such a chilly night. Then he grinned at the stupid idea going through his mind.

The usual regulars were gathered in the Milchhüsli. Luise in her black tulle dress, little Niggi in his far-too-tight confirmation suit, Richard with the black ribbon on his lapel, pale Franz with his black tie. On the table a bottle of Beaujolais Villages with a white paper frill round the neck.

At the bar Joseph the Bavarian with his wife, who was always in a good mood. Senn, the second-hand bookseller, engrossed in a magazine. In the corner an oldish gentleman who seemed familiar to Hunkeler, although he didn't know the man's name.

He sat down at the regulars' table.

"Why didn't you come to the funeral?" Luise asked. "After all, Hardy was a friend of yours."

"No, he wasn't a friend, he was a boozing companion. And I've been excluded from the investigation, anyway."

"Who's going to find the murderer if not you?"

"How should I know? There are enough police officers in Basel."

"We'll find him," pale Franz said, "it's just a question of time. His guilt will bring him back to the scene of his crime."

The door opened and an oldish dark-haired man came in. He looked round to see where he could sit and went to the table to the right of the entrance and ordered a glass of white wine. It was the man Hunkeler had seen walking past on Burgfelderplatz.

"Who's that?" he asked.

"That's Herr Rentschler," Luise said. "He's taken early retirement; his wife died two months ago."

She gave the man a friendly smile.

"And who's the man in the corner back there?" Hunkeler asked.

"Don't you know him? That's Garzoni, Hermine's ex; he owns the pharmacy. He was at the funeral service as well."

Milena came over to take the empty wine bottle away. Luise ordered a camomile tea, Franz a coffee with schnapps, Richard a glass of white wine from Wallis, Niggi a double fruit brandy and Hunkeler a beer.

"The guy isn't kosher," Franz said, "I'm sure of that. I've tried to hack his data. Generally I'm good at that, usually the register of inhabitants is no problem for me. But it didn't work with Garzoni. I can't get through to him. All I know is that he grew up in the Frick valley, in Herznach to be precise. And that his father had a filling station there. There's something secretive about him. He does come over and sit with us now and then, he's very friendly. But he never tells us anything about himself."

"He was really furious with Hardy," Richard said, "because he pinched Hermine from him. But he didn't let on. He's always smiling like a Chinaman, he does yoga."

"Just have a look," little Niggi said to Luise, "to see what kind of guy the murderer was. We have to go about this systematically."

"No," she said, "not here. People are going to laugh at me."

"No one's laughing here," Niggi said. "Go on, do it."

Luise took the silver chain off her neck; it had a green tourmaline attached. Taking a piece of chalk out of her bag, she drew a cross on the table.

"This branch is fire, that one air, that one water and then earth."

She held her hand over the table, closed her eyes and let the stone swing. "Your cigarette," she said, "it's putting me off."

Hunkeler stubbed out his cigarette in the ashtray. Luise's hand was relaxed. For a long time nothing happened. Then the stone moved to the left, so faintly it could hardly be seen, swayed back then swung towards the left again. Luise opened her eyes and hung the chain round her neck again.

"Aquarius," she said. "Opposite him is fire. The fire will try to eat up the water. But the water will win."

Hunkeler picked up his glass and went over to the man in the corner.

"May I?"

"Yes, of course, Herr Hunkeler," Garzoni said. "I'm delighted to get to know you personally at last."

He was very well groomed, his hands neatly manicured, bald head, surrounding hair cropped short. Bright, intelligent eyes.

"I didn't see you at the funeral. You were often together with Hardy."

"True," Hunkeler said. "However, I do wonder how you know that."

"I live on the corner down there, over the Cantonal Bank. I have private means, the pharmacy brings in enough. I have plenty of time for watching what's going on."

He had a glass of mineral water. He put his hand in his jacket pocket, took out a flask and had a swig.

"Irish whiskey," he said. "I can't take Scotch, it makes me aggressive."

There seemed to be a scar on his left ear. But perhaps it was a birthmark.

"You have a good look at me," he said, "it doesn't bother me. I used to have a ring in my left earlobe. The kind of thing you do when you're young; I thought it was great to have gold in my ear. My early life wasn't a bed of roses."

"Garzoni? Where does the name come from?"

"From Lombardy. My father immigrated when he was young and married a woman from Herznach and opened a filling station. Both died young."

He smiled as if it was an interrogation that he was enjoying.

"I worked my way up, studied pharmacy. A few years ago I managed to buy the property on Burgfelderplatz. I'm sure you know that I had a liaison with Hermine, don't you?"

"How should I know that?"

"Because you're interested in me. Oh yes, you're showing interest. Otherwise you wouldn't have come over and sat down at my table. Unfortunately the liaison broke up. *C'est la vie*, isn't it?"

Hunkeler nodded and waited.

"I don't hold it against Hardy. He did take her away from me, but that's just the way love goes."

"I don't know about that," said Hunkeler, "I don't know the way love goes. But all the time I've been asking myself where I've seen you before."

Garzoni smiled, delighted. "There you are, I knew you'd remember me. It was Monday evening, 27 October, almost two weeks ago. I was in the Singerhaus watching the ladies who were good enough to get undressed."

Oh yes, the man in the corner with the newspaper, Hunkeler remembered now. But hadn't his hair been different?

"I didn't notice you," he said.

"Do we need to be noticed? At our age we're happy when we can see a beautiful naked woman now and then, aren't we, Inspector? And sometimes we're fortunate enough to possess a woman, at least for one night. Angel from Seville is really a most beautiful angel."

Hunkeler looked at the man, fury rising inside him. What did this guy know? But he controlled himself and calmly emptied his glass.

"I don't want to put pressure on you in any way," Garzoni said. "On the contrary, I'm happy to communicate with you. Moreover, beautiful Angel told me you were working on the Barbara Amsler case. A terrible crime, really."

Hunkeler was now sitting there quite calm, relaxed and composed. What else was going to come out?

Garzoni took out his flask, had a swig and screwed the top back on.

"Sometimes I feel the need," he said, "to sit down with ordinary people, to feel a bit of human warmth. Basically we're wretched creatures. Too weak for the harshness of today's society, shattered by the unloving nature of the world. All those over at the regulars' table are drawing their pension. I'm afraid there are going to be more and more like that, unable to stand the pressure any longer. In Basel almost every tenth person is living on a disability pension. And a good quarter are foreigners. Unfortunately there are hardly any people left resisting that trend."

"That's enough idle chatter. Your father was a foreigner too. And you aren't working either."

There was a flicker of something in Garzoni's eyes, a brief flash, then he was smiling again.

"Sorry. I thought one could talk quite calmly about anything with a flatfoot."

"A flatfoot?"

"Sorry, that wasn't very polite. I'm a lonely man and you have to be careful that the capacity for love that you do have doesn't turn into hatred. I'll say goodbye now. Perhaps we'll see each other at Herr Laufenburger's place later on."

Out in the street Hunkeler stood for a while breathing in the cool air, which promised snow. There was a light shimmer on the asphalt. He heard the sound of roller skates coming from the town. A figure appeared, striding out, wearing a red jacket, white hair flying, hands clasped behind his back like a speed skater. He braked a little, performed an elegant curve to the left and did a complete circle in the road. Then he disappeared in the direction of Burgfelderplatz.

It had been an old man on in-line skates, a man of Hunkeler's age. Going through the night, he thought, an ice skater, turning Basel's streets into frozen canals. An old city gent rolling across the Rhine bridges, along the Ring under the bare plane trees, across Petersplatz, Kannenfeldplatz, Voltaplatz, now he's speeding down St Johann's- Ring. And at midnight he'll go to bed, tired and contented.

What was he actually doing here? Why was he filling his belly with beer and smoke? Why was he listening to an old man who hated immigrants, who was prophesying the decline of the West?

He wondered whether to go home and lie down, tired and discontented. But he didn't want to do that. He crossed the road and went into the Billiards Centre. He joined Laufenburger, Nana and little Cowboy and ordered a bottle of Beaujolais for them to share. Skender came over to the table, cursing the Basel police, who, he said, were ruining his business. Hunkeler had great difficulty shaking him off.

Laufenburger had fallen asleep in his chair, the Siamese cat in his lap. Cowboy was talking in his lilting local dialect about the valley he came from. About herds of cows with bells ringing, about black quartz crystals, about a meadow full of edelweiss plants that were so big, you could put a coffee cup on them without it falling off. Nana said almost nothing at all, she seldom spoke about herself.

Shortly after twelve Dolly came in from her work in the hospital, she'd had a late shift. Hunkeler got on very well with her. He listened as she talked about a woman with cancer who had died two hours ago in her arms.

At one o'clock he bought another bottle as a carry-out, and they all went together to Laufenburger's apartment. Hunkeler knew it, he'd been there several times before. A kind of Noah's Ark for the shipwrecked, a haven for all kinds of lost nightbirds. It looked out onto Missionsstrasse, which was very busy with traffic until the early morning. A corridor, a bedroom, a kitchen and a bathroom. Piles of magazines in the corridor. The bedroom crammed full of boxes and books the artist had dug out in second-hand bookstores in Paris and intended to sell at a profit. Among them three wire sculptures, really beautiful, meticulously made, the only art objects of his own Laufenburger still possessed. Years before they'd made him one of the most promising of Swiss artists.

Nana put a casserole of goulash down on the table. Hunkeler had a plateful as well; it was excellent. Laufenburger had an attack of drunken misery, he was crying, hands over his face. He was moaning in the most pathetic terms about his mother, who had married for a second time when he was eight. His stepfather had terrorized him and once hit him over the head with the blunt end of an axe. The indentation was still there, they all had to put their hand on the poor artist's head and feel it. They did that, they'd done it several times already.

At half past one Garzoni rang the bell. He sat down at the table without a word, he didn't want anything to eat, he just wanted to sit there and drink his whiskey. Later Hauser arrived bringing a bottle of grappa. He didn't say anything either, he just wanted to drink grappa, and to do so in company.

Once Hunkeler went to the toilet. He had to step over little Cowboy, who was lying on the floor in the corridor, his arms wrapped round his dog.

Around three there was another ring at the door but Nana didn't go to open it. She cleared away the casserole and plates, then started washing up.

"Will you take me home?" Dolly asked. "I don't want to sleep by myself, I'm too sad."

"Of course," Hunkeler said.

"But just an embrace, nothing more."

"If that's what you want," he said.

They went down into the street. The road was quiet, not a sound, no engine noises. One street lamp was swaying a little, its gleam seemed to be dancing. Clearly the wind had dispersed the fog a little. A marten darted across the road in drawn-out wavy movements. It disappeared under a parked car.

There was a figure standing in the entrance to the sex cinema across the road. Just a shadow, but Hunkeler still saw him. It was Richard, the former foreign legionnaire, standing there motionless.

"Clear off," he said. "Don't give me away."

He pointed across the road to the bench in the corner on which Hardy had died. Little Niggi was lying there, apparently asleep. Hunkeler nodded and grinned. So the Milchhüsli regulars were setting a trap for Hardy's murderer.

He felt Dolly's left hand on his hip. That was nice, and he put his hand round her hip as well. And they went on like that to Kannenfeldplatz with its trees towering up into the fog. There was a slight rustling from the wind going through the autumn leaves.

Dolly lived in Ensisheimerstrasse. They went up in the elevator to her apartment. They stood there looking at each other.

"It's difficult," she said, "to accompany someone you don't know to their death. What should you say to them, how should you say farewell?"

They went to bed. He put his arms round her. Then he could hear her calm breathing.

At ten the next morning – it was Tuesday, 11 November – he parked by Allschwil Pond. He didn't go to the water, he didn't want to see another woman's body float to the surface. He went up the stream at the back past the Gypsy caravans, in which there didn't seem to be anything moving at all. He stopped by the horizontal bar in the keep-fit circuit, making sure that he was alone. Then he grasped it and tried to pull himself up. It was impossible, his arms were too weak. He felt a pain in his back, his weak spot, he'd had that for years, the doctor had warned him against doing pull-ups.

Sitting on a bench by the rear pond he saw Sergeant Hasenböhler of the Basel Rural District CID. "Oh, it's Hunkeler," he said grumpily, "who's been suspended and is having a nice day out."

"It's not that nice a day," Hunkeler said. "On the horizontal bar just now I got a real pain in the back."

Hasenböhler grinned maliciously. "At your age you shouldn't be hanging from horizontal bars. At your age you should at most get massaged by a Thai lady."

Hunkeler put a foot on the bench, first the right, then the left. As he did so he pushed his hips forward to ease his back.

"Anything new?" he asked.

"No, nothing new. Apart, that is, from the fact that I'm amazed at how many people there are running round here. Clearly they all want to toughen themselves up, from teenagers to old men. And then the border's up there. Who's actually supposed to be checking that?"

"I mean with the Gypsies. The girl you were observing eating an apple, for example."

"What are you getting at? Are you trying to tick me off?"

"No, of course not, I know how boring your job is."

Hunkeler sat down, lit a cigarette and looked across the pond. The surface was dull in the fog. A pair of ducks paddled across, the female in front, the drake behind.

"I do wonder," he said, "why the drake doesn't get fed up with going along behind the female all the time. Why does he do that?"

"Why are you surprised at that? We do it as well."

111

Hunkeler spat on the ground, on the wet grass. There was something there that caught his eye. He leaned down and saw that it was a pumpkin seed. He picked it up, wrapped it in his handkerchief and put it away.

"What's all that about?" Hasenböhler asked. "What did you find there?"

"Nothing special. Just a snail shell."

"That would be the thing, a shell you could withdraw into. I have great difficulty not popping into the nearest bar to have a coffee with a schnapps or two. What am I doing here? I see some figures appear out of the fog and then disappear again. And almost none of them are carrying an identity card. And why should I keep a watch on the Gypsies? I'm no racist, I'm a decent husband and father."

He took a bag of hazelnuts out of his pocket, put some in his mouth and chewed.

"Heard anything new about Binaku?" Hunkeler asked.

"The lad clearly got burnt to death, in his car near Heiligbronn. The old man, Ismail, was seen at the Römerbad Hotel in Badenweiler. That's a luxury hotel where they know all the tricks. When the police appeared he'd already gone."

"Well I never," Hunkeler said. "In Badenweiler, is he? And I thought he'd be somewhere on the Adriatic."

"Why on the Adriatic?"

"Because that's where the sun shines. Old Binaku is a man of the world. He doesn't hang around in the fog if there's an alternative."

"The Römerbad Hotel," Hasenböhler said, spitting out a hazelnut, probably because it was rancid, "a spa hotel. Just imagine: splashing around in the warm water a bit, then caviar and champagne. Sometimes I wonder whether we aren't fighting on the wrong side."

"Don't say that. It's not a matter of money here, it's about justice."

"Justice, what is that?"

"It's what we live on. We get our wages by seeing to it that there is justice. In your case, justice means that at the moment you have to spend your time getting fed up here in the fog."

"Oh, go on then," Hasenböhler said sadly, "keep on running me down. Go and have a walk, just go."

Hunkeler walked up through the woods to the hill that went across into Alsace. He could feel his heart thumping, he'd smoked too much again the previous day.

It had been a good night of love, he recalled later, sleeping in each other's arms. Nothing more, just that. But warmly and with fondness. He went past an old border-stone. It must have come from the time before 1870; a large F was scratched on the west side. Alsace had belonged to France back then; later to Germany, after 1918 to France, during the Second World War to Germany and now to France again. That was presumably why the people here were so open and peaceable – they were sick to death of frontiers.

He went across empty maize fields, disturbing a flock of crows who were pecking up the last grains, and enjoying the sight of the mistletoe up in the trees. He'd get a clump like that on Christmas Eve and hang it over the door of the house, he did that every Christmas.

He turned off to the right down the valley in which the Alsatian village of Neuwiller lay. Going into Luc Borer's inn, he ordered roast goose, in honour of St Martin, and a glass of Côtes du Rhône. He took out the pumpkin seed and examined it. It was still fresh. Clearly some walker had recently been sitting on the bench, nibbling pumpkin seeds. What was remarkable about that? One man would nibble pumpkin seeds, another hazelnuts. He popped the seed in his mouth. It didn't taste that bad.

Out on the road, he wondered what he should do. Go back to Basel and sit in the kitchen drinking tea? Or continue the walk to his house? He'd be there in two hours and there was always something to do: chop firewood, prune the hornbeam, get the garden ready for winter.

He didn't want to do that, he wanted to have company, talk to someone, and specifically with the old actor. He headed off in a westerly direction, past boggy meadows with black-and-white cows standing around in them, through old mixed woodland with beech, oak, acacias. A rather unkempt area, almost completely undisturbed for centuries and quietly growing rampant, not done up for a quick profit: the tracks full of potholes, the fruit trees unpruned, the fruit rotting on the ground. He recalled the wasp on that apple by Morschwil Pond, the yellow shining in the fog. He thought of Alois Bachmann making the carp dance, gasping for air. He would surely have had to spend several hours in the Waaghof being interrogated by Madörin. Perhaps he'd even had to spend one or two nights in custody. What had he told them? More than Hunkeler knew? That was improbable, he knew that kind of man. They were as tough as old boots, they wouldn't be very impressed by a detective sergeant.

He came to the road between Hagenthal-le-Bas and Leymen, crossed it and went on along the woodland track that seemed to continue unending to the west. He'd never followed it right to the end, it looked as if he would end up in the wilderness. You could get lost here in the trackless waste and disappear. And not even the bones left by the wild animals would be found.

That would have been what the wife of the old actor had felt when she had gone out in the snow on an ice-cold February day to sit down somewhere, to rest and to die. Hunkeler had known her well, they'd liked each other without getting too close. She'd been a creature of the forest, a fairy-tale beast like Master Brock. It was days before her corpse had been found.

Hunkeler was familiar with that feeling. He knew that, especially in November, it could arise from one hour to the next. That it could spread itself through your head and body, seductively inviting you to pause, sit down, wait for the cold gradually creeping into your heart. He also knew that he wouldn't succumb to that feeling, he still enjoyed life too much.

He came to the place where the badger had crossed his path and led him to the burnt-out car. He went over to see if it was still there. It wasn't. The snake scratched on the tree wasn't there any more either, someone had cut it off. It was just the burst-open bark on a few trees that bore witness to the intense heat there had been.

He returned to the track. After a few hundred yards he came to the turn-off that went left down to Heiligbronn. An early holy place with a healing spring, the basin to bathe in, hewn out of the rock, was still there. Beside it was the chapel, through which the place had been Christianized. The old farmhouse from which, in good weather, you had a view out over the whole Leymen valley.

Hunkeler had often come this way. Thick undergrowth blocking the view. Yellow gravel along which rainwater had found its way. Then, suddenly and still surprising, the projecting roof of the farmhouse. The boules court, the damp foundation walls. The lime tree, the cherry tree, the cackling hens.

He knocked on the door and went in. Stallinger was sitting as usual at the table, a book in front of him. He looked to see who it was, got up and in his trained voice declaimed the lines he'd just been reflecting on:

"Sounds of the Night

Tell me the sounds of the night, O Muse,
Waves on the sleepless ear, a flood:
First the wonted barking of the watch-dogs,
Then the clock duly striking the hour,
Then two fishermen chatting by the shore,
Then? Nothing more than the obscure
Ghostly sound of the unbroken hush,
Like the sighs from the breast of a youth,
Like the murmur of a well, deep-hewn,
Like the dull beat of a muffled oar,
Then the unheard step of slumber.

"That's by C. F. Meyer. Incredibly precise, that mood when you're lying awake at night listening to the noises that come to your ear. Since my wife died I can't stand proper music any more. All I can stand now is the music of words."

"I like poems," Hunkeler said. "As far as I'm concerned you can keep on reciting as much as you like."

"Yes, earlier on I could keep on reciting poems I knew off by heart for hours on end. But my wife took my memory with her to the grave. Now I can only read aloud from books. Are you going to have a bottle of wine with me?"

"No, tea, if you don't mind."

"Come on then."

They went into the kitchen, which had been built into the slope. Dark marsh plants with big leaves could be seen through the window. Two black cats sitting by the window put up their tails and miaowed. A limestone sink, a dresser, a wooden range with a gas stove on it. A table with two chairs, on one of which was the urn with the ashes of the creature of the forest.

"Are you actually not going to bury her?" Hunkeler asked.

"No. It's my descendants who're going to do that when I'm dead. Both urns together, on the edge of the woods behind the house."

"But I can sit down?"

"Yes, of course. There you are."

He put the urn in one corner and Hunkeler sat down.

"I just can't part from her," Stallinger said. "Perhaps I could if I were to start a new life. But I'm too old for that."

He went to the small stove and lit it. Then he shuffled across to the sink, put water into a pan, carried it over to the stove and put it on. He opened the dresser, took out a bottle of wine, uncorked it and poured himself a glass. He filled the tea ball with herbs, hung it in a mug, picked up his wine glass and had a drink. He did all that without saying a word; he couldn't do something and talk at the same time any more.

"Let the cats in," Hunkeler said, "they're hungry."

"Nonsense. They know very well that they only get something when I'm having my dinner."

He emptied the hot water into the jug. Hunkeler would very much have liked to ask for some milk, but there probably wasn't any there.

The dresser was still open. On one shelf there was a bottle. On the label it said that it was Albo olive oil.

"That bottle of olive oil," Hunkeler asked, "where did you get it?"

"What do you mean? It's just ordinary olive oil."

"No, that's not ordinary olive oil."

Stallinger refilled his glass. It was the finest Burgundy.

"I do have a problem with you," he said. "Because you're not just my friend but you're a policeman as well. I've had a problem with policemen since I came to Switzerland from Berlin in 1939. They very nearly sent me back again."

"I'm not in the section dealing with immigrants, I'm a detective inspector. I can't do anything about what happened back then."

"There's been enough detectives sniffing round here. They didn't find anything, I didn't tell them anything."

Hunkeler took a sip of tea. It was still too hot and the milk was missing. But if he took it easy, everything would sort itself out.

"I've nothing to do with the Albo firm," he said. "I'm looking for someone who's strangled two people. A whore and an old man. He'll do it again if I don't find him."

Stallinger was still unmoved. "If you've nothing to do with it, then why are you asking?"

Hunkeler thumped the table with his fist, making the wine glass fall over. He just managed to catch it before it fell on the floor. He saw that the cats had disappeared from the window ledge.

"Sorry," he said, "I was unfriendly there. I'm being kept away from my work, first of all by the public prosecutor and then by you. I can't bear it."

Stallinger poured himself more wine. He drank slowly, taking small sips.

"A Monsieur Bardet from Mulhouse was here," he said, "three or four times, a pleasant chap. He asked a lot of questions. But how can I answer them if I know nothing?"

"The guy I'm looking for," Hunkeler said, "seems to be a psychopath. First he strangles his victims, then he cuts open their earlobes."

"Why their earlobes?"

"I don't know."

"He's crazy," Stallinger said. "That's terrible."

Opening the table drawer, he took out a cheroot and lit it. He watched the bluish smoke drifting up to the ceiling.

"A man acting under some kind of compulsion, I suppose?"

Hunkeler shrugged, he really didn't know.

"Right then," Stallinger said, "if you insist. Three weeks ago someone came driving down the forest track. Hardly anyone drives down there. It was a nice young man, very well dressed. Someone from the Balkans, as I immediately realized. But he spoke good Swiss German. He was in a red Punto with Swiss plates. He said he came from Albania and worked in Basel and he had a few bottles of olive oil with him. If he were to import all of them at the same time, he'd have difficulties. One bottle was allowed. Could he leave them here, he'd collect them one by one? I agreed and we hid them in the pigsty. He gave me three bottles, they're in the dresser. It's excellent olive oil, by the way."

"What did the man look like?"

"The way Albanians look. When you found the wrecked car up there I became suspicious. It was said to have been a red Punto. I took out one of the bottles we'd hidden and compared it with those he'd given me. On the label was a little black bird that wasn't on the three others."

"Where is the bottle?"

"I threw it away. In the forest up there, where no one will find it. A few days ago, another car came driving down the forest track. It was another Albanian, also very well dressed. He said he was a cousin of the other one. His task was to collect the bottles. I agreed at once, since I felt there was something fishy about the whole business. He counted them and said one was missing. But I knew nothing about it. He gave me a funny look, as if he distrusted me."

"Would you be able to find the place where you threw the bottle away?"

"Of course. But I don't want to. The bottle stays where it is."

"For goodness' sake," said Hunkeler. "What are you up to? The guy could have killed you."

"Oh come on. Who's going to send an old man like me to his grave?"

"At the place where the burnt-out car was someone carved a snake in the bark of a tree. The snake's not there any more."

"I know. It was two days ago, in the evening. I heard a car's engine, from up there. Then it was quiet. Then the car drove off again. The next morning I went up there. I saw that the snake had been cut out. Somehow or other it reminded me of the falcon. I mean what is that, a falcon and a snake? That's why I took off the label before I threw the bottle away."

He opened the table drawer and took out an Albo label.

"Is that a falcon or not?"

Indeed, at the bottom left, scarcely recognizable, was a black falcon.

"Give it to me," Hunkeler said.

"No," Stallinger said, putting the label in the ashtray and setting it alight. It curled up in the flame. They watched as the fire ate up the paper, leaving ash behind.

"Ashes to ashes, dust to dust, that's the best way," Stallinger said. "Now we'll have something to eat, if that's all right by you. Then we'll have a game of boules."

They had ham and bread. Then they went out to the boules court and threw the boules by the light of a lamp. Now and then they heard the noise of the owls that lived in the rafters of the barn. It sounded like coughing. They played on doggedly until midnight. Hunkeler didn't win one single time.

At around two the next afternoon he went into the Sommereck. Edi was just stirring a white powder into a glass of water. He took a drink and screwed up his face in disgust.

"That's my lunch," he said, "the doctor's prescribed it for me. It's supposed to be everything I need to build up my body. But who's talking about building up bodies? I'm talking about hunger."

"Why are you doing this to yourself?"

"Because the doctor says I have to lose at least ninety pounds if I want to last until retirement age. And I'd certainly like to do that. After all, I've been paying my contributions for years."

He passed the *Basler Zeitung* to Hunkeler. "Look, just read that, it's about where we live. The Wild West was a peaceful place compared with our St Johann."

Hunkeler read a short report about a shoot-out that had taken place shortly after nine in the evening on Kannenfeldplatz two days ago. A man, apparently Turkish, had taken refuge in the former Café Entenweid, now a grocer's, and used it as cover as he shot a pistol across the square. From there someone behind the kiosk had been firing at the store. No one had been injured. The store owner, an Albanian from Kosovo, had informed the police. When they arrived, the Turk had disappeared. There were no clues apart from empty cartridges and bullet holes.

"So," said Edi, "on a quite ordinary evening there were bullets flying all over Kannenfeldplatz, just as in New York during Al Capone's days. And nothing is done about it. For the *BaZ* the shoot-out's worth nothing more than a brief note. What's the point of all this? When are the police finally going to clear all this up? And why is a Kosovo Albanian actually allowed to turn a lovely old local inn into an Albanian store?"

"I'm old and stupid," Hunkeler said, "moreover, I come

from the country and don't understand city life or its outlook at all."

"What? Are you kidding?"

"What makes you say that? I'm just explaining the situation. Anyway, have you got anything to eat?"

"I've got smoked ham from a wild sow, from the landlord of the Angel in Todtnauberg. But I'm not allowed to sell it."

"You want the ham to go off? Off you go, slice it up and serve it up."

Edi disappeared into the kitchen. Hunkeler took out his phone and dialled Lüdi's number.

"You know I can't give you any information," Lüdi said. "Why are you embarrassing me like this?"

"Just a morsel of information. It's nothing to do with Albo. I'd just like to know whether Turkoğlu and Sermeter have left."

"Why do you want to know that?"

"Because on Monday evening, the day before yesterday that is, I saw the pair of them going into town on the number 3 at 10 p.m."

"Oh, now that is interesting. Are you sure?"

"Would I have called you otherwise?"

"OK then. We have made enquiries at the airport. I can tell you for sure that Turkoğlu and Sermeter left from the EuroAirport on Tuesday morning. Anything else?"

"No. Thank you, my angel."

At four that afternoon Hunkeler decided to go to Badenweiler to get some treatment for his lumbago. He crossed the border after Huningue, drove across the old Garnisonsplatz and over the Europa Bridge, then slotted into the northbound traffic going along the autobahn at breakneck speed. They're all crazy, he thought, these German racing drivers in their BMWs and Mercedes, they all believe it should be a clear run for those who can do it, even in thick fog. He pressed his foot right down in his small car but was still constantly overtaken.

One hour later he was parking outside the Römerbad Hotel – a magnificently elaborate building more than a hundred years old, in the spa district with a view over the Rhine plain. A roofed interior courtyard surrounded by balustrades, a Steinway concert grand, lots of marble. At the desk was the receptionist dressed in respectable black, his Mediterranean hair slicked back, otherwise there was not a soul to be seen. Just right for a November-weary Hunkeler.

He took an outrageously expensive room with a view of the park, the Rhine plain and the Vosges hills, as the receptionist had promised. All he could see was the almost bare branches of a plane tree in the fog. He went down in the elevator to the bathing pool and lay in the warm water, where the ancient Romans had lain to strengthen their weary limbs. He swam a few strokes. Then he stayed lying in a niche where the water was bubbling up, seething and swirling. He almost fell asleep there.

Later, after a short nap on a white-sheeted day bed, he sat in an armchair in the entrance hall and looked over at the receptionist, who seemed to be asleep. Also there but a proper distance away, so that hardly any of their quietly spoken words could be heard, were an elderly couple. She was a tall, slim lady with an erotic attractiveness that had not entirely faded, a cool beauty. From North Germany, Friesland perhaps? He was a curly-haired businessman, grey from the harsh struggle for existence, weary and relaxed from the hot spring. There was a bottle of red wine in front of them.

At last the receptionist seemed to wake. He looked up, considered whether he should come over. Then he did come.

"Is there anything you require, sir?"

"Aha," Hunkeler said, recognizing the Italian accent, "*sei Italiano. Da dove?*"

"*Udine. E Lei?*"

"*Basilea, Svizzero.* From Basel. And I'd like some caviar to eat and a glass of champagne to drink."

"Very well, *signore,*" the receptionist said, sketching a bow and disappearing through a door that clearly led to the kitchen.

The caviar was excellent, the champagne likewise. He ate slowly, with a little butter on the toast. He left the little white onions, he didn't like them.

The couple talked very little. Clearly they were speaking some kind of Low German. Around eight they stood up, gave Hunkeler a brief nod and went up in the elevator.

"Who was that?" he asked, simply in order to hear his voice in the silence.

"A businessman with his wife," the receptionist said. "Why?"

"What's your name?"

"Vittorio. *E tu?*"

"Pietro. Can you play cards, jass, for example?"

"No. Backgammon."

"Right then, bring it over. Can one get jasmine tea here?"

"Of course, *signore*. Backgammon and jasmine tea."

He vanished into the kitchen. After a while, during which the drip, drip, drip of the fog could be heard, he reappeared with the backgammon box under his arm and a tray on which was a silver pot with the tea and a bottle of schnapps.

"Grappa," he said, "from home. To help me bear the Schwarzwald melancholy."

"Jasmine tea," Hunkeler said, "to help me bear this Greater German splendour."

They grinned at each other.

"The gentleman is a publisher from Hamburg," the receptionist said, "that's just between the two of us. He's taking the waters, he's had a heart attack. A delightful couple."

They cast the dice and moved the pieces around. It quickly became clear that Hunkeler had no chance at all.

"Why is the hotel so empty?" he asked.

"Magnificence of the past, it's too expensive today. Also, it's November."

At nine Hunkeler interrupted the game and called Hedwig. He heard her voice on the answerphone.

"I'm in a Roman spa with hot springs," he said. "I'm playing backgammon with a magician from Udine. He won't let me win one single time. Otherwise everything's fine."

At eleven he could hardly keep his eyes open any longer. "Before I go to bed," he said, "I have one more request. I'd very much like to see the register."

"The register, certainly. I've already realized that you're a policeman. Actually, it's not permitted. *Però, per te…*"

They went over to the desk and the receptionist put out the register. Hunkeler didn't need to leaf through it for long, there weren't that many entries. On Wednesday, 29 October, an Ismail Zara had checked in, in very legible, straight handwriting. He'd stayed until 2 November. On 9 November a Prenga Guma had checked in. He had only stayed one night.

"This Ismail Zara, what kind of guy was he?" Hunkeler asked.

"Mafia, a padrino. There aren't many of that kind left, unfortunately."

"Why didn't the German police arrest him?"

"The German police won't catch a padrino like that. By the time they'd realized he was the wanted Ismail Binaku, he was gone."

"And this one there, Prenga Guma? What kind of guy was he?"

"Herr Guma's a mafioso as well. His actual name is Prenga Berisha. He eats his caviar with a soup spoon. And he can afford it too. But he's not up to being in a difficult situation. He'll soon get caught. Fortunately – if you'll allow me to say so – there are still just a few civilized Swiss policemen left."

The next morning, after a splendid sleep right through the night, Hunkeler breakfasted at a table with a white cloth, served by Vittorio. He had scrambled eggs with capers, three slices of smoked ham, quark with chives and dark, bitter bread, followed by fresh, juicy pineapple. He felt good, there was hardly any sign of his lumbago. Despite that, he decided to go to the hot spring again and stretch out in the warm bath.

Shortly before twelve he got into his car and drove off, not heading for the autobahn but up the narrow road into the hills. His idea was to have an excursion, an old man's trip through the dark woods. He went along in second gear, bent right forward over the steering wheel, in order to be able to see any approaching headlights as quickly as possible. He didn't meet anyone, he was alone on his journey.

Halfway up, on an almost level stretch through meadows, he was suddenly faced with a wall of snow, grey in the dark fog, white in the glow of his headlights. He pulled onto the right-hand shoulder of the road and waited. The snow was falling so thickly that everything around turned white within seconds. He stayed sitting in the car, the wipers working furiously, hardly able to keep the front window clear. He listened to the wind whistling over the roof of the car, the frozen snow rattling on it. Then all was calm again.

He switched off the wipers and got out. He almost fell over, so icy had the ground suddenly become.

He grinned, contented. So he had his adventure, unexpectedly thrown down from the overcast sky onto the asphalt of the mountain road, on a quite normal weekday. He went to the tailgate, opened it and set about looking for the chains. They were right at the bottom, under cardboard boxes, woollen blankets, old jackets and worn-out shoes he'd intended to throw away ages ago. Kneeling down beside the left front wheel, he tried to fit one of the chains round the tyre. He remembered that he hadn't done this for years. It was all so much like back in the early days, when his wife and little daughter had always waited in the car until, swearing, groaning and eventually almost weeping, he'd managed to attach the two chains. He cut his left hand on the mudguard, his fingers were numb, the rubber band was too short to attach them properly, the hooks were ice-cold. Once he thought he'd done it, but the chain slipped back onto the ground. He worked determinedly, feeling the sweat on his forehead, then he'd managed it. As he drove off, cautiously, he could hear the rattle of the chains on the asphalt: they were holding.

He grinned, proud of his achievement. He was a genuine specimen of pre-war excellence, born shortly before the Second World War, defying snow and storm. He drove on slowly, taking care not to come off the road.

Just before the top the fog was gone. He was driving into sweeping countryside with dark clouds hanging over it. Long ridges, the black of the pines covered over by the brightness of the snow. To the left was the western slope of the Belchen, unexpectedly massive and steep.

He drove down into the Wiese valley, followed the river to the Rhine and crossed the bridge into Alsace. There he carried straight on to Hésingue, then up the rise until he took the turn-off to his house. He lit the stove, fed the cats and set about clearing the garden. The flowers were Hedwig's thing. She was the one who had planted them and lavished her care and attention on them, she knew their names. Most of them had not survived the previous night's frost, the flowers were hanging down slack on their stems.

Once he'd finished he went back into the kitchen, put some more logs in the stove and sat down at the table. He wrote down what he'd been thinking about while he was working in the garden.

Question one: Is the person I'm looking for actually a man? Couldn't it also be a woman? Answer: No. I cannot see a woman cutting open a whore's earlobe.

Supplementary question: Why ever not? Answer: I don't know.

Question two: Was it the same person in both cases? Answer: Yes. The procedure was so specific it must have been the same person.

Question three: What had Hardy Schirmer been hiding? What kind of past did he have? Answer: I'll have to talk to Hermine about that.

Question four: Who was Barbara Amsler's farewell letter intended for? Was it love, was it servitude, was it sexual dependence? Answer: I need to talk to Casali again.

Question five: What kind of scissors were used to cut open the earlobes? Would a pair of nail scissors have been enough? Answer: Yes, probably.

Question six: What kind of person is Skender from the Billiards Centre? Is he genuinely the decent husband and father he appears to be? Is it possible to understand a man from the Balkans? Or does that reservation border on racism?

He hesitated as he wrote down this last question. Basically, he thought the exemplary nature of his outlook was superfluous. But that was the way things were in the Basel police department. No one would have admitted to being racially prejudiced.

He went on writing.

Answer: No, that question does not come close to being racially prejudiced. This reservation has to be taken into account. So that means another discussion with Skender, taking note of what he says.

Question seven: Is it right to exclude the Albanian drug mafia from the equation? Might a falcon, a snake or an eagle be worth considering, e.g. Prenga Berisha? Answer: Yes, that might be worth considering.

Question eight: Was the killing of the man in the red Punto actually part of a blood feud? Was it Gjorg Binaku? Answer: Give Bardet a call.

Question nine: Is anyone from the late-night bars on Missionsstrasse a possible culprit? Laufenburger, Garzoni? Answer: No, that is unlikely.

Question ten: Why does Stallinger recite poetry all the time? Answer: Because a poem is language given form that lives on in time. Stallinger recites poetry because he is afraid of death.

Question eleven: Why am I pursuing a murderer so doggedly? Answer: Because that's my job. And because I want to stop him doing it a third time.

Question twelve: Is the wait-and-see tactic the right one? Answer: Yes, because I have no other choice. That's also the reason why I'm staying here and not going off to Paris. I must be here if and when something happens.

Then he wrote down one more question.

Question thirteen: Why is the rose killed by frost but not the aster? Answer: I don't know. Perhaps because the rose is too beautiful.

That was nonsense, he thought, an aster was beautiful as well.

He picked up his mobile phone and called Bardet.

"Listen, Monsieur," he said, "I have two questions."

"Yes, go ahead."

"Was the corpse in the burnt-out car wearing a ring?"

"What makes you suspect that?"

"I'm assuming it was a ring with a black stone and a falcon engraved on it."

"Perhaps it was an onyx, who knows? Perhaps the heat had made it crack."

"Thank you. At least that point is clear."

"Clear? What is clarity? You can't see your own hand in front of your face in this fog."

"In the second place," Hunkeler said, "I have a piece of information. I've read a book about blood feuds. A novel by Ismail Kadare."

"And the book is called?"

"*Broken April.* It says in the book that it's only a case of blood feud if the victim is shot in the forehead by someone standing in front of them."

"Interesting," said Bardet. "It could well be that a bullet hole in the forehead of that corpse was established. Is there anything else?"

"Yes. It seems that there are three families involved. However, a blood feud is carried out between two families. At least according to the Central European concept."

"That too is an interesting point of view indeed," Bardet said, and it was clear that the formal, stilted mode of expression was amusing him. "Only it is clear that the blood feud carried out here in no way corresponds to the Central European conception of justice."

He giggled. The click of a cigarette lighter could be heard.

"Moreover," he went on, "it seems that in this case other interests are involved, interests that overlap with the family interests. Large-scale financial interests. In any case, a further corpse was pulled out of a pond the day before yesterday in the Petite Camargue near Blotzheim, which is just across the border from Basel. Once again a young man, this time with a stab wound to the heart. A nice piece of work but, according to your definition, not part of a blood feud. And the man had a ring with a snake engraved on it. His name is unknown."

"He could well have been a Prela," Hunkeler said.

"What makes you say that?"

"I'd very much like to know where Ismail Binaku is hanging out. He's said to have been staying in Badenweiler. Do you know anything about that?"

Again Bardet giggled, and Hunkeler could hear him puffing out smoke.

"It could be that his work is done. I've no idea where the falcon is flying now. Presumably to another country. Is that everything?"

"Yes, thank you, Monsieur."

He picked up his notebook again and wrote down one final question.

Question fourteen: How can an old Swiss inspector understand all that? Answer: He can't understand it any more.

He looked out of the window into the fog, watching the hens who were scratching, pecking, scratching again and pecking again. He liked them. Then he phoned Casali and arranged to see him on Sunday evening in the bar at the Klingental. He called the pharmacy on Burgfelderplatz and was told that Hermine Mauch would not be back until Monday.

He stayed in Alsace for three nights, he had no idea what to do in Basel. In the evenings he sat in his neighbours' cowshed and listened to the milking machine, the chomping of the cows and the farmer's wife's moaning. From the farmer he heard that there was someone living in Bisel who had donkeys and might sell one or two. Bisel was a bit to the west, between Feldbach and Seppois-le-Haut. The man even had a small cattle truck and would bring any animals ordered up there, only if paid in cash, of course.

Hunkeler was uncommonly pleased at that. He immediately bought a few bales of straw and hay from the farmer and took it all across the road in the cart to put it in the old pigsty. The straw he scattered around by the hen coop, the hay he piled up in one corner. The straw for them to lie on, the hay to eat.

On Sunday evening he took a taxi across Dreirosenbrücke to the Klingental restaurant. It took its name from a convent that had been established close by in the Middle Ages. It was one of the nicest places in Basel, an inn like the ones you got round Les Halles in Paris fifty years ago, with whores for the simple man and warm food until the early hours. Now, early in the evening, it was only half full: two taxi drivers, an Italian family with whiny children, weary couples. Sitting beside the way through to the bar, where the prostitution business would begin at ten, were two old men Hunkeler knew. They were Jürg Federspiel and Werner Lutz and both were writers; he'd hung around the streets with them when they were all younger. He joined them and said,

Poetry is something
that's there beside us
goes on in parks
in public lavatories
on the trains
at stations of course
seldom at airports.

"Does anyone know how that goes on?"

"No," said Federspiel, "but I do know that it's a poem by Manfred Gilgien. How long is it now since he died?"

"Ten years," said Lutz.

"Then I'll buy a bottle of wine, if that's OK," Hunkeler said.

It was very much OK. And the food Hunkeler ordered was good as well. Sauerkraut with juniper berries and bacon, and watery potatoes to go with it. He liked sitting there and talking to writers. They talked about their fellow author Rainer Brambach, who'd died twenty years ago. Simply fallen off his bicycle and dead, the best of them all. About Dieter Fringeli, who'd drunk himself to death. About Guido Bachmann, who'd succumbed to whiskey. About Adelheid Duvanel, who'd gone out into the wood and lain down to die.

"Basically, Basel's a poet's town," Lutz maintained, "full of hidden beauty, full of poetry. Though hardly anyone notices. That's why the authors in this town come to a bad end."

"That's not right," Hunkeler said, "not all of them come to a bad end. The two of you are still alive. And you have a good life."

"What do you mean by good?" Federspiel asked. "I live to write. I can't write any more because nothing occurs to me any more. What do I have to live for?"

"You've written enough. You've already become a classic."

"What's that to me? I can't live as a classic."

A pensioner had sat down at the neighbouring table with a black lady of the night. He'd ordered spaghetti bolognaise for her and a half-bottle of red wine for the two of them. He watched her lovingly as she ate. He had his hand between her thighs the whole time. That didn't seem to bother her, she ate with great relish. Then they emptied their glasses and went upstairs.

At nine Casali came in, sat down at an empty table and waited. Hunkeler went over.

"Delighted to see that you have time," he said.

"Any time for you," Casali said. "How's business?"

"Business is bad. That's why I'm here. Perhaps you can help me."

"You're a state official with a permanent post, nothing can happen to you. At most you'll be suspended, isn't that right?"

He lifted the espresso the waiter had brought to his lips and emptied it.

"We of the red-light district are entrepreneurs. We are dependent on the economic situation, and that's poor. We suffer from the fear of AIDS, we suffer from Eastern European imports. Fresh goods, stunningly beautiful students who want to earn enough to pay their university fees. They come in on a tourist visa, work here for three months, don't register, don't pay taxes and ruin the market. If one of our ladies insists on a condom she's just laughed at. And then you come here to cry on my shoulder. What's that all about?"

He blew a speck of dust off his left cuff, in which there was a diamond.

"Where did you get that?" Hunkeler asked.

Casali raised his eyes and looked at him astonished, disbelieving. "My God, you're really something," he said softly. "I wonder why I'm wasting my time with you."

"Sorry," Hunkeler said, "it just slipped out. That was really stupid."

Casali thought for a moment. A vertical line appeared on his forehead. "I have heard," he said, "that they fished an Albanian out of a pond in the Petite Camargue Alsacienne. He'd been stabbed. What's the truth about that?"

"I heard about that as well but I don't know any more about it."

"So what have you been doing all this time? Perhaps you know that the Albanian drugs mafia is penetrating the red-light district. They're the worst kind of crooks."

"But you're a crook yourself, aren't you?" Hunkeler tried to smile as sweetly as he could.

"That question should be pointless, actually, shouldn't it? But I will tell you one thing. Although I'm not a pimp, I do look after my two establishments. I protect the ladies who work here. I also protect the customers, otherwise the business would be ruined. I will not tolerate these Albanian swine here. I know how to deal with them. That's something you should be aware of, Inspector."

He got up and was about to leave the table. Hunkeler grasped his arm, holding him back. Casali tore himself away, a thin purple vein appearing on his temple.

"Don't you ever touch me again," he said, almost inaudibly. Then he sat back down. "Ask me your questions."

"If you kill me, I will stay with you for ever," Hunkeler said. "Until now you've always claimed you didn't know who that was addressed to. Did you hit Barbara Amsler?"

Casali lowered his eyes so that his black eyelashes stood out. Not a muscle in his face moved, he didn't seem paler than usual. Despite that, it was suddenly a different face, a face of wax, of stone. He took out a cigarette, lit it with his silver lighter, blew out the smoke.

"Why do you want to know that? Is that not my private business?"

"I just can't get inside the woman's head. I'd like to understand who she was. Why she became a tart. Why she wrote such terrible things."

"You find those things terrible?"

"Yes."

Now a trace of colour appeared in the man's face again. Something like scorn. "I assume," he said, "you grew up in comfortable circumstances."

"It was OK. More or less. I skedaddled to Paris fairly early on."

"With enough money in your pocket to rent one of those cosy little garrets, yes?"

Hunkeler nodded, that was true.

"You see," Casali said, "we of the red-light district are a particular kind of people. Nobody who's not one of us will ever understand us. I'm not talking about the methods by which thousands of girls from Asia or Eastern Europe are forced into prostitution. I'm talking about clean work, about honest business."

"I can't imagine that Angel and Maria became whores of their own free will."

"Have you ever been to the Caribbean?"

"No," Hunkeler said.

"You should go there sometime. Then you'd see that on

the islands prostitution has a very different status from over here. There the whores aren't despised, they're respected. They play an important part in society. That's also the case in Spain, as in other countries where the most valuable dowry a bride can bring is her virginity. Angel and Maria were already whores when they came here. They came because they can earn more over here. When they go back home they'll be rich women."

A likely story, Hunkeler thought cynically, but he didn't say anything.

"Barbara Amsler was different. She was Swiss, from Schinznach Dorf, as you know. She had an unbelievable, insatiable longing for love. Her early life had been very difficult. She always had a runny nose, lived in institutions and homes, was beaten, kicked. I don't like talking about myself, but I will say this. It was like that with me. I've never known my mother."

This Casali had a strange face. Always pale and controlled. And yet curiosity could change to coldness, coldness to scorn, scorn to sorrow.

"When a woman comes in through the door here," he said, "I can tell from the very first look whether she's got what it takes to be a whore or not. I couldn't tell you how I know that, but I can see right away what her attitude to love is. Whether she loves love, whether she hates and despises love. Whether she loves or despises herself. Some women prostitute themselves because they hate themselves. Others so that they can despise men. They're not doing it out of love but out of hate. There are a few who, despite everything, find their great love. They want to debase themselves in the eyes of that love by prostituting themselves with other men. And they are the best whores. As it happens, the same is also true of the men who work in the red-light district. They too hate themselves, despise themselves. That's why they strut about so proudly. They deck themselves out with pearls and diamonds. They behave in an ice-cold manner. But if their beloved dies, they howl like a lonely wolf on a cold polar night. Even if no one can hear it."

He sat there at the table, suddenly slumped, very small, staring at his hands beside each other on the table. He swallowed once. Then he put his hand in his jacket pocket, took out some nail scissors and trimmed his left-hand thumbnail, carefully and precisely. Putting the scissors away again, he looked at Hunkeler out of grey, hard, old eyes.

"I'll tell you this just once. I'm telling you because I want to help you. Barbara's words of farewell were addressed to me. I think that with her death my life is over. She was the flower in my life, the rose. I don't want to live without her, it's too dreary. But there is one thing I will promise you. I won't let one of those bastards get away with strangling my beloved. If you don't find the murderer, I will."

He sat there a while longer, expectant. When Hunkeler said nothing, he got up and went over behind the bar.

Hunkeler went down the stairs to the men's room, stood at the urinal, put his hand against the wall and leaned his head on it. He stood there like that for a while and thought. Should he believe what he'd just heard, that she had been his great love? Had she really been the love of his life? Was a guy like Casali even capable of that? Wasn't it all simply about a commodity called sex, which earned Casali a fortune? And what was all that about a clean business? Hadn't he already seen Polish girls in the Singerhaus?

There was one thing, however, that did seem credible: Casali's threat to find Barbara Amsler's murderer himself. And not because Casali's life had been destroyed by Barbara's death, but because his business was under threat. Hunkeler was still assuming Casali was a pimp. And a pimp who cannot guarantee the safety of his whores loses credibility. Casali certainly would not lack the means of finding the murderer, he'd proved that several times already. He'd often been quicker and better informed than Hunkeler himself.

He went back up the stairs. Up there, right beside the bar, was the landlady, a woman with the figure of the Mother Goddess of Malta and the face of a girl. She was always sitting there, keeping an eye on the whole of the area.

"Please come over and sit with me for a moment," she asked.

Hunkeler sat down.

"I'm still waiting for the guy who went out with Barbara that night to appear again. I'd recognize him right away, even with a different toupee, and I'd call you immediately, I've got your phone number. I wouldn't be happy if Casali were to approach him himself. This is a respectable bar, I want everything to be right and proper. That's what I wanted to tell you."

"If I could prove," Hunkeler said, "that Casali uses violent means to coerce his girls, I could take action against him."

The landlady gave him a truly sweet smile. "Casali is a good manager. He has everything here under control. You don't find people like that very often. That's why I pay him so well. Please just leave it be."

Hunkeler stood up. He gave the woman a slight bow, surprising even himself. He went across to the two writers.

The pensioner returned with the black whore. He tried to kiss her on the lips again. She pushed him away and went behind the bar. He sat down at the table beside it and ordered a large beer. He drank it, slowly, in one go.

The barroom had filled up by now. Tarts from the Caribbean, from Thailand, few Europeans. Men over forty, some of Hunkeler's age and older.

The lounge was full as well. People from Lesser Basel across the river, store assistants with their friends, Swiss from other cantons, playing cards. There was no festive atmosphere; they had Monday morning on their minds.

At half past eleven Angel arrived. She was so beautiful that the eyes of all the men followed her as she disappeared into the barroom. Hunkeler had nodded to her, but she had paid no attention to him.

"I know one more," he said. "It's by Rainer Brambach and is called 'Salt'.

> "We need each other. We are
> the salt of the earth,
> salt, more precious than gold, more necessary,
> a single syllable, white contained in the cellar,
> lost in the Atlantic,
> in our bread, in our tears, in our sweat

> before birth or any other way, any other place,
> we need each other, salt of the earth, salt."

"I was there," Federspiel said, "when he wrote that poem. We were in a bar, there was a salt cellar on the table. Brambach was looking at it all the time, as if spellbound. Then I had to go for a quick pee. When I came back, he'd written it down. In a brief moment, in one brief, precise moment, because the salt cellar was on the table."

Hunkeler got up and went into the barroom. Whores were sitting on high stools at the bar. The throng of men was packed round them. Caribbean music could be heard, no one was making a fuss.

Only one person appeared to be drunk, an oldish, non-descript man who was standing beside Angel. Not tall, not short, not fat, not thin, with strangely bushy black hair. He was bawling the Caribbean song of the island in the sun, though without being able to speak English correctly. His hand went down Angel's low-cut neckline, he slowly grasped her breast. Angel laughed, a vulgar screech such as Hunkeler would not have thought possible from her. She undid his tie, opened his shirt and stroked his right nipple.

That was going too far for Hunkeler. He pushed his way through the men, using all his strength to get beside her, and tapped her on the shoulder.

"Fuck off," she said, "*viejo. Estoy trabajando.*"

It sounded sharp and nasty. He looked closely at the made-up face, the purple eyeshadow, the flaky light-coloured powder, he smelled her sweat. What a disgusting guy, playing with Angel's breasts in public. Why did she allow it? And what was that about his hair?

He put his hand out, grabbed the man's shock of hair and pulled – he had a toupee in his hand. A bald head appeared from underneath it. Angel let out a screech, the man picked up his beer glass and smashed it on the bar so that he was holding a sharp, pointed weapon in his hand.

"Bastard," he said, "you're not getting my Angel. I'll smash your face in."

Hunkeler drew back, his fists raised, ready to fight. But Casali shot between them, an ice-cold look in his eyes and a sharp knife in his hand.

"Off you go," he said, "or I'll call the police. Is that what you want?"

"He's got a toupee," Hunkeler said, "like the murderer. Only black, not grey."

"Nonsense," Casali said, "that's not him, it's someone else. Clear off, or there'll be trouble."

Hunkeler looked at beautiful Angel, who was rearranging her décolleté and staring at him, full of hate. He looked at the baldy, who was clutching the bar with one hand. The other was still holding the broken glass. Hunkeler threw the toupee on the floor and left.

Outside he tried to calm down. What had been going on in there, why had he lost control like that? Had he actually fallen in love with Angel during that night, was he jealous? Nonsense, he knew that she had slept with him on Casali's orders. Had he believed Barbara Amsler's murderer was standing in front of him? That was a piece of bullshit too, he knew he couldn't allow himself to treat any one of the prostitutes' customers as a suspect. Why then had he lost his cool?

Because he couldn't stand all this waiting, that was why. This sitting around and lying around, this waiting for something that didn't come.

He could only hope that neither Casali nor the bald man would call the police. Neither of them would, of that he was almost sure. Not Casali, because he wanted to keep order himself. Nor the bald man, because he'd want to keep his visit to the brothel secret.

Now Inspector Hunkeler was grinning cheekily to himself once again. He'd nearly had a fight in the Klingental, he thought, at his age. It had almost been a duel, with bare fists against sharp glass.

He went down a lane to the Rhine, the water was gliding past, dark in the light of the street lamps. He would find him, the guy, of that he was sure.

At two in the afternoon on Monday, 17 November, Hunkeler went into the Burgfelder Pharmacy. As always when he entered that kind of store, he felt embarrassed. He hated the smell, he hated the medicaments on offer, he hated the white doctors' coats worn by those who worked there.

A young assistant came up to him, a serious expression on her face. "Can I help you?" she asked.

"I would very much like to speak to Frau Hermine Mauch."

"I'm afraid she's not available at the moment."

She looked him straight in the eye and for a moment Hunkeler felt the appraisal of a surgeon who decides on life or death. Astonishing how quickly they learn that, he thought, and already he was stuttering a little.

"I have…" he said, then hesitated. "I have problems with my prostate."

"Do you have a doctor's prescription?"

"No, unfortunately not."

"Then I would recommend pumpkin seeds. They contain an active agent that will not cure your ailment but will certainly alleviate it."

"What does that mean? If I feel the need to pass water there's only one kind of alleviation. I have to pee."

She remained unmoved, went behind the counter and brought out a bag of pumpkin seeds. "You take a teaspoon of them every evening before going to bed."

"Perhaps I'll eat them with a knife and fork. I hope that won't reduce their alleviation effect."

She entered the price on the till and he paid.

"Goodbye," she said.

"I would very much like to speak to Frau Hermine Mauch."

"I'm afraid she's not available at the moment."

"Do you want me to turn the store upside down?"

She almost lost her composure. She probably felt like crying. But she stood her ground and pointed to the door. "That's the way out."

Then Hermine came in from the back. She looked superb. Her ivory face was even paler than usual, her look even cooler. The white doctor's coat gave her a dignity that immediately crushed any resistance.

"What do you want?" she asked.

"I want to invite you to dinner. Out in Alsace."

"You know I'm in mourning."

"That's the very reason why I'm inviting you."

She lowered her eyes, wondering what to do.

"I've given you all the information I have to give," she said. "Herr Madörin advised me not to talk to you."

"Advised? Or did he forbid it?"

She put her beautiful, slim hand to her neck, those delicate, slender fingers. There was a ring on one of them, and in the ring was a pearl.

"Where do you want to take me?" she asked.

"To the Piste du Rhin, outside Village Neuf. It's by the Rhine dam. If the fog isn't too thick, you can see the lights of the ships going past."

She took her hand down and tried a smile. "Right, pick me up at half past seven."

Once outside he went up Colmarerstrasse. He grinned at his awkwardness in dealing with the assistant. He would certainly have been able to buy twice as many pumpkin seeds for half the price in a department store. Moreover, he hadn't actually wanted to buy any pumpkin seeds. But that was just the effect of the white coats. Give them a sore finger and they'd have your whole hand off.

He stopped at the cheese store and looked in. He could see delicious things lying around in there, around a hundred kinds of cheese, a few carefully cut slices neatly set out. Eat cheese, my son, he thought, and you'll stay healthy. He went in and bought a piece of cheese from Mont-Soleil and some sheep's cheese from the Franche-Comté. Then he went into Hauser's news agency next door.

Hauser was sitting at his laptop, writing.

"Sit down," he said, "but don't disturb me."

Hunkeler sat down and waited. He liked what he saw. The worn carpet, the two plastic chairs, the bare walls, the unshaded bulb on the ceiling. Basically, Hauser was OK. He was always on the ball, worked a lot, didn't sleep much. And in the evening he was a good guy to have a drink with.

Hauser got up, came across and sat down in the empty armchair. He seemed to be thinking something over, then he wrinkled his nose. "What's that stench?"

"That's my sheep's cheese," Hunkeler said, "from next door."

"Oh, right. I thought I'd have to get a cleaner to come in. I hate cleaning women, they muddle everything up."

He took a toffee out of the dish, put it in his mouth and sucked it. The he spat it out in his right hand and threw it in the wastepaper basket. "They're no good, they're all too sweet."

"Do you know anything about the corpse in the Petite Camargue?" Hunkeler asked.

"Yes, if you buy me a beer."

Hunkeler nodded.

"The dead man's called Adrian Prela. Stabbed with a switchblade. Used to live in Tirana. Entered the country on a tourist visa. Reason given was to visit relatives. The stupid thing is that there's no Prela registered as living anywhere in Basel and the surrounding area."

"Why near Blotzheim in Alsace? Why not in Weil am Rhein or in Allschwil?"

"That I don't know. The gendarmerie don't seem to know either. Anything else?"

"Yes. What are you working on at the moment?"

Hauser got up, went over to the espresso machine and filled two cups.

"I don't have any sugar," he said, "it's OK without as well."

He emptied his cup.

"Don't you want any?"

Hunkeler shook his head. Hauser drank the second cup as well.

"Basically," he said, "it would be a huge story. A dead tart in the pond, a strangled pensioner outside the Cantonal Bank, a charred body on the edge of the woods, a drowned corpse in the conservation area. It's got everything: sex and drugs and murder. And all this either side of the border in an area where the three countries meet. It's an area that doesn't get enough coverage in our paper. And besides that, what's happening here is something that points to the future. The area is actually coming together, slowly and unspectacularly. And not only in the sphere of criminality."

"But?" Hunkeler asked.

"I'd need facts. I can publish conjectures and hints now and then, I can tart up the story a bit, that kind of thing, but it can only go so far. There comes a point when you have to start dealing in facts. And facts are what I don't have. I'm almost certain that the police don't have them either. And that Madörin's an absolute idiot. He goes for the Albanians like a mad bull, locks a few up, drives the rest away and he's got absolutely nothing to show for it. What do you think?"

"I think that one story has nothing to do with the rest."

"Oh, you do, do you? That's something at least. Get your cheese out."

He took a packet of crackers down from the shelf, tore it open and spread some sheep's cheese on one. He took a bite and started chewing.

"I'm writing a series about the St Johann district. Hardy's murder is the starting point. But that's just the plug. The

149

new editor doesn't want that much blood in the paper. He wants more social stuff, the real problems in present-day society, whatever that might be. He didn't like my photo of the dead Hardy. Times change."

He cut off a piece of the Mont-Soleil and ate it, this time without the cracker.

"In the St Johann district," he said, "forty-seven per cent of the population are foreigners. Any number of social problems, therefore: disturbed, furious Swiss pensioners, kindergartens and schools where no one can speak German. And among all this block after block is being torn down for an autobahn tunnel to be built. Clearly the kind of story our editor wants to use to soothe his social conscience. A man who lives in a villa above Lake Zurich with a view of the Alps."

"Please leave a bit of the Mont-Soleil," Hunkeler begged. "The sheep's cheese you can keep, I only bought it for reasons of nostalgia."

"Longing for what?"

"Actually, I could keep sheep out in the Franche-Comté," Hunkeler said. "That would be a quiet, peaceful life. Or don't you think so?"

"No," Hauser said, "take it with you. It stinks too much."

That evening, shortly before eight, Hunkeler drove with Hermine out through the customs post at Huningue. The road was empty, the commuters were sitting at home. The fog had thinned, you could see the brightly lit factories that Basler Chemie had moved out into the EU. They drove at twenty miles per hour through the old garrison town with the little bars and grocery stores, on the left the closed-down station, on the right cheap high-rise housing. Then came the elongated fishponds, all that was left of the old arm of the river. The sandy fields in which asparagus was grown in the spring. Now there were Brussels sprouts and leeks in them. Then the narrow strip of woodland that went down as far as the Petite Camargue.

He turned off up to the dam that canalized the Rhine and parked close to the water. The lights of the weir could be seen faintly across on the other side. There were swans on the bank and ducks, which had flown down from the far north to overwinter there. On the right was the Piste du Rhin restaurant.

During the journey Hermine had sat unmoving in the passenger seat. Not once had she turned her head towards Hunkeler. He'd said a few things, asked how she was. She had remained silent.

They sat at a table looking out over the river. Hermine wanted to keep her coat on, it was too chilly for her, she said.

"You have to eat the simple dishes here," he said. "They do them very well."

She still wasn't saying anything. She was pale and very thin.

"Eat something, drink something," he said, "otherwise your clothes will start falling off. I suggest sirloin with chips and salad. With a half-bottle of Bordeaux to go with it."

She nodded and he placed the order.

"I knew Hardy as a pleasant, sociable guy," he said. "But basically I had no idea what kind of person he was."

151

He looked out over the dark water, on which the rear light of a barge was going past.

She had put her hands on the table, neatly beside each other.

"I've never seen a pearl like that," he said. "It has a dark glow. Where did you get it?"

"It's a Tahiti pearl," she said, "they're very rare. Hardy gave it to me. For our engagement."

"Did he now? I never knew you two were engaged."

He watched as the woman who was serving them poured the wine.

"Cheers," he said.

Hermine picked up her glass, clinked his and tried to smile. "I'm so done in," she said. "The feelings of guilt are almost killing me."

"I can understand that very well. But it's wrong."

"If I hadn't thrown him out, he'd still be alive."

Two tears appeared in her eyes, stayed hanging there for a moment and then ran down her cheeks. She didn't wipe them away.

"When someone dies," he said, "the people closest to them almost always feel guilty. Because they hadn't paid enough attention, they think. But no one expects their partner to die. You couldn't live, couldn't love like that. And suddenly death comes along."

He would have liked to say something more fitting, but he couldn't think of anything.

"I'm aware of that in theory," she said. "But it doesn't help. I imagine him dropping off on that bench and a man coming along and strangling him. And thirty yards away I'm asleep in my bed."

"It's tough, that thought. I can understand that."

He shifted to the side a bit to make room for the woman bringing the food.

"How did you get to know each other?"

"It was nine years ago. I'd given up my job as a pharmacist and was working as a bartender in the Express Bar. I wanted to have normal conversations again, not all that doctor-chat any more. At the time I was together with Garzoni. Then, one evening, Hardy came in and sat at the bar where I was. I liked him immediately. He didn't drink much, just two or three beers. There was something optimistic about him, he was something of a cheeky guy. He told me he'd had stomach cancer and was on a disability pension. That despite that he still drove trucks now and then, moonlighting, of course. He was so trusting. He said he was divorced and had a daughter he'd lost contact with. He wanted to enjoy the time that was left to him, he wanted to get something off the ground. After that he came every evening. A week later I took him home with me. By the very next morning we were already engaged. He went to a jeweller's with me and bought me the ring. It was a lovely time."

She was sawing away at her sirloin a bit. It was clear that she didn't feel like eating meat.

"And Garzoni," Hunkeler asked. "how did he take it?"

"He felt insulted. He didn't actually admit that, but I noticed. He continued to fight to get me back. A few months later he bought the Burgfelder Pharmacy and appointed me. To help me, as he said. In fact, he did it so that he could keep me under control. Garzoni is a cruel man for whom power is everything, and he can't accept any kind of defeat."

"Why did you go along with it then?"

"Because it made things easy. I'm very well paid at Garzoni's."

She looked out of the window at the river, where a boat was appearing out of the darkness, a passenger ship with long, shining rows of windows. It was gliding upriver incredibly quickly, you could see the white foam of the propeller.

"Tell me something about Hardy," Hunkeler asked. "What kind of person was he?"

"I thought you'd been taken off the case. Or is that not true any more?"

"It is true. I'm just asking as a friend."

She gave him a thoughtful look. Then she nodded. "He was a charming vagrant, a gambler who hated nothing more than boredom. It was never boring with him. That's probably why I loved him so much. He was a lost soul."

She watched the ship go, with yearning, lips slightly apart.

"He was full of longing for love. He looked forward to every day that lay ahead of him. He was disappointed again and again."

"By you?"

She gave him an astonished look, slightly shocked.

"No, definitely not by me. I never gave him any cause for that. I was faithful to him."

She lowered her eyes. Once more two tears appeared, hanging from her closed lids. She took out a tissue and wiped them away.

"Who was he disappointed by, then?"

"By people in general. There was something wild about him, something alien that didn't fit into our world. He kept on trying to fit back in. He never entirely succeeded."

"Do you know anything about his family?"

154

"No, almost nothing. He rarely talked about his past. There must have been a dark point somewhere."

"What kind of dark point could that have been?"

She shook her head. Then she looked up again, showing him her sad eyes, watery bright.

"I don't think," she said, "he ever knew his mother. His father, yes, he talked about him. He had a filling station in Herznach, he said. He died early and then Hardy came to Basel and did an apprenticeship as a mechanic. More I don't know. Now I'd like a coffee so I don't fall asleep. It's so stressful."

Hunkeler ordered coffee.

"You assume he never knew his mother. Why do you think that was?"

"I don't know. She must have come from Bern canton – he hated that area. Why, I can't really say. He was a lonely soul."

She slowly sipped her hot coffee. No sugar, no milk.

"When did he start doing these Balkan trips?" he asked.

"Do you have to ask all these questions? They hurt, now he's dead."

"It's just because he's dead that I'd like to know."

She put her cup down and looked out at the dark Rhine once more.

"I don't know. It must have been before my time. He kept going away for a few days. He never told me why. He said it was better for me if I didn't know. Once he told me he'd been in Zagreb. I was scared, I can remember that. Back then it was dangerous in that region. He just laughed at that. Nothing would happen to him, he said, he'd managed to slip off the devil's cart several times. Somehow that was part of him, that aura of mystery, of a vagabond."

"Did you know that he was regularly carrying drugs on the return journey?"

"No, but I suspected he might be. It was no concern of mine."

"If he was carrying drugs," Hunkeler insisted, "he would have been well paid for it. You didn't know anything about that either?"

She looked at him anxiously, stroked her lips with her index finger, then slowly shook her head.

"And Garzoni? Do you still see him now and then? I mean just the two of you together?"

She stared at him, stunned. There was a trace of fury in her eyes, which she immediately wiped away.

"I beg you to take my mourning seriously and to respect it," she said softly. "Please take me home now."

Shortly before midnight he was sitting on the bench where Hardy had died, looking across the fogbound square. He saw the faint light shining in Hermine's apartment opposite, he saw it go out. Now she'd presumably gone to bed. The last number 3 came from the border, heading into town. He saw the pensioner who had recently lost his wife sitting in the front carriage; he seemed to be asleep. Hunkeler had forgotten his name.

He went over to the little tree and pissed on the cracked bark. It had to be, he wanted it to be that way. And his thinking was excellent as he did so. He sat back down on the bench and called Hedwig.

"Yes," she breathed.

"Sorry for calling so late. Were you already asleep?"

"No. I've just got in. From the Relais de l'Odéon, where the black people go. Well-dressed men, each and every one of them a beauty. We must go there together sometime. Are you coming at the weekend?"

"I don't know yet. I can't get away from here very easily, I've got any number of problems."

"Oh."

"Don't hang up," he said. "You have to help me. I need your advice."

"Go ahead."

"Hardy," he said, "the man who was killed, you know his lover Hermine?"

"Yes. What's the problem with her?"

"Is she a woman capable of love? I mean, is she the kind of woman who can lose herself in her love?"

"Oh, you men are all so stupid," she said. "You fall for every woman with a complexion like Dresden china."

"Not me," he said. "If I've fallen for anyone at all, it's you I've fallen for."

Now she giggled. She liked to hear that.

"You can fall for me because I'll catch you. She's cold right down to the bottom of her heart. She always knows precisely what she's doing. She only does things that are to her advantage."

"Well, at least she's a good actress."

"All of us women are. That's the way you lot want it, because you can't stand the truth."

"What truth?"

She paused for effect. He knew that now something beautiful was to come.

"The truth is that I have a yen for you," she breathed.

He stayed sitting there for a while, thinking of the yen Hedwig had. A nice word, he too had a yen.

He heard the sound of a dynamo turning, it was approaching from the town. A bicycle appeared out of the fog, he saw its thin light. A lassie with an orange knitted cap and a blonde ponytail was riding on it. White woollen gloves, a blue jacket. She was cycling cautiously, carefully, that struck Hunkeler. She halted at the stop light and put both feet on the ground. When the light went green, she got back on the saddle and disappeared in the direction of the border.

A comforting apparition. Lassie was a lovely word, just like yen.

He took out his phone again and tapped in Lüdi's secret number. It rang twelve times before he got an answer.

"*Oui, mon chouchou*, are you coming round?"

"I'm not your *chouchou*," Hunkeler said. "I'm your colleague Hunkeler."

"Oh right, just a minute."

He could hear Lüdi sitting up and the click of a lighter. "So what's this all about?"

"Two questions. Firstly, I'd like to know about Hardy Schirmer's past. Where he came from, what he did. Secondly, what his financial circumstances were."

"I can answer your second question. We were interested in them too. He had a considerable stock portfolio with a major bank, which he hadn't declared. Otherwise he wouldn't have got a disability pension."

"What does 'considerable' mean?"

"It means that before the stock exchange crash it was worth almost a million francs. How much it's worth today is difficult to say. Perhaps half that."

"You don't say," said Hunkeler. "And who will inherit this block of shares?"

"Hermine Mauch."

A marten appeared on the pavement opposite. It slowly went along the gutter. Then it crossed the road and disappeared down a passage.

"Are you still there?" Lüdi asked.

"Yes. I'm amazed."

"We were amazed too. As far as Hardy Schirmer's past is concerned, there's nothing I can do. I can't find anything in the population register. An FA in capital letters, nothing else."

"What does that mean?"

"That means that I don't know. I can't get at the data. And I don't know what FA signifies."

"Can't you do anything about it?"

"Yes, I could. I could make enquiries. Or I could try to find out on my own, but that wouldn't be entirely legal."

"But his prehistory, the stuff you can't get at, is important after all."

"Not for Madörin. He's concentrating entirely on the drugs business. Is that all?"

Hunkeler thought. He almost broke off the connection. But then something else occurred to him.

"I'd like to know the same about Thomas Garzoni."

"Why Garzoni?"

"I don't know. I'll be able to tell you when you've had a look."

"I'll try. Don't call me until the day after tomorrow. I've got a visitor tomorrow."

"Thank you, my angel."

"I'm not an angel. I have a yen for an angel."

After this conversation Hunkeler popped over to the Billiards Centre for a quick beer. Hauser was at the bar.

"These women," Hunkeler said, "what man can understand them? They tell you something, clear tears in their pure eyes. You try to comfort them and already you're being hoodwinked."

"Sounds bitter," said Hauser, "very bitter, but sounds about right."

"Grappa or beer?"

"Grappa, if I may."

As always, men were playing on the billiards tables. In the corner at the back a few Albanian couples were holding hands. Laufenburger, little Cowboy and Nana were sitting at the regulars' table. Senn, the second-hand bookseller, was there too.

"What's he doing here?" Hunkeler asked.

"He wants to get drunk. He's sold his store."

"Why?"

"He simply had to. A second-hand bookstore in a district like this'll never work. It's a crackpot idea."

He drained his glass and ordered a grappa, on Hunkeler's tab.

"If a pharmacy can pay its way," Hunkeler said, "a second-hand bookstore ought to as well. Pills and romantic novels keep people in a good mood."

"Wrong. People have to pay for their romantic novels themselves, the insurance pays for the pills."

Hunkeler slowly drank his beer, one sip after another. It tasted good, calming and bitter.

"Where did Garzoni actually get the money," he asked, "to buy the pharmacy?"

"I'd like to know that too. It was several years ago, for 1.4 million, the pharmacy plus two apartments."

"That's a lot of money," Hunkeler said. "Sometimes I have the feeling I'm doing something wrong."

He went to the bathroom at the back. The place had previously been a grocer's and this had been the store-room. There were two toilets, one for women, one for men. A young man came out of the ladies' room, clearly an Albanian. He seemed to be startled. But then he gave a friendly smile. He went across to the mirror over the basin, took out a comb and carefully combed his hair. Hunkeler would have liked to tell him that it was the wrong bathroom but he had no time, he was too desperate for a pee.

When he came out again, someone had sprayed a picture on the mirror. It must have been done very quickly but it was clearly a bird. An eagle with wings outspread.

He went back into the barroom and looked round. There was a sports bag beside the little potted tree. The zip was half open. He was about to go over and take a look at the bag when there was a hissing noise, a dull bang, not loud but clear. A murky cloud came out of the bag, clearly tear gas. The men playing billiards looked over to see what was going on. They started to cough and choke and ran out. In a few seconds the place was empty, they were all standing in the street outside, only the Albanians had run off. Nana was holding her Siamese cat tight under her jacket. Skender was crying – it wasn't clear whether because of the gas or with rage – but he definitely didn't want the police to be called. Laufenburger was sick in the gutter. The bookseller was cursing the Balkan riff-raff in a hoarse voice.

Richard came over from the entrance to the sex cinema across the road. Little Niggi was there as well.

"I saw him come out," Richard said, "I was standing at the entrance over there. I'd recognize him again at once if he came here again."

"I saw him too," said Niggi. "He ran off in the direction of the border."

They decided to go across to the Milchhüsli for one last glass. Hunkeler didn't go with them, he was too tired.

Over the next few days he was driven by increasing restlessness. He didn't like this sudden nervousness. He tried to keep it under control by going for walks in the Allschwil woods followed by a visit to Harry's sauna. He wanted to clear his head and think of nothing. He couldn't manage that. He felt as if he was close to a breakthrough that would light up the darkness all around at one blow, and that it would come from a completely unexpected direction. He suspected he ought to take precautions but had no idea against what.

At lunchtime he joined the two advertising men, who were close friends, in the Art Gallery cafe and had the set meal of roast beef, mashed potatoes and carrots. He listened to the two of them discussing the coming return leg of FC Basel's match against a top English club. They thought it possible that Basel would be successful and go on to the next round. A difficult task, but achievable. The previous season the team had at least achieved the almost impossible and qualified for the intermediate stage of the Champions League. They talked themselves into such a state of enthusiasm about soccer, as if they were going to turn out on the pitch themselves shortly. Like little boys, Hunkeler thought.

He too liked watching soccer. He used to play himself, every evening after dinner on an old disused tennis court until it was so dark they couldn't see the ball. Now he didn't take part in the conversation, it seemed so trivial.

He walked back to his apartment, across Barfüsserplatz and Marktplatz, then up Spalenberg to Petersplatz. The first Christmas decorations were shining in the store windows, with Father Christmases and fir trees covered in glittering snow. There were a surprising number of people out, grumpy-faced as always in November. People kept to themselves, avoiding each other as best they could. It was always like that in Basel, Hunkeler had got used to it.

On Petersplatz council workers were taking down the stands of the autumn fair. They were loading light-coloured boards into a ten-foot stack on a trailer. Hunkeler stopped and watched them. That was honest, clean work: first set up the market stalls, shelter them from the rain with waterproof sheets. Then offer all kinds of goods for sale, books and gloves, leather belts and raclette. Then take the stalls down again and store them away until the next autumn.

He looked up into the leafless elm trees to see if the crows were already there, having flown into town for the winter. They were there, dark and motionless in the trees, as if they were sleeping in the fog.

He spent Wednesday night in Alsace. He went to bed early and fell asleep straight away. He woke up once, it must have been close to morning. He thought he'd heard a cock crow. But it stayed quiet and calm outside. There was a bright light coming in through the window, as with a full moon, but it was diffuse, with no shadows. He got up and went outside. He stepped into new snow as deep as a man's hand; it was what had made the night white. Grey flakes were falling from the sky, wet and cold and silent, as if it had to be that way and no other.

At ten on Thursday evening he was sitting outside the Cantonal Bank again. It had been snowing there as well, but it had melted, apart from a few patches on the pavement. The air was clear, the fog had risen, well above the town.

There were only a few cars driving past, most heading for the border. The number 3 that went past was almost empty.

He was thinking about the next day, about his visit to Dr Naef. What would he do if he got bad news? Danger of a heart attack, constriction of the blood vessels, for example, because of all the smoking, cardiac arrhythmia? Would he agree to open-heart surgery, the insertion of bypasses or a new heart valve? There presumably wouldn't be anything else for it.

He called Hedwig and heard her voice on the answerphone. He'd been fortunate with that love, a rare piece of good fortune. Mostly, it seemed to him, he'd had bad luck. He'd attracted bad luck, like a magnet attracting iron, through his intransigence, his pig-headedness, as some people called it. He thought he wasn't pig-headed. He thought he was precise. That precision was presumably the reason why Hedwig loved him. He had no other explanation for her love. But perhaps that wasn't right either. Could you love someone for their precision? He'd no idea.

"It's me," he said on the answerphone, "your Peter. It's snowing and I'm feeling melancholy. I'm wondering how anyone can love a man such as I am."

He looked across to Hermine's apartment, where the light from the TV was moving. He saw that it was starting to snow again, big damp flakes. They melted immediately on the asphalt.

Shortly before twelve little Niggi came round the corner and joined him on the bench. He was wearing a winter coat and a woolly hat.

"Go to bed," he said. "I'll take over the watch."

"How will you do that? Who do you want to catch?"

"I'll lie down, as if I was asleep. Richard's over there. And when the guy comes, we'll grab him."

"That's not allowed. Anyway, he won't come again, he'll try it somewhere else."

"Go home now. You're old and tired."

It was true, Hunkeler did feel old and tired. He went down St Johann's-Ring, home to his apartment. Past the grocer's, where an Indian family had recently decided to try their luck. Past the second-hand bookstore, which would soon be cleared out. Past the Café Oldsmobile, which was dark and deserted. The Sommereck was closed as well, Edi was probably sitting in his apartment upstairs watching TV.

At the junction with Mittlere Strasse Hunkeler went over to the twelve-sided fountain there. He listened to the water trickling out of the three pipes into the trough. He didn't want to go home yet. He would have much rather driven out to Alsace. He wiped the snow off the wooden bench under the plane tree and sat down. Then he took out his phone and tapped in Lüdi's number. He replied immediately, he could well have been expecting the call.

"Listen," said Lüdi, "you seem to have hit the bullseye again."

"How come?"

"This morning I tried to get at Garzoni's particulars. And do you know what?"

No, Hunkeler had no idea. Perhaps he suspected something, but he didn't know precisely what.

Lüdi giggled, almost inaudibly. "Where are you, actually? I can hear water splashing."

"At the fountain on Mittlere Strasse. Get on with it."

"For Garzoni it's also restricted access. And I can't crack that one either. And he also has the initials FA."

"What does it mean, FA?"

"That's what I don't know. But what's striking is that both are restricted access and both have an FA. What made you think of Garzoni?"

"He was Hermine's lover before Hardy came along. He bought the pharmacy where Hermine works. He lives on the third floor of the Cantonal Bank building. And he goes to the Milchhüsli now and then."

"Interesting," said Lüdi. "So it could be a crime of passion?"

"What could that FA mean?" Hunkeler asked. "Have you any idea?"

"I really don't know."

"Can't you find out, for God's sake?"

"FA must mean Federal something. But that's all a little police corporal like me gets: sweet FA."

On the morning of Friday, 21 November, at ten on the dot, Hunkeler went into the joint practice of Dr Naef and Dr Gelpcke. He'd had a bad night, had stayed awake until three and then taken a sedative. He felt tired and listless. He had to start by sitting in the waiting room for half an hour with four other men, who looked pale and wan. Then he had to strip to the waist and sit on a kind of exercise bike. A young lady who, judging by her accent, came from Markgräflerland just north of the Rhine, stuck a couple of probes on his chest and belly. They felt strangely intimate, which he found slightly disturbing.

"How often a day do you do that?" he asked.

"What?"

"What you're doing here."

"I don't know. I'm just doing my job."

She's in a bad mood, he thought, perhaps her lover's run off. He could have understood that, she seemed to be angry.

He pedalled away, cheerful and happy at first, then panting and sweating as the resistance of the machine increased. As the first drops of sweat started to drip off his forehead, Dr Naef came in, a slim young man with the professional expression of an undertaker. He looked at a screen and waited until Hunkeler's legs tired.

"Not bad," he said. "Ten per cent over the average for people your age. Stand over here now, please."

Hunkeler let the angry lady show him where he was to stand. He did it like a good boy and waited to see what would happen. He heard the phone in his pocket ringing. He didn't dare respond.

Dr Naef sat down at another machine and seemed to be observing something. That lasted a few minutes, then he stood up again.

"What's actually going on in our city?" he asked. "You work for the police, don't you? Why aren't these murderers being found?"

"What murderers?"

"Don't you read newspapers? That Zurich rag has a long article about the St Johann district. It seems to be the law of the jungle that operates there. A shoot-out practically every day, people from black Africa selling drugs with impunity. Why aren't the police doing anything about it?"

"Where do you live?" Hunkeler asked.

"Bruderholz. Why?"

"Very nice too. Why are you interested in St Johann then?"

Two furrows appeared on the doctor's brow, he shook his head indignantly. He was probably not accustomed to people asking questions of him.

"You can get dressed again," he said. Then he sat at a little table and wrote something down.

"When will I get the report?" Hunkeler asked.

"You can have it right now. You're basically healthy, that is, healthy for your age. I've noticed that you smoke. You shouldn't."

"Yes, Doctor. Anything else?"

"What else?"

"There's nothing wrong with me inside?"

"I haven't seen anything wrong. Apart from the aorta, which is a bit dilated. The best thing would be for you to come back in a couple of years' time, then we'll have another look at it."

"Thank you, Doctor."

In the corridor outside he remembered that he'd left his raincoat hanging up in the waiting room. He went to get it, relieved and happy. He surveyed the men sitting there. None of them looked up. He felt like giving a whoop of joy, but he didn't bother because he thought it wouldn't be appropriate there.

He went into the nearest cafe and ordered a special sausage salad with a beer. He lit a cigarette, drawing in the smoke greedily. It was marvellous, he wasn't condemned to death, he had a life ahead of him. He took the tabloid out of the newspaper rack and read Hauser's article. So the St Johann district was a hotbed of criminality. It was dangerous to go out alone at night there. It was seething with sly Negroes, and if you didn't take care you could end up with a knife in your back before you knew what was happening.

That stuff was just too stupid, he felt. He took a sip of beer, fresh from the keg. Then he took out his phone to give Hedwig a call. There was a message and he listened to it. It was Füglistaller, telling him to come to Allschwil Pond at once. A woman had been pulled out of the water there; she'd been almost strangled.

Hunkeler parked at Allschwil Pond. He would have liked to drive up to the nature reserve to get there more quickly.

He was prevented by a barrier guarded by two colleagues from Allschwil.

He went up along the stream. He could still feel all the pedalling for Dr Naef in his legs. There was a group of Gypsies by the caravans outside the Rifle Club. They shouted something to him he couldn't understand, presumably insults. They shook their fists at him.

Parts of the path were covered in slush, the rest was clear. He could see his breath in the cold air. He glanced up at the sky. The clouds were low up there.

A dozen cars were parked by the nature reserve. Hunkeler saw at once that there was no ambulance there. They'd presumably already got the woman to the hospital. Which almost certainly meant she was still alive.

The cars of the two forensic squads were there, three of the crime-scene detachment, some other cars and a fire engine. There were a few men standing on the edge of the pond, watching two divers looking for something. By the little bench at the back specialists were scouring the ground. They were being very careful; they probably didn't want to tread on any possible evidence.

Sergeant Hasenböhler was leaning against the trunk of a beech tree, being sick.

"It's not my fault," he spluttered. "I can't be everywhere at once."

"Is she still alive?" Hunkeler asked.

Hasenböhler nodded and had to spew up again.

"Is she a Gypsy?"

"Yes. You know her. We both watched her sitting on the caravan steps eating an apple."

"Who found her?"

"That jogger over there."

Hasenböhler pointed to a man in the yellow outfit of a cross-country skier. "He was training for the winter season, he said, he wants to do the Engadin Skimarathon. He was running along by the pond and saw her floating in it. He pulled her out, put her across his knee to get the water to run out of her lungs. He shouted out loud and I came running. I called immediately. What else could I have done?"

"What about her ear?"

"That's it, that was the horrible bit. Someone had torn open her earlobe."

"Did she have anything in it?" Hunkeler asked. "A ring, that kind of thing?"

Hasenböhler wiped his mouth and chin with his handkerchief. "I don't think so. Or did you see a ring in her ear before?"

Hunkeler went over to the men by the side of the pond. Füglistaller was there with his team, plus Suter, Ryhiner, Haller and Lüdi. They gave each other a quick nod. There was also a woman of around fifty there, clearly a Gypsy. They were all watching the two divers floating in the shallow water.

"I have two questions," said Hunkeler, "if that's permitted."

Suter gave him a venomous look, but didn't say anything.

"Go ahead," said Füglistaller. "This is in the Basel Rural District area, so I make the decisions."

"Did the young woman say anything? Or was she unconscious? And secondly, did the woman have anything in her earlobe?"

"Ask Frau Căldăraru, she's her mother."

Hunkeler turned to the woman to repeat his question. But she'd understood it.

"When I came up to the pond," she said, "Eva was lying unconscious on the ground. I talked to her quietly and she opened her eyes. I asked her who it was. She said she saw a shock of red hair. That was all she said."

"That's right," the man in the yellow outfit said. "They spoke briefly to each other. I couldn't understand, it was in a foreign language."

"Eva didn't have anything in her ear," the woman said. "She's only sixteen. But he'd slit her."

"Where did you learn to speak such good German?" Hunkeler asked.

"Transylvania. We used to go there often. If she dies," she went on, "then the beauty's gone from my life. Then I'll curse this inhuman city."

"In all probability she won't die," said Dr Ryhiner. "He did try to strangle her, but he didn't quite succeed. The cervical vertebrae, artery and windpipe do seem to have been crushed but have suffered no terminal damage. And she'd only been in the water for two or three minutes."

"Who would do a thing like that?" the woman asked. "A young, innocent girl?"

Her whole body suddenly started quivering. She seemed to be swaying, but she managed to stay on her feet.

"Come with me," Haller said. "There's no more help you can give us here. I'll take you to your family."

He went away with her.

"I'm glad you're here," Füglistaller said to Hunkeler. "You're the one who's most familiar with the Barbara Amsler case. I'd like to work with you on the Eva Căldăraru case, if that's possible."

He looked across at Suter, who briefly snorted, as if a fly had flown into his nose.

"Right," said Suter, "that's agreed. I'll expect to see you in my office at five o'clock this afternoon, Inspector Hunkeler."

"Unfortunately that's not possible this afternoon," he said. "Could it not be tomorrow morning?"

"Why? Tomorrow's Saturday."

"I've things to do this afternoon. Until late in the night."

"If you insist. Tomorrow, Saturday, my office."

Hunkeler went through the slush to his car. He suddenly felt dead tired. Most of all he'd have liked to lie back against a tree stump here in the woods and have a little sleep. Then he realized that he wasn't just tired but also very calm. He was sure of what he was going to do now.

He went to the nearest bookstore and asked for an etymological dictionary, just to consult it. He looked up the word *Schlitzohr*. "Slit-ear, to slit", it said: a punishment in the Middle Ages for thieves whose ears were slit open. It was also used to identify Travellers.

"Do you have a book about Gypsies in Switzerland?" he asked the assistant.

"You mean Travellers?" she asked.

"If you like. You know what I mean."

"Yes," she said. "There's an excellent standard work, published in 1987. I haven't got it in stock. I can have it here by midday tomorrow," she said.

In the grocer's next door he bought three bananas and a bar of milk chocolate, went to sit in his car and started to eat the chocolate, slowly and with pleasure. Then he called Enrico Casali and asked for Angel's number.

"I don't like giving those out," Casali said. "I have to safeguard my girls' privacy."

"I've no time for jokes," Hunkeler said. "And since you're not her pimp, I'm sure you can have no objection to private contacts."

He was given the number and called it. Angel was at home.

"*Hola, hombre,*" she said, "*qué pasa? Quieres hacer el amor?*"

"No, I'm calling on business. Back then, when I visited you in the Singerhaus, what was it you said about Barbara Amsler? That she was a puta?"

"*Por amor, hombre,* definitely not. That's not a nice word."

"What was it then?"

"*Fuera una gitana.* Didn't you know that?"

No, he hadn't known that. He'd been too stupid.

He started the car and drove off. He went across the viaduct, past the station and out onto the autobahn. He grinned bitterly, he was furious with himself. Why had he forgotten the word *gitana*? It was a lovely word, he'd known it since he was young, when he'd discovered flamenco. And why hadn't he looked up the term *Schlitzohr* ages ago to see what that meant? Because he was pig-headed, stubborn, a mule from the Aargau.

After Rheinfelden he was driving into thick fog. He took his foot off the gas and switched on the headlights. Schirmer, he thought, had he not been a *gitano*? A vagabond, as Hermine had said? That meant there must be a man in Basel who had it in for Gypsies or travelling folk. Who punished them with death by strangulation and then marked them by slitting them. That was the word the Gypsy woman had used, up there in the nature reserve. "He'd slit her," she'd said.

Who was this man? What made someone at the beginning of the twenty-first century carry out such cruel punishments, like some kind of medieval kangaroo court? Where did such hatred come from?

He almost missed the rear lights of a truck flashing in front of him in the fog. He slammed on the brakes, pulled over to the right and parked on the shoulder. There he switched off the engine. He waited until his pulse had calmed down. And he decided that from now on he'd drive slowly and cautiously.

After Frick he left the autobahn and headed off towards Staffelegg. Ueken appeared: long rows of farmhouses, two inns. Empty, foggy fields, then came Herznach. He saw a small filling station with the Adler Inn right after it. He pulled up and went in.

There were three old men sitting at the table beside the bar. They turned their heads to see who was coming in. They didn't say a word. He went over to them, rubbing his hands as if he felt cold.

"Chilly outside, isn't it?" he said.

The one smoking a Brissago cigar nodded slowly. The two others just stared.

"May I?" Hunkeler asked, sitting down with them. The one with the Brissago nodded.

"Bloody fog," Hunkeler said, "you can't even see your hand in front of your face."

"The sun's shining up there on the Staffelegg. Are you going to Aarau?"

"No, to Schinznach Dorf."

"Why to Schinznach Dorf?" the one in the cardigan asked.

"Visiting relatives."

"Really? What are your relatives called?"

"Amsler," Hunkeler said.

"Aha, the Amslers," the man in the woolly hat said. "One lives in the upper village, Walter, he's as old as me. Is that the one?"

Hunkeler nodded and ordered a coffee from the waitress.

"He recently lost his daughter," the one in the cardigan said, "she was a tart."

"No, that was the other one. That was Werner," said the one in the woolly hat. "He lived in the Römerhof up there and he died five years ago."

"But his daughter was a tart all the same."

"She was a streetwalker," the man with the Brissago said.

"The filling station over there," Hunkeler said, "it used to belong to a Garzoni, didn't it?"

"I've no idea," the one with the woolly hat said, "who the filling station used to belong to."

Hunkeler stirred three sugar cubes into his coffee, nice and slowly so that they'd dissolve completely.

"I heard," he said, "that old Garzoni immigrated from Lombardy."

"Really, from Lombardy," the man with the Brissago said. "Why on earth? Why would he move here from Lombardy, to the back of beyond?"

Hunkeler sipped his hot coffee. He was going to have to be careful if he wanted to learn anything here.

"I know his son," he said, "he lives quite close to me, in Basel. He's the one who owns the Burgfelder Pharmacy."

"We don't know anyone called Garzoni," the man in the cardigan said. "Or am I wrong there? Do we know anyone called Garzoni?"

"No, we don't know a Garzoni," the man in the woolly hat said.

Hunkeler looked at the three men, sitting motionless by half-empty beer glasses, their eyes on the ashtray with the glimmer of the Brissago. He emptied his cup.

"The bill," he shouted.

"Already settled," the man in the cardigan said. "We don't like policemen here."

After Densbüren the climb up to the Jura heights began. Hunkeler grinned, partly out of rage but also out of amusement. He liked talking to people, especially country people. But here, with the men from Herznach, he'd been banging his head against a brick wall once again.

Up high, at Asp, he drove into bright sunshine. He was almost dazzled, the light was so glaring. He put his foot down, letting the engine show what it could do, which wasn't all that much. At the top of the Staffelegg pass he took the left bend, heading off in the direction of the Schenkenberg valley. He stopped, parked and got out his old walking boots. He put them on and set off, at first over meadows with a thin layer of snow, then through woods with spruce and pine trees. He reached the top of the ridge after an hour, sat down on a limestone rock and looked at what he could see.

The sun was low in the west, casting its light straight out over the sea of fog filling the valley of the Aare and the relatively flat part of Switzerland. The eastern cliffs of the Wasserfluh on the right were in shadow, the Alps to the south gleamed white. He could only see the spur of the Gislifluh. Beyond it the dark ridge of the Lägerns emerged from the fog.

He stayed sitting there for half an hour, enjoying what he could see. Then he set off back to the car and drove down into the Schenkenberg valley.

When he came to the first vines the fog started again. Thalheim, Kasteln Castle, Oberflachs, old villages of the Jura with limestone walls three feet thick. Then Schinznach Dorf. He drove through the upper village, turned off down to the church and stopped outside the Hirzen Inn.

He sat down at one of the long wooden tables. Outside it was gradually getting dark. He saw the fog illuminated by a tractor's headlights.

There were framed photos on the wall by the stove. He went over to have a look at them. The Men's Gymnastic Club of 1928 could be seen, men with moustaches in white clothes. The women's squad of 1944. The male voice choir of 1952. The wine press of 1914. The fire brigade of 1963. Beside them was a notice about the local rules for playing jass.

Hunkeler ordered a glass of white wine from the wood, and to eat: black pudding and liver sausage with sauerkraut and slices of dried apple. On the table next to his was a cloth for playing jass, a pack of cards and a slate with two chalks and a sponge.

He remembered that he had a dentist's appointment the next day. She intended to insert two screws for implants. He called her, recording his message on her answerphone.

"Good evening, Frau Dr Steinle. Hunkeler here. Unfortunately I can't come tomorrow, I have too much to do."

That wasn't entirely correct. The truth was that he was afraid of the noise of the drill, of the buzzing in his bones.

He ate slowly and carefully, chewing on the right side alone. Black pudding with apples, liver sausage with sauerkraut, it was pure poetry.

The place began to fill up around eight. A larger group of three oldish couples, presumably coming from outside the area. They also ordered the assorted cold cooked meats and sausages with sauerkraut. A younger couple, oddly nervous and fidgety, dressed like hippies from the sixties. Three young men speaking a language Hunkeler couldn't understand. An old man with a strangely anaemic-looking face, whom the waitress addressed as Cousin Sepp. He ordered the meat soup.

Three men of Hunkeler's age had taken the table beside his. They had come to play cards but took their time getting down to it. They ordered a half-litre of red wine and talked about Ernst Wiesel in the house across the road, who was now confined to his bed; about the farmer down by the bend in the road who had now also given up farming. There were only a few dairy cows left in the village and their days were numbered too. There used to be one dung heap after the other, in both the upper and the lower village. The jangle of bells could be heard throughout the village when the cows came down from the meadows in the evening. Now all you could hear was the through traffic.

Hunkeler stood up, put his card on their table and introduced himself.

"Weren't you here a few months ago?" one asked. "You were sitting over there with the mayor. It was because of Barbara Amsler."

"That's right," Hunkeler said, "but he wouldn't really say anything."

"That's the way he is, our Alois, a real politician. What do you want to ask us?"

"I'm looking for a serial killer. Three people strangled."

"Really? Wasn't there something again, yesterday I think, just outside Basel? I read something about it."

Hunkeler nodded.

"Join us if you like. I'm Fritz Riniker, that's Jakob Zulauf and that's Gottlieb Hartmann. Let's have a drink together."

Hunkeler let him fill his glass and all four drank to each other.

"Right then," Hunkeler said, "I'd like to know if Barbara Amsler was a Traveller."

They were silent for a while. It almost looked as if they were going to break off the conversation.

"She certainly wasn't a Traveller any more," Fritz said. "But what has that got to do with it?"

"She, like the two other victims, had had one earlobe slit open. In the past they used to punish Travellers that way to mark them out."

"Oh."

They were thinking about what to say. Fritz was the first to make up his mind.

"There used to be a lot of Gypsies around here. They were mainly Yenish folk who'd been here for ages. The Aargau used to be a kind of no-man's-land where there was no centralized power. The Frick valley, ruled by the Habsburgs, was a long way away from the centre of power. The federal governors in the Confederation changed every year. They didn't bother much with the Travellers. The Bernese did, though, they tried to keep the Travellers out of their district. But their power didn't extend to the out-of-the-way valleys of the Jura. Moreover, it was pretty easy to keep out of the way of their country policemen. You just had to cross over into the valley or the Confederation."

"How do you know all this?" Hunkeler asked.

"I was a primary school teacher here for forty-two years. As a teacher you had to give talks and write things for the New Year edition of the paper. You automatically become a local historian."

"The Hartmanns are also partly descended from the Yenish people," Gottlieb said. "My great-grandmother was an Amsler. I got that from old Marie who lived over there in the Rinikers' house. We all went to her school."

"True," said Jakob, "and we always had to pray with her. Then we got a stick of liquorice from her to suck – we used to call them bear turds."

They all three nodded, presumably remembering the late Marie and the liquorice.

"So the Amslers are a Yenish family," Hunkeler said, trying to get the conversation back on track.

"Originally, yes," said Fritz, "but they have long since merged with the settled population. Barbara's mother, she was Yenish. She was called Rosa Minder and originally came from the old part of the Aargau. She went to school with us but often played truant."

"Roseli," Gottlieb said, "she was a lovely girl. She had very bright eyes and laughed a lot. Sometimes she'd tear her handkerchief apart in front of us to show off to us lads. She was born in the Aarau cantonal hospital. Because her mother suffered from depression."

"Oh come on," Fritz said, "she didn't have depression. She was forcibly interned in Königsfelden by the anti-Yenish aid organization Children of the Road, who worked on behalf of the government. Little Rosa was taken away from her immediately after birth and taken to a foster family in Aarau. She never saw her mother again. At least that's what she told us."

"So what happened to her mother?"

"She died of grief, people said, but no one knew anything precise. What's more, that so-called aid organization was partly financed by the Pro Juventute charitable foundation, above all through the sale of postage stamps."

"I took part in that," Hunkeler said.

"We all did," said Jakob, "we went from house to house selling those Pro Juventute stamps. We all thought what we collected was to go to the poor orphans."

"That was Dr Siegfried," Gottlieb said, "he thought that up."

"Why have we never heard about this?" Hunkeler asked.

"People do know," Fritz said, "if they want to know. But they're ashamed of what happened."

"What happened to Rosa?"

Rosa came to our village when she was around eight. They lodged her with Stephan Müry, down by the stream, he was paid for her maintenance. But he wasn't good to her, she kept on running away. Once she got over the Staffelegg and down as far as the Rhine. The police brought her back. The pastor then went to see how she was and looked for a better place for her."

"That's right," said Gottlieb, "with my relatives. She grew up with their son, Werner Amsler. She married him later on. He treated her well, but she never became a proper farmer's wife."

"She was very beautiful," Jakob said, "and she really loved dancing."

"But things didn't work out with Werner," Gottlieb said. "He'd had polio and was lame in one leg. And then she had Barbara, her only child. She was just like her mother. She also liked to take things too far."

"I taught her at primary school," Fritz said. "I liked her very much. She was actually quite clever, but she hardly ever did her homework. She could easily have got into the district school that prepared kids for high school, but she wasn't interested in that. At twelve she went off on foot and got as far as the French-speaking region. She was picked up there and put away in various institutions. We here in the village lost touch with her. Once she worked as a waitress in the railway station up by the Bözberg tunnel, for three months. Another time we heard that she was in Thailand. Eleven years ago she returned to Switzerland and worked as a store assistant in Basel. Then we heard she'd become a prostitute. That was the way things were for Barbara, she didn't have much luck."

"And her parents?" Hunkeler asked. "What happened to them?"

"They were pleased when she came back. Rosa went to see her in Basel a couple of times. Not Werner though, he wasn't going out any more. Once, about seven years ago, Barbara turned up in the village with her fiancé. He was a smartly dressed, elegant Italian. It was early summer, they came in a convertible with the top down and drove very slowly through the village. They brought Barbara's parents down from their farm, the Römerhof, and they all had a meal here, in the Hirzen."

"Over there in the corner," Jakob said, "that's where they had their meal. Barbara had a really beautiful pearl in her ear."

"That's right," said Gottlieb. "The place was packed. They'd all come to congratulate the young couple. And the Italian paid for everything."

"And then we heard she'd become a prostitute. That broke Rosa's heart. We didn't see her in the village any more and she died soon after."

"From what?" Hunkeler asked.

"From melancholia. They say she stopped eating and slowly starved to death."

"Werner," Gottlieb said, "didn't survive that for long. He started drinking – schnapps. We drove him up to the Römerhof a few times when he'd stayed on in the inn after closing time. We did try to talk him out of it, but we couldn't help him. One night he went down to the Aare to drown himself. And he succeeded, we couldn't keep an eye on him all round the clock. They're lying next to each other in the graveyard."

"Yes," said Fritz, "that's the way it was, just as we've told you. A sad story, wasn't it? But we can't put right all the mistakes that were made in the treatment of the Yenish people at one blow. We're an open, tolerant village. Perhaps that comes from the fact that as a south-facing valley we get a lot of sunshine. But the crimes committed against many of the Yenish people sixty, seventy years ago are still having their effect today. Even though they're not our fault."

They fell silent for a while. The sad story had exhausted all four of them.

"Despite that I'd like to pay for another half-litre," Hunkeler said. "The wine is excellent."

"Good," said Jakob, "Let's play jass for a half-litre."

Each one took a card to see who was playing with whom. Hunkeler was with Gottlieb.

They played jass slowly and carefully. They gave themselves plenty of time to think. Only now and then was there a touch of venom, in a quick look at one's partner or an almost inaudible curse. A few times Hunkeler was close to screaming at Gottlieb Hartmann. But he kept himself under control.

"Are you playing the wrong card," he asked in as friendly a tone as he could manage, "or are you showing me a suit when you throw it away?"

"It all depends," Gottlieb said firmly. "You're meant to notice it, but you don't notice anything at all."

At ten a dozen women came in. They were carrying sports bags that they deposited by the stove. They all seemed to be fit as a fiddle, bursting with *joie de vivre*. They sat at the table in the corner and ordered mineral water, coffee and beer. They were chattering and laughing away so merrily that Hunkeler, delighted, kept looking across at them.

"Hey, you just keep your eye on the game," Gottlieb said venomously. "That's just the ladies' squad. Keep a better eye on the card I'm playing."

They played for three half litres. And each time it was Gottlieb Hartmann and Inspector Hunkeler who had to pay for it.

They said goodbye around twelve. It had been a lovely game, said Jakob Zulauf, he should come again and be sure to bring enough money with him.

Hunkeler got back into his car and drove through the village. Then he saw the vines appear in his headlights. After Thalheim he was driving through a starry night. He saw the snow crystals glittering in the meadows.

The next morning at eleven he collected the volume he'd ordered from the bookshop. Back home he lay down on his bed with it and started to read. He read that the aid organization Children of the Road had been set up in 1926 and lasted until 1973; that it was the aim of that organization to make Travellers sedentary in Switzerland; that they hoped to achieve this by taking the children away from Travellers; that they had not revealed to the parents where the children had been taken; that they hadn't told the children who their actual parents were; that they had imprisoned mothers and fathers in institutions, prisons and psychiatric clinics if they refused to accept this and tried to find their children; that the new 1980 Canton of Argau constitution officially recognized "non-sedentary ethnic minorities" for the first time; that the files of the aid organization were sealed in 1986 and transferred to the Federal Archives in 1987; that in 1988 the federal government awarded the Arise Yenish Foundation three and a half million francs in compensation.

Hunkeler also read a couple of the attached transcripts of statements by people who had been directly affected. They were so terribly sad that he gave up.

He put the book away, went into the kitchen and ate the three bananas, one after another. He put on some water to make tea and waited until it was hot. He drank three cups of tea. Then he lay back down again and tried to get to sleep. He didn't manage to do so for a long time. How could someone deprive a mother of her child, he wondered. How could they stop her searching for her stolen child? What did they have against these people who travelled round the country? Why had they been so cruel to them? After all, Switzerland was a democracy. And democracy didn't mean the dictatorship of the majority, but protection for the minority and the right to participate in decision-making. At least that was what Hunkeler had learned.

How did it come about that people tried so desperately to force a particular way of life on others? Why couldn't everyone live the way they wanted?

But that was how it had always been in the history of the world. Individual people kept on gaining power over the rest. Once they were in power, they went over the top and became crazy. For there was nothing so hard to bear as power. And many of the powerless had to suffer from that.

With such unavailing philosophical thoughts, Hunkeler fell into a short sleep.

*

Shortly before five that evening he was outside the Waaghof and ringing the bell. He had to wait for several minutes before Kaelin, the attendant, came and opened the door.

"What are you doing here?" he asked. "Firstly, it's Saturday evening, and secondly you're not allowed in here at all."

"You just shut your trap," said Hunkeler, "otherwise I'll give you a kick in the balls."

Kaelin's jaw dropped and he drew back, allowing him in. Hunkeler went up the stairs to Suter's office and knocked. Suter was sitting at his desk reading a newspaper, the *Frankfurter Allgemeine* in fact. He stood up and took Hunkeler's arm.

"Come on, let's sit down and talk like sensible men."

Hunkeler sat in one of the armchairs.

"Would you like to smoke?" Suter asked.

"Not at the moment, no."

"I'd quite like to have coffee sent up, but as you will know, the cafeteria's closed because it's Saturday. Even though we're all hard at work here."

He waited to see if Hunkeler would say anything, but he didn't.

"I've made enquiries," Suter said, "to find out how little Eva Căldăraru is, and I was delighted to hear that she's out of danger. She's in Bruderholz Hospital. There's a guard on her round the clock. There's also someone from her clan with her. Naturally, you can go and see her any time."

"I thought the case was under the jurisdiction of the Rural District CID."

Suter gave a brief snort. "Of course," he said. "But I'm in constant contact with Füglistaller. There are clear parallels with the Schirmer and Amsler cases. We can only solve the case through trans-cantonal cooperation, even though our country colleagues can still be stubborn at times. But that will sort itself out."

Hunkeler was leaning right back in the armchair but his oblique position didn't bother him at all this time. "What has Madörin actually found out?" he asked.

"Madörin's getting on with it. He seems to be close to a breakthrough. But it appears to be the way you thought. Albo, which is clearly dealing in drugs, doesn't seem to have anything to do with the murder of Bernhard Schirmer."

He flicked a speck of dust off the lapel of his cinnamon jacket. Then he looked Hunkeler in the eye with a man-to-man expression.

"As you know, the senior prosecutor has instituted proceedings against you. There are plenty of reasons for that. Letting Ismail Binaku escape really was a piece of incompetence. He could have given us some decisive help in our investigations."

"No," Hunkeler said, "that man would never have talked under pressure."

"Be that as it may. Nevertheless, I've been holding a protective hand over you, if I may put it like that. I've seen to it that the procedure against you has not got under way. I stand by my men, even if they don't always make it easy for me."

"Good," Hunkeler said, "then I'll come back to work again."

"That would be my wish, yes. You can pick up your keys and go back to your office."

"And I'll work just in the way I see fit?"

"That's what you've been doing all the time. Even while you were under suspension, haven't you?"

Now Suter did indeed smile, an honest, heartfelt smile. "Lord above," Hunkeler thought, "the man must be in a bad way."

"Has Madörin actually got nothing concrete to go on?"

"Not at the moment," Suter said.

"What's the situation with the corpse in the red Punto outside Heiligbronn and the one in the Petite Camargue? Have they been identified?"

Suter lowered his eyes. He clearly felt uncomfortable talking about it. "I suspect you already know that. You're our best man. Devil only knows how you keep on managing it."

He leaned forward, as if he was going to get up. But then he didn't.

"They are Gjorg Binaku and Adrian Prela. But they come under Monsieur Bardet's authority. And he's getting nowhere either."

Hunkeler took a cigarette out of the box and lit it. He had all the time in the world.

"We can't get at Bernhard Schirmer's data," he said. "Why?"

"Go on," said Suter, very quietly.

"Likewise, we can't get at Thomas Garzoni's data."

"Why Garzoni?" Suter asked. "Why are you bringing him into it?"

"Because the details of the two of them have the same note: FA."

"Garzoni, isn't that the man who owns the Burgfelder Pharmacy?"

"Yes. And he was Hermine Mauch's lover before Hardy turned up."

"So a crime of passion? What do you think?"

Hunkeler shook his head slowly. He didn't know.

Suter leaned forward. "How did you find out about the notes?" he asked. "In general you're not one for computers."

"I have a colleague."

Suter considered this. Now he'd gone very pale. "So there are people in my team stabbing me in the back."

"No, that's not true, no one's stabbing you in the back. We're searching by different routes. But we all have the same goal."

"Is it Lüdi?"

"In our profession there's an unwritten rule, which you know very well. You don't reveal the names of informers."

Suter thought, eyes down. Then he nodded.

"Right then. You have to work as is best for you. Anyway, I've also made enquiries in Aarau about Barbara Amsler and her mother. Her mother's maiden name was Minder. And Rosa Minder's data also has the note FA."

"And what do those two letters signify?" Hunkeler asked.

Suter had gone even paler. Hunkeler had never seen him like that. The state prosecutor was having a hard time of it.

"FA means the Federal Archives. They have the files of the Children of the Road. I have that from a Party colleague in the Department of Justice and Police. I ask you to treat that information accordingly."

"I wouldn't have got that," Hunkeler said, "even though it's pretty obvious."

"What's pretty obvious?"

"I've found out that Barbara Amsler had a Yenish mother who got into the hands of that aid organization. Schirmer is also originally a Yenish name. Eva Căldăraru comes from a family of Travellers."

"Oh my God," Suter said. "What has the past got in for us? Visiting the iniquity of the fathers unto the third and fourth generation. We can't do anything about the iniquities of our fathers. We try to repress and forget them. But they come back to us."

They both fell silent. Hunkeler knew that he was at one with his superior again. "I have to access those details," he said. "They're the key to solving these three cases."

"Right, what has to be has to be," Suter said. "The files are in Bern. I'll call Elvira Hebeisen. She'll get in touch with you."

On Sunday morning Hunkeler drove to Bruderholz Hospital. There was a strong headwind blowing. The snow had gone, the meadows were in bright shafts of sunlight coming down through white clouds. Clearly it was föhn weather. At the reception desk he asked for Eva Căldăraru's room. He bought seven roses and took the elevator up to the eighth floor. Sergeant Hasenböhler of the Rural District CID was out in the corridor, asleep on a chair. There was a torn-open packet of hazelnuts on the floor beside him. Hunkeler woke him up.

"Oh, it's you, Hunkeler," he said, bending down for the nuts. "What are you doing here? I thought you were suspended."

"Is this what you call exemplary devotion to duty, Sergeant Hasenböhler? Sleeping while on guard?"

"I can't sleep at night any more, that's why I'm so tired during the day. I've got such a guilty conscience. But I just can't be everywhere at once."

"How's the patient? Has she had many visitors?"

"Fat Hauser was here. He wanted to take a photo. I got rid of him. Otherwise there's any number of women who've come. Gypsies all of them. You can't understand a word they say."

He stuck a couple of nuts in his mouth and chewed nervously.

"By the way, I'm glad you're here. One of us has to catch the bastard. Only you can do that."

Hunkeler opened the door and went in. He was immediately taken with the solemn mood in the room. Eva was lying in a bed, her face white and her eyes closed. There was a tube going into her open mouth and down her windpipe, a machine was pumping in a regular rhythm. Four Gypsy women were sitting neatly beside each other on the other bed, wrapped in black coats. One was Frau Căldăraru. They were all sitting in such a way that they could see Eva's face. Hunkeler waited a while, then went over to a table and put the flowers down. Then he looked at Eva. She had a white bandage around her neck and a dressing on her left ear. Her face was haggard.

He went over to the big window that took in the whole south side of the room. The sun had gone, the sky had clouded over. In the west he could see the tree-covered Blauen hill, looking almost close enough to touch; to the left were the individual hills of the Jura range, which went down to Gempenstollen.

Frau Căldăraru stood up and signed to him to step out of the room with her.

"Will you come and have a coffee with me?" he asked.

She nodded. They went down to the cafeteria and he fetched two cups.

"She won't get stolen," he said, "we're keeping a good eye on her."

She sipped her hot coffee.

"We haven't come here because we're afraid she might get stolen," she said. "We're all here so that she has company, so she's not alone."

"From what I've heard her condition isn't critical any more."

The woman shook her head a little. Then the tears started to run down her cheeks. It happened very suddenly, her expression didn't change.

"Would you like my handkerchief?"

She took it and wiped the tears away.

"What kind of country is this," she said, "where someone tries to throttle a young girl? What kind of people are they, who look on us with nothing but contempt and hostility? Aren't we God's children as well?"

"Yes," Hunkeler said, "you are just as much God's children as we are."

"We're going to stay here until Eva comes out of the hospital. Then we're going away, across the border."

"Where do you intend to go?"

"We'll keep going until we find a country where we can live in peace, the way we want to. We will find such a country, I'm sure of that."

He looked out of the window, embarrassed, not knowing what he could say. He saw that it had started to rain outside. The drops were splattering on the windows, whipped along by the wind.

"I will find the man who did this to your daughter," he said. "Perhaps you can help me."

"How could I do that?"

"By telling me what you saw."

She thought, shook her head.

"I have to go through everything first to bring it back to mind. We had breakfast, as always. Eva went out with the dog. She always does that after breakfast. I heard her talking to the girl next door. The dog barked. Then everything went quiet. I assumed she'd gone over to the ponds at the back. She often went there, she likes being by the water. Then, around half an hour later, the dog was at the door yowling. I let it in. It immediately crept under the bench. That was when I knew something had happened. I ran out the back and saw her lying on the ground. The ambulance arrived immediately, the police a little later."

"Is there anything that's struck you during the last few days? Some figure? Some man?"

"Yes, the policeman who's sitting outside Eva's room. He's been watching us all the time."

"Anyone else? It could, for example, have been a man of my age. Perhaps one with striking hair."

"The same people appeared every day. Lots with dogs. I notice that every time when our Kaló gives a warning bark. The keep-fit trail starts a bit further back. Several older men run past every day. Oh yes, one did strike me because he had such strange light-blonde hair. I've seen him two or three times. He's roughly your age. But his hair's almost yellow."

"Is there anything else that struck you about that man?"

"No, nothing else. Apart from his hair there was nothing particularly striking about him – not tall, not short, not fat, not thin either. But he took a good look at us every time."

"When did he come every day?"

"Usually on the dot of nine. You could have set the clock by him. I always noticed when he ran past. Kaló doesn't like him. He started growling every time."

"Would you recognize that man, in a photo for example?"

She thought. "No, I don't think so. There was nothing special about him, I can't even remember what he used to wear. Just his light-blonde hair, that stood out."

That Sunday evening he went down to Burgfelderplatz to sit outside the Cantonal Bank. It was raining too hard, the föhn wind was making the drops splatter almost horizontally against the walls. He stood in the entrance of the sex cinema, waiting for the wind to die down. A young couple walked past. They were arm in arm, the man carrying a red umbrella that was suddenly swept up and flew away through the air. They both whooped, laughed and ran after the umbrella until they caught it. Then they linked arms again and went on in the direction of the border.

Hunkeler tapped in Hedwig's number. She answered.

"Good that you've called," she said. "I've made a wonderful discovery. Do you know Marie Laurencin?"

He remembered vaguely having heard the name once. Hadn't it been in Paris when he was reading Apollinaire, *Ombre de mon amour?*

"I'm not sure," he said. "Who's that now?"

"Just like a man. You only know the big boys, Picasso and Apollinaire."

"What do you mean 'just like a man'?" he shouted. "I have to go and see the urologist tomorrow. He might cut out my prostate because I've got cancer."

"Oh dear. I didn't mean to upset you. Is it really that bad?"

"That I don't know yet. I'll be able to tell you tomorrow evening."

She waited, she was thinking.

"I don't think you've got prostate cancer. You're not the type for that. And anyway, it would be a great pity."

Yes, that was his opinion too: that it would be a great pity.

"Nothing doing there," she said, "you haven't got cancer. If I were to drink as much beer as you, I'd be dashing off to pee all the time."

"Only you haven't got a prostate. A prostate's 'just like a man'."

She decided to laugh, she was simply enchanting.

"This is what we'll do. Tomorrow you'll go to the urologist and get examined. He'll confirm that you have a somewhat enlarged prostate. Perhaps he'll prescribe some medicine. You'll swallow it like a good boy. Then you'll come to Paris and go and see the Laurencin exhibition with me. She spent all her life painting the same picture. A young, beautiful, bewitched and unreal young woman. Actually, it's a picture of a woman who doesn't exist at all."

"Agreed," he said, "I'll come if I've found this guy. He almost killed a girl a couple of days ago."

She was horrified, he could tell from the way she gasped.

"I thought you were suspended?"

"Not any more. I'm back at work."

"My God," she said," what a terrible profession you have. Listen – the Laurencin exhibition goes on until 9 December. If you can't find time for me by then, we go our separate ways."

He stood in the cinema entrance for a while longer thinking about what Hedwig had said. She was right, his profession was terrible, just now at least. And what would he do if he was diagnosed with cancer in the morning? He'd no idea what he'd do in that case. All he knew was that he had to find the guy who'd slit Eva Căldăraru.

Which direction had the unknown man come from, on that night of 26 to 27 October, to go up to Hardy while he was asleep? From St Johann's-Ring? From the border? Down from Colmarerstrasse? From the town centre? Had he walked past the Billiards Centre? Had he seen the glitter of the diamond by the light of the street lamp? Had he known Hardy?

He heard footsteps. They were coming from the right, from the town centre. They were so soft he could hardly hear them. He withdrew into the darkness of the cinema entrance. The footsteps stopped, there was nothing to be heard for a while. Then they started up again, coming closer.

It was Richard who came round the corner. Going very slowly, as if he was stalking something. He looked ahead, to the square, as if something was moving there. Then he turned round and stopped in surprise.

"My God, Hunkeler, what are you doing here? You gave me a fright."

"You gave me one too," Hunkeler said. "Why are you creeping around?"

"I come here every night. I'll keep coming here until I catch the guy."

"You shouldn't be doing that, as you very well know. Please leave it to the police."

"No, I'm not going to do that. Because the police can't find him."

"If you use violence," Hunkeler said, "there be one hell of a row."

"So what? What kind of place do you think we live in? We're not going to let someone get away with strangling a young girl and throwing her in the water."

"I'll have you locked up," Hunkeler said, "if you lay just one finger on anyone."

He went across the road to the Billiards Centre.

He sat down with Laufenburger, Nana and little Cowboy. Also at the table were Senn, the second-hand bookseller, the pensioner Rentschler, and Joseph the Bavarian with his wife. Unusually, she didn't seem to be cheerful. She was sitting there motionless, very upright, stony-faced. No one at the table was saying anything.

Across the room at the bar were two well-dressed men of around forty. They seemed to be very fit. They had cups of coffee before them and at regular intervals kept breaking out into loud laughter, a little too loud, it seemed. Presumably two Albanians who were telling each other jokes.

Hunkeler looked at Joseph the Bavarian and then his wife. There was something wrong there. He leaned forward and quickly grasped Joseph's collar, picking off something he'd seen shining there.

"That's a lovely blonde hair," he said. "Perhaps a touch too blonde, too yellow. I assume it's a woman's hair. Or is it from a wig?"

Joseph went pale. He grasped Hunkeler's hand, he was very strong. He took the hair and got a lighter out of his pocket. In a second the hair was gone.

His wife stood up and left without a word.

"Did you have to?" Joseph asked. "She'd already noticed it anyway. You didn't have to point it out to her specifically."

"What had she noticed? That you've been going round in a blonde wig so no one will recognize you?"

Joseph looked at him dumbfounded. "Tell me, have you gone crazy?"

"He's got a girlfriend who's a blonde," Senn said. "His old woman's noticed and now she's mad."

Hunkeler got up. He really should have gone home to get some sleep, so that he'd be ready for work in the morning. But he didn't feel like it.

He went down the long corridor at the back to the men's room. He supported himself with one hand on the wall and rested his head on it. Clearly he was close to cracking up. Why? Was it seeing Eva Căldăraru in the hospital bed that had hit him hard? Or was it because he was afraid of the diagnosis he'd get in the morning? He put the lid of the lavatory bowl down and sat on it. He tried to breathe calmly – first breathe in, then breathe out, fill your lungs then empty them, all in one flowing movement.

After a few minutes he went back into the barroom and sat down at a little table by the aquarium. He ordered a second beer and watched the fish swimming round lethargically, opening and closing their mouths as if they were breathing. They must have been some kind of carp, grey goldfish, always swimming up and down the same stretch, pointlessly and stupidly.

Then Skender came over and joined him. "I heard," he said, "that a girl was strangled over by Allschwil Pond. Who would do a thing like that?"

"She wasn't strangled, she'll survive. As to who would do that kind of thing, I've no idea."

"And Hardy? Who strangled him?"

"I don't know that either."

Skender got up, went over to the bar and came back with two espressos. "There, you drink that. It'll do you good."

Hunkeler emptied his cup.

"Who are those two guys over there at the bar?" he asked. "Have you taken them on?"

"They're friends. If the police can't protect me, then I have to do it myself."

Hunkeler thumped the table with his first, making his beer glass topple over. "Have you all gone mad?" he shouted. "Are we living in Chicago?"

Skender took the empty glass, went over to the tap and refilled it.

"Your good health. Perhaps you should have another two or three beers so you can get to sleep."

"Thanks. How are your children?"

"The older one's doing very well at school. He wants to be a doctor."

"And your younger son?"

"He's still at kindergarten, he doesn't know yet. They're both talking Basel German, just like real Baselers."

"Well obviously. After all, your wife's from Basel."

"Actually, we did intend to go back to Albania and buy a hotel there. But that will probably not be possible."

"Really. Why ever not?"

Skender lowered his voice, as if he'd revealed a secret. "We thought things would be better after the collapse of the old government. But things have all just got worse. The health service, the legal system, the schools and the economy."

"The economy was already kaput under the old government, otherwise the regime wouldn't have collapsed."

"Perhaps. But back then at least the police functioned. Today there's no security in the country. There are the old blood feuds again. That's too dangerous for me."

"Really? So that's why you're employing those two thugs over there to protect your family and business."

"No, of course not, they're two of my cousins."

"Really? And what's the name of the young guy who set off a tear-gas grenade a few days ago? Isn't he called Prenga Berisha?"

Skender remained quite calm. "That I don't know, Inspector. I don't even know whether it was a man or a woman."

He leaned forward, concern written all over his face. "You should go home and lie down. You're talking gibberish."

The next morning at nine Hunkeler went into the joint practice of Dr Sommer and Dr von Dach. The receptionist directed him into the waiting room. He went in and sat down without looking up. There were more men there, all of around his age, or so it seemed. He kept his head down and tried to curl up in his chair.

"Well, it's Hunkeler," the man beside him said. "Welcome to the dripper club."

It was Thomas Garzoni. He seemed to be pleased to meet someone he knew there.

"Keep your mouth shut," said Hunkeler, "I don't feel like talking at all."

Garzoni nodded and remained silent, but not for long. "Your first time here?"

Hunkeler nodded.

"The first time is always the most difficult," Garzoni said. "You think you're going to die right away. But it doesn't go that fast. And we're not going to live for more than twenty years anyway."

"Do stop going on like that."

Garzoni gave a friendly smile. He put his hand in his jacket pocket and took something out. "There, take these. They're the best medicine against the drips. Everything else you can buy in the pharmacy is rubbish."

He gave Hunkeler a handful of pumpkin seeds.

"Thank you very much," Hunkeler said, immediately wide awake. "The active agent of the pumpkin seed that doesn't cure the ailment but alleviates it."

"I know. The lady told me. I had a good laugh."

Hunkeler put three seeds in his mouth, the rest in his jacket pocket.

"Now I know why you only drink whiskey. So that you don't have to keep going to the loo all the time, as you do with beer."

"Precisely. I've already had two operations. A third wouldn't be possible without the removal of the prostate gland. Then goodbye Angel, goodbye Maria la Guapa. Sad, isn't it? Will we see each other sometime soon?"

"I hope so. Perhaps tomorrow evening."

When Hunkeler came out from the examination Garzoni was no longer there. He would have liked to tell him that he'd had good news. His prostate was indeed considerably enlarged, Dr von Dach had told him, but there was no carcinoma. For the moment an operation was not necessary. Furthermore, Dr von Dach had given him some good advice: drink a lot of water, he'd said. If you drink alcohol, then just the best Bordeaux.

Once out in the street he called Hedwig. He got her answerphone.

"It's all gone well," he said, "you can keep me for a bit."

He drove back to his apartment and went upstairs. He put two of the pumpkin seeds he'd bought in the pharmacy on the kitchen table, placing two of Garzoni's beside them. They looked the same.

He went back downstairs and bought a packet of pumpkin seeds in the department store on Burgfelderstrasse and did the same in the pharmacy next door. He took them down St Johann's-Ring and went into the Sommereck. Edi, a grumpy look on his face, was sitting with a glass of water containing a white powder. "Bring me a glass of Bordeaux," Hunkeler said, "and don't look over at me."

He tore open the two packets, took the other seeds out

of his jacket pocket and made four little piles nicely laid out in front of him.

"Cheers," he said, as Edi put his wine glass down. He took a sip. "Now have a good look," he said. "There are four little piles here. Can you see any differences?"

"Pumpkin seeds," Edi said. "They all look the same. They all come from the same producer in Styria. How can there be differences?"

"It was just a question."

"If they're fresh," Edi said, "they taste really good." He pushed the four little piles together and started to eat them. "They're still fresh. Have you got any more of them?"

"Yes, here." He emptied the two packets out on the table.

He went back to his apartment and looked at the chairs round the kitchen table. He'd bought them years ago in the Brockenstube, five of them. Why had he done that, he wondered, there were never five people sitting round the table. He selected one, dark-stained oak with a pine seat. He fetched the plastic bag with his notes that had been on his office desk. He took both down to the car and drove to the Waaghof.

Frau Held's smile lit up her face when she handed him his key. "It's nice to see you back," she said. "I've missed you."

"I've missed you too."

"What are you going to do with that chair?"

"Sit on it. I like sitting on wood."

He went up the stairs to his office. It was just the way he'd left it two weeks ago. The swivel chair was in the corner, the box files on the shelves, the computer on the desk. He emptied out the plastic bag and arranged the slips of paper. He put the photo of Crete in the drawer, set the chair by the desk and sat down on it.

He recalled that in the last four weeks some things had happened that he didn't like at all. On 27 October he'd found Hardy dead. On 29 October he'd let old Binaku knock him out. On 30 October Hedwig had come to see him in the cantonal hospital. She'd stayed for three days, then she'd gone back to Paris. He hadn't seen her since then, far too long a time, it seemed to him.

Following that, he'd gone to Alsace to recover from the concussion. He'd been informed of his immediate suspension from duty. On 7 November he'd found the burnt-out Punto near Heiligbronn. On 10 November he'd cleared out his office. And on 21 November Eva Căldăraru had been found in the pond.

So one catastrophe after the other.

Today was Monday, 24 November. And at last the series of catastrophes seemed to be coming to an end. In the first place he was still reasonably healthy. In the second an image of a possible suspect was slowly forming. In the third place he was back sitting in his office – and in the fourth he enjoyed sitting in his office.

He pushed the chair back and rested his feet on the edge of his desk, first the left one, then the right. He tipped the chair back, very slowly, unsure whether that still worked. It worked well, and he clasped his arms round his knees and laid his head on them. He stayed sitting like that for a while, concentrating entirely on his breathing.

There was a knock on the door. He started, he'd almost fallen asleep. It was Lüdi.

"Are you doing yoga?"

"No. I'm putting myself in a state of suspense. So that I can think better."

"And what have you found out?"

"Nothing much so far."

"There's a meeting this evening at five. We have to be prepared for that. Just read this."

He put the tabloid down on the desk. The front page had a photo of the pond where Eva Căldăraru had been found. The place was marked with a black cross. Above it in large letters was the question: "Who knows the Basel strangler?" Subtitle: "Has the Basel CID run out of ideas?"

Hunkeler turned to the second page and scanned a longish article by Hauser. It ended with three questions: "Are the Basel police stuck in their own sleaze? Who will be the fourth victim? When will heads finally start to roll?"

"As expected," Hunkeler said. "That snoop Hauser's not going to let an opportunity like this go begging. At least it doesn't have a photo of Eva Căldăraru."

"Because they haven't got one. Otherwise it would be there."

"I don't believe they haven't got one. They usually get everything they want. They could have had a picture of the Gypsies' caravans in it. But they didn't do that either."

"At the very least they're making a political statement out of it: Zurich against Basel. The vigorous metropolis against the dozy, sleazy provincial town."

"Obviously. And they're right about that."

"But Suter won't enjoy reading that. Nor the senior prosecutor."

He sat down on the swivel chair in the corner and folded his arms.

"Suter had a talk with me," he said. "He asked me if I gave you the information."

"He didn't get that from me."

"Doesn't matter. I admitted it. He went very pale, was very dejected."

"I had to have the information," Hunkeler said. "There was no other way."

"I know. He told me that Barbara Amsler's mother's details also had an FA. And he told me it means Federal Archives. Apparently the files of the Children of the Road are there."

He paused for a while. Then he spoke, his voice very quiet.

"I'm wondering what's so sensational about someone coming from a family of Travellers. My grandmother on my mother's side was called Moser and she was Yenish too. I was very fond of her."

"Don't start crying now. The whole business is sad enough."

Lüdi nodded.

"What made you think of Garzoni?"

"I was up at the Allschwil nature reserve a few days ago. There's a little bench by the pond there. There was a pumpkin seed on the ground."

"Have you still got it?"

"No. I ate it. This morning I was at the urologist's. Garzoni was in the waiting room. He gave me a handful of pumpkin seeds."

"At least you'll still have those?"

"No, Edi ate them all."

"Who's Edi?"

"The landlord of the Sommereck. I bought pumpkin seeds in three different stores. We compared them, they all look the same."

"Have another look. Perhaps you've still got one."

Hunkeler felt in his right-hand jacket pocket. He found two seeds.

"There you are. I got these from Garzoni."

"Good. We'll compare them with those we found at the crime scene outside the Cantonal Bank. Perhaps that will give us something."

"OK. But we say nothing about Garzoni at the meeting. It's still too soon."

Once Lüdi had left, Hunkeler called the Federal Archives in Bern and asked for Frau Hebeisen. He had to wait several minutes before he was put through to her.

"Hebeisen."

"Peter Hunkeler here. I'm an inspector with the Basel CID. I assume Suter, the state prosecutor, has already spoken to you."

"Oh yes. I had a call this morning. There's a huge amount going on here, you know. I don't know whether I'm coming or going."

"What's keeping you so busy? The files aren't going to run away."

Silence. Hunkeler waited. Then her voice had changed, had lost its Bernese charm.

"What is this about?"

"What it's about is the fact that here in Basel we're looking for someone who strangles people and slits open one of their earlobes. The files of the first victims are marked FA. We know that these documents are in the Federal

Archives. The third victim is called Eva Căldăraru and she's a Romanian Gypsy."

"I read about that. It's incredible that something like that can happen in the old humanist city of Basel."

"I would like to have the files of three people: Barbara Amsler, born 1971; Bernhard Schirmer, born 1940; and Thomas Garzoni, born 1941."

"I won't be able to give you any information on Barbara Amsler," she said.

"Why not?"

"Because she's too young. No new cases from the aid organization were accepted after 1971."

"Then please look under her mother, Rosa Minder."

There was a pause. She was presumably thinking.

"Why Thomas Garzoni?"

"Because his files are also marked FA."

"I'm sure you will know," Frau Hebeisen then said, "that we are only allowed to issue the files to those directly involved. And only while respecting the privacy of third parties. That means that certain names are blacked out."

She was a tough cookie, but presumably she had to be. Hunkeler tried to adopt as friendly a tone as possible.

"I know. And naturally I accept that. But I would ask you to bear the following in mind: firstly, it looks as if we're dealing with a serial killer. Secondly, the FA mark appears to play a decisive role."

"Right. If it looks as if it's a murder suspect, then I assume I will have to release the files. When can you come to Bern?"

"I can't come to Bern," he said. "I'm needed urgently here. I'm asking you to come to Basel, and as soon as possible."

"Is it so urgent?"

He gave no answer to that.

"If you insist," she said. "What are you suggesting?"

"I'm suggesting we meet tomorrow, Thursday, at midday in the Birseckerhof restaurant. That's on Heuwaage, five minutes' walk from the station."

"Right. I'll be there."

Shortly before five he got a cup of coffee from the cafeteria and went with it to the meeting, which involved the restricted group. Suter was there, Dr Ryhiner, Dr de Ville, Haller, Lüdi, Madörin and, as a guest, Füglistaller, the head of the Basel Rural District CID. Hunkeler went straight over to Madörin and shook his hand. Madörin gave a brief nod, apparently pleased by the gesture, then went on sitting there, looking crestfallen.

At five Suter opened the meeting. He was sad, he said, deeply moved. That morning he'd been to see Eva Căldăraru in Bruderholz Hospital. He'd seen her lying there in an induced coma, attached to a respirator. And he wished to take this opportunity to express his profound sympathy to the whole family. The main cause of his sadness was not the anti-Basel reporting of the Zurich gutter press, he was used to that by now. It was the awful deed itself through which a young, innocent life had been almost extinguished. It was absolutely necessary to ensure that there wasn't a fourth victim. He was asking all of those gathered together in the group to devote their every effort to that common goal and be sure to set aside any rivalries that might exist.

He thanked Detective Sergeant Madörin for the great commitment he had shown in the Bernhard Schirmer case. Such commitment had been necessary in that case, even though it had turned out to be a false trail. At least now that was something they knew. And at least a gang of drug dealers had been broken up, even if it had not yet been possible to apprehend the guilty parties.

Furthermore, he was asking them not to pass on the things that were being discussed there. It was absolutely necessary to ensure that old wounds in recent Swiss history would not be opened up again.

Then Füglistaller took the floor. He read out a report by the Basel District specialist in forensic medicine, which said that Eva Căldăraru's injuries had only been life-threatening for a brief while, that by now it had been possible to stabilize her condition. However, it was highly likely that she would have to spend a few more days in an induced coma. After that, though, it would presumably be possible to discontinue the artificial respiration.

As far as the forensic evidence was concerned, it was not possible to say anything precise at the moment. In particular, it was impossible to give any precise information as to the means used to strangle the victim. They had to be patient on that, the victim's return to a stable condition naturally took priority. They could at least say that no traces of a struggle were found on the victim's body. The attack had been sudden and the victim taken by surprise. In all probability her earlobe had been cut open with a small pair of slightly curved nail scissors.

As far as forensics were concerned, Füglistaller went on, very few facts had been established. Nothing had come from the divers. As for the tracks in the snow, a few prints had been obtained. However, the snow on the path round the bank had already been stamped down, either by joggers or by the police who had been called in. Naturally there had been a wide-ranging search of the whole area. No traces indicating a struggle had been found.

It was impossible to say where the culprit had attacked his victim. According to her mother's statement, Eva had liked to spend time close to the water, so it at least seemed highly likely that the attack had taken place near the side of the pond.

There was also very little available as far as witness statements were concerned. Probably of great importance was Eva's statement that the man had had a shock of red hair. That was quite striking. She had clearly spoken not of red hair but of a shock of red hair. This could indicate that the perpetrator had worn a red wig in order to make himself unrecognizable. He was laying great emphasis on that detail because, according to the statements of some of the ladies in the Klingental, the man who had strangled Barbara Amsler might have worn a toupee. What's more, a number of the people living in the caravans had stated that several times an oldish jogger with striking blonde hair had been on the keep-fit course, always at nine in the morning. Blonde wasn't the same as red, but firstly the time fitted precisely, and secondly it could have been the same man wearing a blonde wig several times, the red wig just the once.

Several witness statements were about the Căldăraru family's dog Kaló, all agreeing that the dog had growled in a striking way when the blonde jogger ran past. The dog had gone with Eva to the pond shortly before the crime.

Sometime later, clearly after the deed, it had come back with its tail between its legs. It was therefore entirely possible that Kaló knew the perpetrator.

Very little had been learned from the man who had found Eva Căldăraru and pulled her out of the water. He had been entirely concentrating on saving the young woman and hadn't paid attention to anything else.

That was all the information he could give them. Unfortunately, it wasn't very much. With the little they knew it would presumably be very difficult to draw up a profile of the offender that was in any way precise. This might be made easier with a comparative analysis of the Amsler and Schirmer murder cases. The parallels were striking. And their colleague Hunkeler was going to say something about that now.

Hunkeler was as brief as possible. There were indeed several parallels between the Amsler, Schirmer and Eva Căldăraru cases. Firstly the strangulation, secondly the slitting of the left ear, thirdly the wearing of a wig the murderer might well have used to disguise himself. Fourthly, it was particularly notable that all three victims came from Traveller families. The perpetrator was therefore possibly a person who had something against Travellers, the Yenish, Gypsies and the Sinti. There was therefore a definite suspicion that a man was going round Basel who had pronounced and carried out his own death sentence on Travellers, marked them out by slitting their ears and was actually trying to wipe them out. This was putting it strongly, he was well aware of that. But it was justified. As his esteemed colleagues were perhaps aware, Children of the Road had been established in 1926. This so-called aid organization had the aim of wiping out not these people themselves, but their travelling way of life. To that end over six hundred Yenish children had been torn away from their parents and put in homes or with settled families. Tomorrow at lunchtime he was meeting a woman from the Federal Archives, where the files of the above-mentioned aid organization had been deposited. He hoped his discussion with her would bring some light into the darkness in which they were all groping for clues. He couldn't say any more about that for the moment, apart from reminding them that the police had to do everything to protect the Travellers wherever they were, as the perpetrator would doubtless continue with his work. He would definitely have read in the newspaper that his most recent victim was still alive. He would come back and try again. That was the law of all serial offenders. If they were able to stop, they would never have started at all.

There was silence in the room for a while. They were all thinking over what they'd just heard. It was a quietness of concentration, it was clear to everyone that the team would once more have to work together as a unit.

In the corridor de Ville came over to Hunkeler and took his arm. "Mon Dieu, you talked well, Hünkelé," he said. "I'd no idea Switzerland had had its own problems with Travellers."

"No," Hunkeler said, "Switzerland hasn't had problems with Travellers. It's had problems with itself. Because it can't stand its own foreignness."

"*Comme partout, hélas.* People can't stand their own smell. By the way, I have compared the pumpkin seeds. They're all alike as two peas. You can't use them to prove anything, so you'll have to find another clue."

*

At nine that evening Hunkeler went down Mittlere Strasse, heading for the town centre. The föhn had relaxed its grip, it had become colder again. It was overcast.

In one of the little front gardens he saw a rose bush with three open yellow flowers. They'd survived the recent frost, perhaps it hadn't been that cold in the town. He wondered whether to cut one off and take it with him. He didn't bother.

He went past the university library, where two thousand years of philosophy were stored. From Heraclitus to Plato, from Spinoza to Kant. He had read something of those men, he'd listened to lectures there on the light of knowledge, on tolerance. But things were just as de Ville had said. People couldn't stand their own smell, which was why they couldn't stand the smell of others either.

On Petersplatz he heard two screech owls. They were up there in the elms, perhaps a hundred yards from each other. He wished he could understand their language, the way Francis of Assisi had been able to. But how could he understand the language of the birds when he couldn't even understand the language of his fellow human beings? And then there were pitch-black crows perched up there. They probably wanted to sleep during the night and regarded the screeching owls as troublemakers.

He went down Totengässlein to the Hasenburg and looked in through the large front window. He saw a few people he knew in there, drinking pals from earlier when they could still make a night of it without batting an eyelid. He would have liked to join them and forget the sadness for a while. But he continued on his way to the Singerhaus and went up to the first floor.

There was nothing on that evening. Apart from a naked woman on the dance floor, nothing was moving. Three men were at a table with an ice bucket, Angel and Maria la Guapa at the bar, Casali beside them.

Hunkeler sat down at the little table in the corner and ordered a glass of Bordeaux from Ismelda. They didn't have any, only a local red from Maisprach. Hunkeler was happy with that.

The dancer had gone, the music had stopped. Only the spotlight continued to turn. Then Casali came over to his table.

"What can you do," he said, "it's Monday, and in November there's not much going on here anyway. I could just as well close the place."

He waited to see if Hunkeler would say anything. But he remained silent.

"I understood what you meant," Casali said, "a week ago yesterday over there in the Klingental. The guy was indeed repulsive. But we can't always choose our customers. Naturally, I didn't report it."

Hunkeler nodded. Casali blew a speck of dust off his left cuff; he had a ruby in it today.

"Sometimes, as you know, we have to put up with a police officer, without them even paying. Which is against our business philosophy. But beggars can't be choosers."

What was up with the guy? Was he trying to provoke him? That wasn't so easy with Hunkeler, who was quietly taking a sip of Maispracher.

"By the way," Casali said, "word has got round that there's a man at work who's strangling women. It's said that he likes hanging around in the red light district. I read that in the Zurich rag. He's said to wear a red wig some-times."

"That's wrong. It's not there. And it's not in the *Basler Zeitung* either."

"Then I suppose I must have dreamed it."

Casali smiled his subtle smile. He took out a cigarette and clicked his lighter on.

"I just wonder what's actually going on. It's completely unacceptable for a man to strangle a woman and throw her into a pond. We men are here to protect women. Or do you see things differently?"

"I'm wondering," said Hunkeler, "what you know and what you don't. Where did you get that about the red wig?"

"So it is true." Casali shook his head in disgust. Then he stubbed out his cigarette. "That's what I wanted to know."

"Just be careful what you do, Casali. Private revenge is not allowed. Tell me what you know."

The music started up again, a lady appeared on the dance floor once more. Strangely enough, she was wearing a dirndl, which she began to take off.

"I don't know," Casali said, "what problems the men here in Greater Basel have. We have a decent range of things on offer, night after night. It works across the river in Lesser Basel, the men there have normal reactions. In Greater Basel they're clearly too inhibited. They've got enough money to spend the night in bed with one of our ladies. But they prefer to go round in a red wig and slit earlobes open."

"But the guy who killed Barbara Amsler approached her in Lesser Basel. Or was that not the case?"

"That wasn't a man from Lesser Basel."

"How do you know that?"

Casali smiled, a nice, charming smile. "It's merely a hunch. Unfortunately I don't actually know anything, otherwise I would take action."

Hunkeler felt weary and despondent. It just came over him out of the dark November night. He would have liked to have taken action himself, but he knew almost nothing either. He recalled the yellow roses in the front garden. He would have liked to have one now, he could have given it to Angel.

"There's nothing sadder than a brothel with no customers," he said.

The next morning he parked out by Allschwil Pond and went up to the nature reserve. Single shots rang out from the pistol-shooting gallery. There was no one to be seen round the caravans. Only the Călăraru family's dog was there and it didn't quite know whether to growl or wag its tail.

Up in the nature reserve Hunkeler sat down on the little bench. There were lots of flowers where Eva Călăraru had lain, roses and asters and others he didn't know the names of. They had been put in vases or laid down by children from the Allschwil schools. There were candles among them, two still burning. Beside them were letters of sympathy, written in red, blue, green crayon. *Dear Eva*, he read, *I'm keeping all my fingers crossed for you. Come and see us when you've recovered.* And: *My dear friend Eva, please stay with us.*

He looked out across the water, which seemed to have a faint mist rising from it. A pair of ducks swam past along the opposite bank, the female in front, behind her the male with the crest on its head.

At twelve he was in the Birseckerhof waiting for Frau Hebeisen. He'd studied the menu and decided on tripe with beans and Parmesan, but he wasn't going to order yet. He'd read through the papers, the *BaZ* and the Zurich rag. There was nothing in them to arouse his interest.

She arrived at half past twelve. She was a lady of about thirty, very slim and pale. She was wearing stockings with coloured stripes, which she'd presumably knitted herself. She was also wearing horn-rimmed spectacles that concealed her eyes. She immediately apologized for the delay, she'd unfortunately missed the train she'd intended to take. She ordered tomato salad and camomile tea.

"Tripe," she said, "how can anyone eat something as revolting as that? Just looking at it makes me want to spew."

"Then you'd better not watch." She sat there, very upright; she had two severe lines going down to the bridge of her nose.

"Right then, what's this all about?"

"I told you that on the telephone. We're looking for a serial killer."

"What has that to do with Rosa Minder?"

"She was the mother of the murder victim Barbara Amsler."

"But she presumably had no immediate connection with the murder?"

"No," Hunkeler said.

"Right then. We'll leave Frau Minder out for the moment. What does Thomas Garzoni have to do with your serial murderer?"

"That's precisely what I'd like to know."

She wrinkled her brow, the two lines became even deeper.

"I'd like to hear a plausible reason. These files are very problematic."

"Why are they? What happened back then has long since been in the public domain."

"In the first place, the Travellers had to fight for years to get access to them. They were given that. Then the umbrella organization for Travellers decided that the files were not to be published, out of consideration for people who knew nothing of their past and didn't want to know. There are people who don't know that they were taken away from a Traveller mother. Those people have to be protected."

"How is it possible to withhold knowledge of someone's own mother from them?"

She took the teabag out of the glass that the waiter had brought.

"A lot has happened in this business," she said, "that people today consider impossible. The whole problem has not yet been sorted out. There's still a lot that has been swept under the carpet that ought to come to light. And it was very highly respected people who were responsible for it. There are various parties who are trying to keep those respected people out of the discussion."

"That is a point that surprises me. Why have those responsible not been brought to account?"

"The federal ministers Pilet-Golaz and Motta and the later Lieutenant General Ulrich Wille were all on the committee of Pro Juventute, which partially financed the baby-snatching. They were such highly respected people that they couldn't be called to account. We can't do that even today."

"But baby-snatching is a criminal act," Hunkeler cried.

The waiter brought the tomato and the tripe.

"I'm sorry," Hunkeler said, "for shouting like that."

She giggled merrily.

"You are a one. Nobody would think you'd been working for the police for fifty years."

"Not quite, just thirty-two."

He stuffed a forkful of tripe in his mouth.

"Don't slurp like that," she said. "You're bolting your food. It's revolting."

"There aren't just beans in it. There's also celery. And a shot of white wine. Together with the Parmesan it's a symphony of flavours."

"Then eat it just the way you like."

"Thank you," he said. "Where are the files?"

"They're in Bern. But I've learned the important bits off by heart."

He spluttered. Then he took his glass of wine to wash it down.

"You're a strange old bird."

"And you're eating like a pig."

He finished all the tripe on his plate then cleared up the tomato sauce with bread.

"Fair enough," he said. "Let's start then. I'll presumably not get to hear anything about Rosa Minder then. Is that the way things are?"

She shook her head firmly.

"That's not a problem," he said. "I know what I need to about Barbara Amsler. Grew up in Schinznach Dorf, difficult early years, father a farmer and wine-grower. Ran away from home when young, clearly a wild thing. Later on became a prostitute in Basel. All that's clear as far as it goes."

She nodded, pushing away her plate, on which there were still several slices of tomato.

"What about Bernhard Schirmer?" he asked.

"Born 1940, in the Muri/Aargau District Hospital. Mother unmarried. After the birth was sent to the care home of the former convent. Bernhard was sent to an adoptive family in Hägglingen/Aargau. At three ended up in the St Benedikt children's home in Hermetschwil/Aargau. Run by Benedictine nuns of the Melchtal Institute. Purpose of the home: to bring up and educate poor children in need (boys and girls) in the spirit of Christian love according to the principle of the founder of the order: pray and work. Room for 120 boarders. School education in the home. At sixteen started an apprenticeship as a car mechanic in Wohlen/Aargau. Completed the apprenticeship at twenty. The following four years not accounted for. From twenty-five training as a truck driver in Liestal. Followed by work as a truck driver for a haulage company in Basel. Regular trips to Turkey. The file ends in 1971."

"So what should be secret about that life? The man seems to have made a decent show of it."

"Don't ask such stupid questions. I need to concentrate."

"Right then. The Thomas Garzoni file, please."

She closed her eyes and recited off by heart what she had learned.

"Born 1941 in Lucerne Cantonal Hospital. Mother's maiden name Waser, married to Adrian Gerzner."

"Sorry?"

"Don't keep interrupting. So, mother married to an Adrian Gerzner. After birth assigned to the foster home of the former St Ulrich Monastery. At the time of his birth his father was in the Herdern/Steckborn District work camp. That institution was a place for men who had become temporarily unemployed through no fault of their own – an institution, that is, where those who were in danger of sinking into a life of idleness and vagrancy could be reaccustomed to an ordered way of life. On entry each colonist had to undergo an inspection of body and clothes."

"Blah-blah-blah. Can't you just get down to the main point?"

She opened her eyes and gave him a very severe look. Then she started reciting again.

"Thomas Garzoni was sent to a foster family in Sursee/Lucerne. At eight he was sent to the Sonnenberg/Lucerne reformatory, an institution run by three teachers. Those admitted had to be Swiss, or homeless children in need of moral improvement for whom a Swiss canton bore responsibility. They had to be physically healthy and mentally able to cope with an education. Lessons in handicraft and housework. At sixteen started an apprenticeship as an installation engineer in Emmenbrücke/Lucerne. At twenty completed his apprenticeship. Basic and NCO training in Brugg/Aargau with the Pioneers, who specialized in river-crossing. At twenty-three his father found him. Moved to Herznach/Aargau. Worked in his father's business, a filling station in Herznach/Aargau that also disposed of used oil. 1966 father died. 1967 moved to Basel. Changed surname from Gerzner to Garzoni. The file ends in 1972."

"Thank you," Hunkeler said. "Will you join me in a coffee now?"

"Of course. But decaffeinated, please."

He ordered two coffees.

"Is Gerzner not a Yenish name?"

"Yes, of course. Waser too. Otherwise he wouldn't be in our files."

"Have you any idea why he might have changed his name?"

"I couldn't say exactly, but I do have a hunch. Perhaps he no longer could or wanted to stick with his Yenish origins. Could I please have your sugar?"

"Why?"

"Because otherwise the coffee will taste too bitter for me. Basically, I don't like coffee."

"Oh, sorry."

He watched her stir four lumps of sugar into her coffee.

"Can you imagine that Travellers might have a longing for a settled existence?"

She took a drink, she nodded.

"The longing of settled folk for the adventure of travelling corresponds to the longing of Travellers for the normality of a settled existence."

The lady really was astonishing. Hunkeler took a sip of his bitter coffee.

"Can you imagine a Traveller suddenly beginning to hate his own origins?"

Again the two lines over the bridge of her nose appeared.

She was thinking. Then she looked up and scrutinized Hunkeler through her horn-rimmed spectacles.

"Oh right. So you think Thomas Garzoni could be the culprit?"

"What makes you say that?"

"How does that work? Are you at all allowed to express such a terrible suspicion publicly?"

"I haven't expressed anything."

She emptied her cup, then put it down in a decisive gesture.

"After everything the young Thomas Gerzner must have experienced with his foster parents and in the reformatory," she said, "I can well imagine that he was brought to hate himself and his origins. What had he been hearing all the time? That he came from an inferior family. That he belonged to the work-shy riff-raff. That he was scoundrel, a vagabond. That his parents, grandparents and great-grandparents had thieved and stolen like magpies. That he absolutely had to make himself a better person by praying and working. It is quite possible that these reproaches and demands became internalized. A child cannot be so self-confident as to be able to resist these reproaches in the long run. Perhaps that was why he wanted to get rid of his name and background."

Hunkeler nodded. He found the lady immensely impressive.

"How ever did you find that position in the Central Archives?" he asked. "And why did you take it?"

"I'm writing a book."

"What about?"

"About the relatively recent phenomenon of a settled existence among Europeans. It only started in the New

Stone Age, when the shepherds and nomads became farmers. They learned back then that you could sow and harvest. For that, however, they had to wait for the seeds to sprout and ripen until they could be harvested. And for the harvest they had to build houses in which to store it. That meant a settled existence. But even today there are still nomads, for example the shepherds in the Swiss Alps, who founded the Confederation. From spring to autumn they follow their cattle from one grazing area to the next. Down in the valley over the winter, up to the alpine pastures in the late spring. It's called transhumance. With my book I want to prove that the ancient culture of the Swiss is a culture of Travellers."

Hunkeler grinned with delight. He beamed at the lady. "I'll buy that book," he said. "And I'll read it."

"I studied history and philosophy. During the first semesters I believed everything we were told. Then we had a seminar on the Travellers in Bern Canton. The writer Sergius Golowin came and told us about his research. That was an eye-opener for me. I realized that nothing at all was right about the view of history we were taught at the university. I gave up the university at once. And now I want to write this book. We have to tear this bourgeois-patriarchal view of history apart, we women have to do that. You men can't, because you're all a product of precisely that bourgeois-patriarchal upbringing."

"That could well be," he said, "but we can't do anything about it."

She gave him a very severe look through her horn-rimmed glasses. Then she glanced at her watch. "Oh my goodness, my train's leaving. I'm always getting there too late."

She picked up her bag and ran out. He followed her to say goodbye. He saw her running up to the station.

He went across the Heuwaage to the high-rise building and took the elevator up to Harry's sauna. First of all he lay down in the rest room to digest what he'd eaten and learned. He fell asleep at once.

Later he had two sessions in the steam room. He enjoyed the heat, the sweat coming out of his pores. Then the cold in the pool, the warm shower, shampooing his hair. He was pleased that he could afford that luxury, he, Peter Hunkeler, presumably a product of bourgeois-patriarchal miseducation.

He went up onto the roof terrace. The town was once more enveloped in fog. Just a few headlights could be seen up there.

He settled on one of the damp loungers and thought of his mother. He'd loved her above all else, he still loved her. She came from a village in the Schenkenberg valley and had taken a course for women teachers in Aarau. At twenty she had returned to the valley, to Kasteln Castle, where there was a home for problem children. She had told him about the boys who were locked up there. About the bed-wetters whose sheets were hung up in the playground. And the bed-wetters had always had to stand by their wet sheets during the break. The poor boys, she'd said.

He wondered if among them there'd been a few boys from Children of the Road, who'd been taken away from their parents. Whether his mother had known about that. He couldn't imagine that, surely she wouldn't have gone along with it. Or would she? Perhaps she'd been happy just to find a position as teacher and hadn't asked any questions.

Moreover, she had never, at any point in her life, had any power at all, not even over her children. His father had had the power. It was the men who had had the power. They had set up Pro Juventute and Children of the Road. They'd taken the children away from their mothers. Hunkeler could not imagine a woman being capable of that. Or would they be? Had Frau Hebeisen not said that the St Benedict children's home was run by Benedictine nuns?

He lay on his lounger and looked up into the fog. He thought about Thomas Gerzner, who had changed his name.

At ten in the evening he went into the Billiards Centre and sat down at the regulars' table. Laufenburger was there. He was asleep and in his lap the Siamese cat was asleep too. Beside him were Nana, little Cowboy with his dog on the floor, Rentschler the pensioner, Senn the second-hand bookseller and Joseph the Bavarian, alone this time.

Standing at the bar were the two well-dressed Albanian gentlemen. At the back on the left were a few couples, on the right the billiards players. An evening like most in November, dull and stale, it was the month of depression.

The second-hand bookseller was moaning about the department stores that were ruining the small, honest stores in the quarters outside the city centre. Joseph the Bavarian was cursing women in general, pensioner Rentschler complaining about pensions in particular.

The two Albanians at the bar seemed to be nervous. They kept looking across at the entrance, as if they were expecting someone.

Once again Hunkeler was asking himself why he was there anyway. He knew the conversations off by heart, there was nothing new to be heard. He didn't want to get drunk, he didn't feel hungry at all. Anyway, there would have been nothing to eat apart from a packet of peanuts from the bar. So why was he sitting there as unmoving as a raven and mute as a fish? Because he couldn't stand the lonely waiting in his empty apartment, the prattle from the TV, the darkness on the ceiling.

Shortly after eleven shouts could be heard from outside. A man seemed to be calling for help in a foreign language. Swiss German curses could be heard mingling with it.

Hunkeler was up on his feet at once. He rushed to the exit. Out of the corner of his eye he saw that the Albanians were also heading for the way out. He turned round and showed his gun.

"The two of you will stay in here. And please take your hands out of your pockets."

They stopped. Slowly they took their hands out of their pockets.

Hunkeler went out into the street. Richard was standing on the pavement with a young man. He'd grasped him from behind and was trying to choke him with his left elbow. It was the man Hunkeler had seen coming out of the ladies' room. Little Niggi was standing beside them and punched him several times in the belly.

"You bastard," he said, "you fucker, you filthy swine."

"Stop," Hunkeler said, "stop hitting him. What's the problem?"

"That's the one," Niggi said, "I recognized him at once. He was the one who set off the tear-gas grenade."

"I'm not letting go of him," Richard panted, squeezing him even tighter, making the young man's knees give way. "He's going to be handed over to the police. And then he'll be locked up."

Hunkeler took out his phone.

"I already called them," Niggi said, "as soon as I recognized him. I did it very quietly so he wouldn't hear me. He ran straight into Richard."

"Let him get some air," Hunkeler said, "otherwise he's going to suffocate."

"He wouldn't be any great loss," Richard said, "he's played his last dirty trick, the bastard."

"Stop it! I've a question to ask him."

Richard released his grip slightly.

"Are you Prenga Berisha?" Hunkeler asked.

Gasping for breath, the man nodded. "Yes," he croaked. "Please save me."

"Right," Hunkeler said, "keep him until the patrol car arrives. But God help you if anything happens to him."

He went back into the Billiards Centre. The customers were all standing at the window to see what was going on outside. The two Albanians were missing.

"Where are those two?" he asked Skender. "Is there a rear exit?"

"Yes, there is. But it's locked."

Hunkeler went to the men's room at the back. There was a door out into the courtyard there. It was locked. Beside it was a window. That was open.

He went back to the barroom and out into the street. A blue light appeared out of the fog, a car stopped with a squeal of tyres. Three men leapt out, among them Sergeant Schaub.

"Handcuff him," Hunkeler said, "and take him to the Waaghof. Inform Madörin. And take those two with him."

Across the road, in the entrance to the sex cinema, Hauser was taking photographs.

"Bugger off, bastard!" Hunkeler shouted at him. Hauser nodded and disappeared.

"What's the guy called?" Schaub asked.

"I assume he's called Prenga Berisha. He's from Albania. But I assume he'll very soon be unable to remember what his name is."

"Are we to take those two there along with him?" Schaub asked.

"Yes please."

"Unfortunately that's not possible, the car's too small. Should we call for someone else to come?"

"Yes, of course. The two of them caught him. They're to make a statement. And you can lock them up for the night."

"Sorry, what did you say?" Richard asked. "The two of us have to go to jail? Is that all the thanks we get?"

"Just for the night. And there'll be breakfast in the morning at seven."

"What? At seven, as early as that?" Richard moaned. "I sleep until midday."

Hunkeler went across the road and into the Milchhüsli. Luise was sitting there with pale Franz and Hauser.

"You swine," Hunkeler said to Hauser. "I'll break every bone in your body."

"Oh come on, Hunki, we're both just doing our job."

"The St Johann district as a mini Chicago where no one dares to go out in the street in the evening? What are we doing here then? Didn't we come on foot?"

"There was something going on there just now," Hauser said, "outside, I mean. Or was it nothing?"

"An Albanian in handcuffs, with an upstanding Swiss police officer beside him. How exciting."

"That would be something. If they'd publish it, but I bet they won't."

The door opened and Garzoni came in. He gave Milena a brief nod and sat down at the table in the corner at the back.

"Just a minute," Hunkeler said and went over to him.

"What was going on out there just now?" Garzoni asked. "Would you like to sit down?"

"Certainly, thank you. Richard and Niggi caught an Albanian. It's presumably the one who set off the tear gas in the Billiards Centre a few days ago."

"Can't the police do that themselves? What's the man called?"

"Apparently he's a Berisha."

Milena brought a glass of mineral water. Hunkeler ordered a glass of red wine.

"Well, well, well," Garzoni said, "the things these Albanians have the nerve to get up to in our district. First Hardy, then the tear gas. What's the situation with the Gypsy girl in the Allschwil nature reserve?"

Hunkeler didn't know.

"There's a lot of discontent in our town. Too many foreigners, too few police. Aren't you drinking beer any more?"

"Not just at the moment, no."

"Did Dr von Dach find anything?"

"Nothing serious, fortunately."

"So no operation?"

Hunkeler shook his head. Garzoni took his bottle out of his pocket and had a swig.

"There's nothing more they can do for me. Either get rid of it, which means the carcinoma will be gone but my potency with it. Or radiotherapy. In which case I'll retain my potency. Since I value my potency, I've decided on the second option, even though it will shorten my life."

He took a sip of water.

"Why aren't you saying anything?"

"I keep asking myself why you changed your name."

Garzoni gave a friendly smile. Then he shook his head, in amusement, it seemed.

"For years I've been doing yoga every day," he said. "It has helped me in many situations during my life. I don't lose my composure so quickly any more. But is that not something that is supposed to remain secret?"

Hunkeler smiled too, a sickly-sweet smile. He didn't know whether that actually was something that ought to have remained secret.

"How did you find out?"

"We checked in your file. We found that those files had a FA and were blocked. FA means Federal Archives and they contain the files of the Children of the Road."

"I thought that was over and done with. But it's not over and done with. Once a Gypsy, always a Gypsy."

He was still trying to say this with a polite smile. But he'd gone very pale.

"So I'm under suspicion. Why?"

"You're not directly under suspicion. We're simply look-ing into Hardy's background. And you're part of that. You were Hermine Mauch's lover. Afterwards that was Hardy

Schirmer. You own the pharmacy where Hermine Mauch works, the apartment where she lives. Our interest in you is clearly logical."

"That is understandable, yes."

"But it doesn't explain why you changed your name."

"But it does contain an explanation. I decided very early on to make a career for myself. And I have done so. I was in a relationship with a really beautiful, successful woman. I've made money and purchased a property in an excellent location. That wouldn't have been possible for me under my original name."

"Why not? Gerzner doesn't sound all that bad."

"Possibly not for you. But for a lot of other, important people it is. They would have been wondering what kind of person I was. Perhaps they would have done some research. And if they'd found out how I'd grown up, they would have turned away from me at once."

Perhaps, Hunkeler thought, perhaps some people would actually have behaved like that.

"What is your specific suspicion?" Garzoni asked.

"There's no specific suspicion. I would just like to get to know you better."

"And to do that you go nosing round in my past and open my file, which presumably was secret? Do I not, like any other citizen, have a right to my private life?"

"As far as our research is concerned, the obligation to maintain secrecy will naturally be maintained."

Garzoni shook his head indignantly. The colour had returned to his face.

"Maintaining secrecy, what does that mean? The only effective maintenance of secrecy I've come across was the maintenance of secrecy about where my parents lived. I've no idea whether my mother's still alive. And I was twenty-three before I found my father. I've always considered you a reasonable man who treats people without prejudice. Now I see that you're just a lousy little cop, out for what he can get. And you're just wrong in what you think about me. I'm not some poor jailbird you can make into a galley slave. I know how to deal with that kind of thing. Now I'm asking you to leave my table."

Hunkeler got up, made a slight bow and went out. There he saw the number 3 heading for the border. Across the road a car was parked with some young people in it and excessively loud music booming out into the night. He could hear laughter. The car started up again and zoomed off in the direction of the town centre.

He felt wretched. Like some bastard, a lousy, devious cop who was going after a man simply because he'd a Yenish mother. Who was he anyway? A country policeman pursuing the Travellers into the depths of the forest then giving them their marching orders to send them on a specific route across the border? Someone hunting out beggars who would hand over the Gypsies to the executioner if they caught them a second time?

And yet it had to be.

He crossed the road and had a look in the Billiards Centre. The regulars' table was empty. He carried on a few steps to where Laufenburger lived and rang the bell. The door opened. Up in the kitchen he joined the others and had a dish of pureed peas that Nana had made. There was a lively discussion going on as to whether or not the Albanian caught by Richard was the man who had murdered Hardy.

If he was the murderer, the bookseller said, he wouldn't have come back. Oh yes, he would have, Joseph maintained, murderers always returned to the scene of their crime.

At one in the morning Hauser and pale Franz joined them. At half past Garzoni came. He sat down at the table without a word and drank some of his whiskey.

Hunkeler felt worn-out and tired. But he stayed there in his chair. Once he thought he'd heard himself snore. He started, Nana had given him a dig in the ribs.

"Go home," she said, "and lie down in bed. Then go and see Hedwig tomorrow."

He looked at the faces all round him. The glasses on the table. The light from the bulb. The tobacco smoke hanging in the light. But he stayed there.

Finally Garzoni got up. "OK," he said, "come with me."

He went on ahead down the stairs and out into the street. The Billiards Centre was dark, as was the Milchhüsli across the road. It must have been after three but that didn't bother Hunkeler. He realized that Garzoni was drunk. He was walking without swaying, but his movements looked as if he was consciously controlling them.

He lived just round the corner, on the fourth floor, next to a Heinz Marti. It was a very large room with steel and black leather furniture. In one corner was a light-coloured mat on the floor. Beside it was a coat stand with a white outfit hanging on it. It consisted of a jacket, trousers and a belt.

"Is that not a judo outfit?" he asked.

"Could be," Garzoni said. "But I use it for yoga."

"Linen or silk?"

"Whichever."

He opened a cupboard in which there were some thirty bottles and filled two glasses. On a glass-and-steel stand beside it was an aquarium. Hunkeler went over and saw that there were tiny turtles in it. They were lying in the tank, motionless, their heads just above the water. They seemed to be asleep. At the bottom was the glitter of coarse-grained sand.

"That's the best Irish whiskey there is," Garzoni said, putting the glasses on a little table. "May I ask you to take a seat?"

Hunkeler did so, picked up one of the glasses and took a sip. He didn't like whiskey.

"You don't like whiskey," Garzoni said. "I can tell from the expression on your face. You ought to stick to beer, or red wine if you like. Only I haven't got any."

"Why do you keep turtles? You can't talk to them."

"I don't want to talk. I just want to have something living in the room."

He raised his glass to his nose, sniffed, then drank.

"I can drink this round the clock, it tastes like honey. And I don't get drunk. As least not so drunk that it becomes noticeable."

He put his glass down again.

"May I ask why you came up to my apartment with me at this late hour?"

"Of course you may. I have no answer to that. But I am wondering why you asked me."

"Because I want to tell you something. Do you have a spare moment?"

Hunkeler nodded and was about to light a cigarette.

"Please don't smoke in here. This room is clean and should stay that way."

Hunkeler put the cigarette back in the packet.

"I'm sure you know," Garzoni said, "that I did an apprenticeship as a fitter in Emmenbrücke. That will have been in my file. What is not in it is the fact that I had a sister. At the time I was seventeen. One evening the pastor came round and told me she had been sent by the authorities to live with a farmer in the neighbouring village. The next Sunday I went there and found her. She was twelve at the time. She knew no more about me than I had about her. We went for a walk up in the woods. We talked a lot and told each other about our experiences. We were delighted to have each other. We agreed to meet again on the Sunday in three weeks' time. Three weeks later I went there. She wasn't there any more. The farmer said a man had come and taken her away. He had no idea where. I've never seen my sister again."

He closed his eyes and seemed to be concentrating entirely on his breathing. His face slackened, the blood drained from his lips. Then he looked up again.

"In the Sonnenberg reformatory we often had to do work outside. The skin on our hands was always rough. We could wash them as often as we liked, we could never get them clean. On Sunday mornings the governor would come. We had to stand in a row and show him our hands. He had a stiff brush that was usually used for scrubbing the floor. If he found someone he thought hadn't washed their hands clean enough, he would scrub them with the brush until they were dripping with blood."

Again he closed his eyes. He was breathing very quickly.

"The dirt sticks to us," he said quietly. "It's stuck there inside us. You can scrub as much as you like. We're like the plague that can't be eradicated. They were trying to re-educate us by putting us in institutions and reformatories. They tore our families apart in order to isolate us. They thought that that way we would adjust to normality. They wanted to save us from ourselves. They didn't succeed."

He took up his glass and downed it in in one. He refilled it.

"How I hate them for not succeeding. I could kill the lot of them for the botched job they made of it. I hate myself, I hate my people for being the way they are. As tough as old boots, you can hit them as much and as hard as you like, they won't change, they can't change. Even though the way things are at present they have no chance at all. They should see that it's the way things are, they aren't welcome anywhere on earth. That they're driven out from one country to the next, across every border to the next border. They ought to finally understand that, but they're too stupid, too idiotic. What's going round in the streets is poor-quality goods. It has to be got rid of, root and branch."

He leaned back in his chair. He was panting as if he were close to suffocating.

"I can't understand how a person can so demean themselves the way I have. How can a person despise his origins, his own mother, his own sister? Just now you had a look at my turtles, showed an interest in them. That delighted me. They're the only living beings I can live with. They're the only reason I can stand it in this apartment. They respect me and I respect them."

He stretched out his hands.

"Look at my hands. Is there anything that strikes you about them?"

Hunkeler looked at the hands Garzoni was holding out towards him. They were soft, well-groomed hands, the nails neatly manicured.

"No," Hunkeler said, "there's nothing that strikes me."

"Have a closer look. It must strike you."

"Oh yes," Hunkeler said, feeling really rotten, "now I can see it. That one, the middle finger of the right hand, there's some dirt on it."

"Where?"

"There, under the nail. You ought to cut it again sometime."

Garzoni had gone deathly pale. He put his hand in his right jacket pocket and took out a pair of scissors in a case. They were small, curved nail scissors and he used them to cut off a piece of the nail on his middle finger. He made such a deep cut that the blood started to flow. He put his finger in his mouth and sucked it.

"Now it's OK," he said, "now it's clean."

He stopped sucking and took his finger out of his mouth. He looked at his guest as if he was surprised to see him there.

"May I ask what you're doing here in my apartment? Who are you actually?"

"You invited me up. Don't you remember?"

Garzoni made an effort to think, but he couldn't remember. He picked up his glass to have a drink. But his glass was empty.

"I must ask you to leave this room," he said slowly, as if he had to search for every word. "You're a stranger here. This apartment belongs to me."

Hunkeler got up and went out quietly.

*

The next morning he was woken by the striking from the nearby clock tower. He counted along with it: eleven o'clock. He felt light and as if floating on air – it was presumably the Irish whiskey that made him feel like that.

As he drank his tea at the kitchen table it seemed as if there was a stench hanging round the apartment. He opened the cupboard and the cooker. Then he looked in the waste bin. It was the remains of the sheep's cheese he'd thrown away. He took out the bin liner, tied it shut and carried it down and out onto the pavement. It was Wednesday morning, 26 November. The rubbish collection was on Thursday morning.

He got into his car and drove up to the Spitzwald restaurant. He tried to park there, but it wasn't possible. Two men were constructing something: two uprights, one on either side, and a crossbeam six and a half feet above the ground.

"What are you doing here?" Hunkeler asked.

"We're doing what we've been told to do," the foreman, a fat man of around sixty, said.

"What's it supposed to be?"

"That's a tramp barrier."

"What's that?"

"Gypsies are tramps. And the point of the barrier's to stop the tramps driving in here with their caravans. Otherwise they'll stay here for months on end. Leaving us with the filth to clear up."

"But that would be a good place for Gypsies."

"No, nowhere's a good place for Gypsies."

Hunkeler closed the window and drove slowly to the edge of the woods at the back. He turned left up to the water tower, rising up high above the beech trees. He parked and put his card on the dashboard.

He took the footpath through the trees, very quickly, he needed to calm down, get some air. Merry are the woods so green, he thought, where the Gypsies are to be seen. The nursery rhyme came back to mind. He was panting, he'd smoked too much again the previous evening. What was supposed to be so merry about the woods, he thought, when behind every oak tree there was a gendarme lying in wait with a loaded shotgun?

He came to the edge of the woods, where the border across into Alsace was. There was a notice there that said crossing the border was only permissible with a valid identity card and not carrying any goods. Hunkeler had a valid identity card on him, he was a worthy, respectable, sedentary Swiss citizen. Tramp barrier, he thought, why not tramp gallows?

He passed an apple tree with mistletoe growing among its branches. The white berries were glistening, looking like something from a fairy tale. He decided to get a bunch down. Three times he tried to climb up, but slid back down with aching knees. So he couldn't manage that any more.

By the time he reached the first houses of Neuwiller he'd calmed down. There was a smell of chopped mangolds, of maize cut for silage, of smoke from the chimneys. Once a dog barked at him. It could go fuck itself, it was chained up.

He went into Luc Borer's inn and ordered half a Münster cheese with caraway seeds and white bread, and a bottle of water to go with it. He ate with pleasure, dabbing his bread in the seeds and washing what was left of the whiskey out of his limbs with the water.

*

At three in the afternoon he called Suter and asked for a meeting, it was urgent.

At four they were sitting facing each other in Suter's office. Hunkeler told him what he'd heard from Garzoni. He needed a search warrant, and immediately.

"I do wonder how you manage to get close to these people," Suter said. "As it happens, I've been wondering that for a long time. No one would ever tell me such intimate personal details."

"I've got eyes in my head, and I've got ears as well."

"And you love people."

"That may well be. Even if there are times when I find it very difficult."

"Is he the one?"

"I think so."

"That is a dreadful suspicion, as you well know. How could someone kill his own people?"

"Out of perversion. After the things he went through when he was young, we can't exclude the possibility that his pride in his own origins has become perverted into hatred of his origins, hatred of himself."

Suter had put his hands together and was looking at his fingertips.

"Why do people do all these things to themselves?" he asked. "Surely it could turn out differently. We're living in a Christian culture, a culture of 'love thy neighbour'. My God, what a difficult profession we have. We have to pay for the sins of our fathers, even though we weren't responsible for them. What did those gentlemen think they were doing sixty years ago? Surely you can't take a child away from its mother."

"I think it always gets dangerous when people try to impose their opinions on others, and do so with force."

"So it's that straightforward, is it? Aren't you making things a bit easy for yourself?"

"It's neither straightforward nor easy. It can even get extremely complicated. It can lead to extreme perversion when people are humiliated in such an inhuman way."

Suter thought for a long time.

"Why don't you just arrest the man?"

"Right now? That's not possible. On what grounds? First of all, I have to get into his apartment. I think there must be evidence lying around there."

"OK then, you can collect your search warrant tomorrow morning."

"Is today not possible?"

"First of all I have to talk to the senior prosecutor. He's not always that well disposed towards you. Anyway, you ought to take things easy for a bit. You look very tired. You ought to take some leave. Not immediately, of course, but once you've tied this case up."

"How about three months' sabbatical?"

Suter gave a hearty laugh.

"Like your Hedwig, yes? It would certainly be possible. But first of all you must catch this madman. You will get any support you need from me."

Shortly before nine that same evening Hunkeler was sitting at the television in his apartment watching the match between FC Basel and a top English team. He saw at once that the English team, playing at home, were more confident, calmer in the build-up, giving themselves more time. Then a high cross from the right came over the Basel goal-mouth, the keeper missed it, the ball hit the leg of a Basel defender and went into the goal. That was it, Hunkeler switched off.

How should he spend the evening now? Go to bed, read a book?

He called Hedwig and left a message on her answerphone. "Where are you again? Watching what film? In which merry bar? I tried to climb an apple tree today to get a bunch of mistletoe and I kept on slipping back down. That's the way things are. Best wishes from your old Peter."

Then he went down and out into the street. The Sommereck was closed, the Oldsmobile too. There were old editions of the classics in the window of the second-hand bookstore. *Everything must go*, it said. *Once-in-a-lifetime low prices.* The light was still on in the Indian grocer's opposite, they were still hoping for customers. There were several rubbish sacks on the pavement outside.

He went round the corner and sat down on the bench. It was wet from the fog, but that didn't bother him. He looked across at the pharmacy. Hermine's apartment could just be made out, the changing light on the ceiling. Hermine was a rich woman now, he didn't begrudge her that. What would she do with the money? Buy a country cottage, hook a mature man who would stay with her for good? Or take a cruise round the world?

He wondered whether he should call Hedwig again. He took out his phone and switched it off. Then he went into the Billiards Centre.

Shortly after midnight Dolly came in. She joined him and drank an espresso.

"Come home with me," she said, "and hold me tight. But it'll just be kisses tonight."

They went out together, arms round each other. He could feel her hips swaying. They came to Kannenfeld Park, with its trees shimmering in the bright fog. They went up in the elevator.

Shortly before six the next morning he was going back along Burgfelderstrasse. He felt comfortable, he felt warm. They'd kissed until they got tired. Then they'd slept for a few hours until he'd woken up. He'd slowly taken his arm away from under her and got dressed, closed the door quietly. He'd had an almost solemn feeling as he went down the stairs.

He went across Burgfelderplatz and came to the door of the place where Garzoni lived. He saw the rubbish sacks by the grocer's in front. Something was moving there. He stood, waiting. He could hear a scratching and tearing. When he went on he saw a marten running off. Some of the sacks had been torn open, there were chicken bones on the asphalt, beside them the tinfoil they'd been wrapped in. It was gleaming like silver in the light of the street lamp. Beside it was something with a yellow shimmer, like fine, artificial straw. He bent down to see what it was. It was a yellow wig, which had been in the rubbish sack. He picked it up and went back to the door of the house where Garzoni lived. He wondered what to do. He rang Heinz Marti's bell and waited for the door to open. Then he rushed up the stairs to the fourth floor. An old man in a red tracksuit was waiting there for him.

"What is it?" he asked. "What's the rush?"

Hunkeler showed him his ID and thumped on the door to Garzoni's apartment until he realized there was no point. There seemed to be no one in at all.

"Herr Garzoni went out at nine," Herr Marti said. "I'm fairly sure he hasn't come back. I don't sleep very well, you know. I hear everything that's going on in the building."

Hunkeler took two or three steps back and hit the door with his right shoulder. It hurt, he rubbed his sore side.

"That's no use," Herr Marti said, "the door's too solid. Anyway, weren't you here yesterday evening?"

"Yes, but that's not the point now. Please help me to break down the door."

"Have you got a search warrant?"

"Tomorrow," Hunkeler panted, "I'll have one tomorrow. Today, that is, at midday."

Herr Marti slowly shook his head. "What a way of going about things. Though he's an odd fellow, that Garzoni. What has he done?"

"Oh come on, man," Hunkeler said. "Stop yakking. Do you have anything we can use to break open the door?"

"Well, if needs be, I'm happy to help. My hobby's looking for rock crystals. I've got a whole display cabinet full of them."

He went into his apartment, he could be heard rummaging round. Then he appeared with a three-foot-long crowbar. "It'll be child's play with that, I've broken open whole walls of granite with it."

He rammed the bar between the door and its frame and pushed against it. The door sprang open. Hunkeler went in and switched on the light. He opened all the doors and looked round. Garzoni wasn't there.

Hunkeler went over to the coat stand by the light-coloured mat and took the belt. It was made of silk. He went over to the aquarium and searched through the glittering sand until he had what he was looking for. There was a pearl in his hand and a diamond. He put everything on the table: belt, pearl, diamond and yellow wig. Then he called for the nearest patrol car. "Come here at once," he ordered. "And tell Madörin and Suter immediately."

"You, Herr Marti, will go and stand there by the door and make sure that no one comes into the apartment, apart from the police."

He went down the stairs, as quickly as he could, and over to his car.

He parked by Allschwil Pond. It was pitch-dark all around, the fog swallowing up any light. He switched on his flashlight; it shone a few yards ahead. He took the things he needed – gun and handcuffs – with him.

The hum of generators could be heard from behind. He went along the path and came to the stream. Across in one of the caravans he saw a light go on, presumably someone making coffee.

He saw a man sitting on a tree trunk, heard him pour something out. It was Hasenböhler, drinking coffee from a Thermos flask.

"My God, Hunkeler," he said, "you did give me a fright. What are you doing wandering round in the dark here, why aren't you in bed?"

"It's the morning, man. The sun'll soon be up."

"Can you see any light round here? It's like sitting inside a cow. How am I supposed to observe anything when it's like this?"

He emptied his cup.

"Like some?"

"Please. What's the situation? Is it quiet?"

"No, quiet it is not. Since about four there's been something going on, but I've no idea what."

"Sorry? What have you heard?"

"I've been hearing things, but I couldn't say what. Footsteps, branches creaking. The fog seems to be alive. It's pure horror."

"Let's get this clear," Hunkeler said. "Have you heard footsteps?"

"Yes."

"From which direction?"

"That's very difficult to say. I think they're from back over there." He pointed back down into the valley.

"Have you seen anyone leave the caravan?"

"Yes, a dog. And perhaps a small female figure, but I'm not quite sure."

"My God, why didn't you say so?"

He took out his phone and called headquarters. "Please send all available forces to Allschwil Pond, to the nature reserve. The Rural District forces as well. Ambulances too."

Then he headed off to the back, as quietly and quickly as was possible in the darkness. He got to the end of the caravan park and went into the woods. He saw a gleam on the trunks of a few beeches. He heard a soft splashing sound. It was a girl, perhaps twelve years old. She was squatting there having a pee. Behind her a dog barked.

"Hi," he said, "please don't be afraid. I'm just a policeman."

She looked at him, rigid with fear. She waited until she'd finished peeing.

"Right, go home now," he ordered. "At once, and straight home. Then go to bed and stay there until it gets light."

He couldn't say whether she'd understood, but she nodded and headed off in the direction of the caravans.

The dog beyond him barked, it was more of a panic-stricken howl. Then all was quiet.

Hunkeler panted up the slope, his flashlight illuminating the way ahead. He heard something like footsteps. He drew his gun and waited. A dog appeared in the beam. It was Kaló. It gave a brief howl then trotted past Hunkeler, tail between its legs. The distant siren of an ambulance could be heard.

Then there was a shot, short and sharp, as if from a pistol. Hunkeler flinched, as if the shot had been aimed at him.

He continued up the slope, cautiously and quietly so as not to give himself away. He heard the siren of the ambulance coming closer.

He reached a plateau surrounded by beech trees. There was a man standing there, motionless, as if he'd been waiting for someone. In the beam of the flashlight it could be seen that he had a gun in his right hand, its barrel pointing forwards at Hunkeler, who slowly crept closer. Then the man dropped the gun. It was Casali. Lying in front of him was a figure in a red wig.

"Just come closer," Casali said. "It's all over."

Hunkeler put his gun back in its holster and went over. The man on the ground was Thomas Garzoni. He'd been hit in the middle of the forehead. His wig was shining like red straw.

"You could have saved the ambulance," Casali said. "He's dead."

Hunkeler knelt down and closed the dead man's eyelids. It was a rigid face, controlled even in death. The ambulance had switched off its siren. It was suddenly very quiet.

"If you want you can handcuff me," Casali said. "It's not actually necessary. I want some peace at last."

"Be quiet now," Hunkeler said. "You can talk later."

He turned the dead body over on its back and folded the soft fingers back together.

"It's all over, Thomas Gerzner," he said, "the end of your sufferings. Death has taken you home."

He heard calls from below, they were approaching. Clearly the men had heard the gunshot.

"There's one thing I'd like to know, Casali," Hunkeler said. "How did you find out about the man?"

"It was Maria la Guapa, she noticed it when he'd been with her. She found two red hairs on her pillow. We've kept a watch on him every night. This morning at four I got a call saying he was at Allschwil Pond. So I came. I wanted him to die by my hand. And that's what I've achieved."

"You could still run off over the border," Hunkeler said. "There's still time."

"Would you let me escape?"

"You'd just have to see, wouldn't you?"

Casali tried to smile. He did it quite well. "No," he said, "I'm staying here."

Steps could be heard coming closer. The beam of a flashlight appeared out of the fog.

"Over here," Hunkeler said. "Arrest that man. And take the corpse down to the ambulance."

On Monday, 1 December, Hunkeler got on the direct train to Paris at the SNCF railway station. He sought out an empty compartment in the rear carriage, closed the curtains, lay down on one of the seats and pulled his cap down over his ears and eyes.

When he woke there was a canal outside in the foggy landscape. A boat was floating on the water, a barge with a woman hanging up the laundry. She looked across at the train hurtling past, presumably about to wave, but she was already swallowed up in the darkness of a tunnel.

Hunkeler went along through the empty corridors to the front of the train. Between each carriage he put his hands to the walls to keep his balance. He could feel the airstream from below and thought he could smell the brake pads rubbing against the wheels.

He got a coffee and ordered a croque-monsieur in the Bar Coraille. He sat down at one of the little tables, watched the meadows slip past and sipped his coffee. When the woman at the counter waved to him he went over to fetch his toast. Thinly sliced ham with melted cheese on crispy grilled white bread. It was, he thought, superb.

He stayed in the bar until Vesoul, where recruits came on board, tired, bleary-eyed lads. He went back along the corridor to his compartment. It was full. He stood in the corridor and looked out of the window. Woods with bare trees, flooded fields, now and then a couple of white cows. Then they were out of the fog. High up on the left he saw the white cathedral of Langres shining in the sunlight.

He saw Hedwig from a long way off. She was standing at the end of the platform wearing a bright-yellow jacket. They embraced at once, he could smell her familiar perfume. They went down to take the Porte d'Orléans line on the *Métro*. They were lucky, they found two seats next to each other. He embraced her, kissed her lustfully. She pushed him away a bit in order to take a good look at him.

"My God," she said, "just look at you. You've gone really grey, even in your face."

"Oh come on," he said, "it's just two missing teeth. Everything else is in order."

"What? Haven't you had them put in yet? How on earth are you going to eat?"

"I'll just have to bolt my food down if there's no other way. And the oysters will simply slip down anyway."

She laid her head on his shoulder and stroked his neck. "How long can you stay?" she asked.

"Three months. I've got a sabbatical."

Startled, she pulled her head away. "What? For so long? I won't be in Paris all that time."

"Doesn't matter. I'll stay in Alsace. I've ordered two donkeys."

"No," she said, "have you gone out of your mind? What are you going to do with two donkeys?"

"Go for walks with them."

CPSIA information can be obtained
at www.ICGtesting.com
Printed in the USA
LVHW051245200921
698250LV00005B/8